W9-COM-344

SENSE AND SENSUALITY

Richard was everything a sensible woman could want—mature, handsome, brilliant, considerate, level-headed, understanding, and even good in bed.

And his twenty-three-year-old son Wendell was everything Richard was not—adventurous, emotional, creative, poetic, and outrageously erotic enough to match a woman's most uninhibited fantasies.

With two such wonderful men why would Emma dream of anything more? But she did. . . .

WOMAN WANTED

"A gem of a novel!"
—United Press International

⊘ SIGNET BOOKS

WOMEN OF PASSION

(0451)

☐ **SMALL WORLD by Tabitha King.** Dolly, an ex-president's daughter, has an obsessive passion for dollhouses. With the help of Roger Tinker's camera-like minimizer Dolly satisfies her lust for revenge by cutting a statuesque and snotty anchorwoman down to size and making her their first "house guest"... "Sex and evil that packs a punch"—*Kirkus Reviews*   (136330—$3.95)*

☐ **THE TWELVE APOSTLES by William J. Coughlin.** A scorching novel about the ravenous new breed of lawyers... big, juicy... This portrait of modern life oozes with sex and scandal, glamour and greed... and all the other things that go along with the world of money and power. A Literary Guild Alternate Selection.   (136047—$3.95)*

☐ **THE OTHER WOMAN by Joy Fielding.** "Hello, I'm Nicole Clark. I'm going to marry your husband." The message was clear, but what wasn't clear was what Jill could do to save her perfect marriage and her attractive husband from the sexy and clever Nicole. Jill knew what it meant to be David's mistress, she knew everything that could happen. But she didn't know what to do about it...   (125509—$3.95)

☐ **GOLDEN TRIPLE TIME by Zoe Garrison.** Kit Ransome's life had always been more sensational than any of her pictures, but now she is threatened with the revelation of a secret from her past, a scandal that would shock even Hollywood. In just five days she must save the biggest picture in her career... and the love of the only man who ever really made her feel like a woman...   (141504—$3.95)*

*Prices slightly higher in Canada

Buy them at your local bookstore or use this convenient coupon for ordering.

NEW AMERICAN LIBRARY,
P.O. Box 999, Bergenfield, New Jersey 07621

Please send me the books I have checked above. I am enclosing $_____ (please add $1.00 to this order to cover postage and handling). Send check or money order—no cash or C.O.D.'s. Prices and numbers are subject to change without notice.

Name_____

Address_____

City_____State_____Zip Code_____

Allow 4-6 weeks for delivery.
This offer is subject to withdrawal without notice.

Woman Wanted

Joanna McClelland Glass

A SIGNET BOOK
Published by
The New American Library of Canada Limited
Scarborough, Ontario

PUBLISHER'S NOTE

This novel is a work of fiction. Names, characters, places, and incidents either are the product of the author's imagination or are used fictitiously, and any resemblance to actual persons, living or dead, events, or locales is entirely coincidental.

NAL BOOKS ARE AVAILABLE AT QUANTITY DISCOUNTS
WHEN USED TO PROMOTE PRODUCTS OR SERVICES.
FOR INFORMATION PLEASE WRITE TO PREMIUM MARKETING DIVISION.
NEW AMERICAN LIBRARY, 1633 BROADWAY.
NEW YORK, NEW YORK 10019.

Copyright © 1985 by Joanna McClelland Glass.

All rights reserved. No part of this book may be used or reproduced in any manner whatsoever without written permission except in the case of brief quotations embodied in critical articles or reviews. For information address St. Martin's Press, 175 Fifth Avenue, New York, New York 10010.

ACKNOWLEDGMENTS

"What a Diff'rence a Day Made" (Stanley Adams/Maria Grever). © Copyright 1934 Edward B. Marks Music Corporation. Copyright renewed by Edward B. Marks Music Company and Stanley Adams Music, Inc. Used by Permission. All Rights Reserved.

"Housewife" from *All My Pretty Ones* by Anne Sexton. Copyright © 1962 by Anne Sexton. Reprinted by permission of Houghton Mifflin Company.

Having It All. Copyright © 1982 by Helen Gurley Brown. Reprinted by permission of Simon & Schuster, Inc.

"Second Fig" from *Collected Poems,* Harper & Row. Copyright 1922, 1950 by Edna St. Vincent Millay.

"Save the Last Dance for Me" by Doc Pomus and Mort Shuman. © Copyright 1960 by Rumbalero Music, Inc. Assigned to Unichappell Music, Inc. (Rightsong Music, Publisher). International Copyright Secured. All Rights Reserved. Used by Permission.

This is an authorized reprint of a hardcover edition published by St. Martin's Press.

SIGNET TRADEMARK REG. U.S. PAT. OFF. AND FOREIGN COUNTRIES
REGISTERED TRADEMARK—MARCA REGISTRADA
HECHO EN WINNIPEG, CANADA

SIGNET, SIGNET CLASSIC, MENTOR, PLUME, MERIDIAN AND NAL BOOKS
are published in Canada by The New American Library of Canada, Limited,
81 Mack Avenue, Scarborough, Ontario, Canada M1L 1M8

PRINTED IN CANADA

COVER PRINTED IN U.S.A.

1   2   3   4   5   6   7   8   9

To
George Athanasios Sperdakos

The author would like to thank the librarians at the Guilford Public Library for their assistance with this book.

HOUSEWIFE

Some women marry houses.
It's another kind of skin; it has a heart,
a mouth, a liver and bowel movements.
The walls are permanent and pink.
See how she sits on her knees all day,
faithfully washing herself down.
Men enter by force, drawn back like Jonah
into their fleshy mothers.
A woman *is* her mother.
That's the main thing.

ANNE SEXTON

One

Emma Rowena Riley presently walks to South Station lugging a dead dog in a Samsonite suitcase. There is autumn in the air and madness in the world, and although her heart is heavy, it is helium compared to the deadweight of Bitsy. The dog has been dead for three days and it was an odious undertaking, lifting him from the floor of Madeline's flat and placing him in all his stiffness in the suitcase. Emma's mother, Peg, once went all the way to Montreal with half her ample bra dangling out of a similar Samsonite. Best not make the approach to South Station with erect tail protruding.

Bitsy was, or had been, a Sealyham terrier and Emma knew little of his history except that he was given to massive, mephitic shit-fits when there happened to be horsemeat in his food. Madeline was Emma's friend, and Emma was not too familiar with her history either, but she did know that Madeline had a habit of referring to this canine as ITSY Bitsy. She called him that once when Michael was present and Michael turned to Emma and whispered, "It is to puke."

And as she walks, all is not well in her world and she has been preoccupied of late with thoughts flat, stale and unprofitable. But it's a Boston dusk and the sun has settled over the Common and tinted the grand old Ritz with shades recalled from an oilpaint kit: yellow ochre and burnt sienna. The sun's reflection in a high Ritz window caused a brief, blinding gleam of deep vermilion. Would she miss the Ritz when she went to live in New Haven?

Surely, for in the Ritz was Firestone and Parson, where she'd gone nearly every Saturday of her life to ogle the jumbles of diamonds and rubies and emeralds that cost seven-thousand-five-hundred dollars a jumble. When she was little she would be accompanied by her Dad, old Kevin, and the two would stick their noses against the F & P windows and Kevin would peer at the price cards and exclaim:

"Jazus Murphy! If I had seventy-five hundred, I'd go into real estate!"

Friend Madeline is due on the Amtrak Colonial at 7:49 from New York City and this whole morbid enterprise is happening because Madeline insisted, over the phone, that she have a last look at Itsy Bitsy prior to Bitsy's disposal at the S.P.C.A. Here is what Emma is thinking as she goes to the station:

This is precisely what happens when you try to be the good guy. Wench calls up needing a favor and isn't even a friend, barely an acquaintance from the one damn time I worked at Filene's. Has to go to the Apple on a buying trip and would I mind awfully going to the flat Monday and Thursday to feed Bitsy? And this must seem crass as hell to ask just when Michael's moved in with Daniel and your life's come apart, but the only other person who might even consider is brother Allan, and he'd have to come all the way from Tufts and the floor has rusted out of his old VW.

"But Madeline, who will walk him daily so he can make his drops?"

Oh, she'll leave the sliding door to the balcony open and he can make his poo-poos out there in the geranium bed so all he needs, really, is fresh food twice, and if you feel so disposed, a hug and a cuddle, and if you wouldn't mind, please rinse out the cans or they'll stink up the garbage and maybe mold

if there's humidity. Forever indebted and *so* grateful,
very deeply appreciative and, really, I would have
asked brother Allan but he'd have to come all—.

Dutifully, she went Monday and opened the cans and
rinsed them and checked the geranium beds to be sure they
were indeed liberally laced with Bitsy's poo, and in the
meantime Daniel came to collect Michael with a Hertz
U-Haul. And Michael came out of the closet and moved
out of the apartment forever. Dutifully, she went on
Thursday to find Bitsy dead as a doornail right in the
geranium bed on the balcony, and it reminded her of old
Kevin who always said if there was one damn thing he
wanted to do before he died it was have a good shit and
die empty.

Panic, then. A call to Madeline, tracked down in the
Apple. Terribly bad news, best sit down for it, Madz,
Bitsy's dead on the balcony, yes, I know, all you had in
the world, yes, like a death in the family, no, peacefully,
no anguish on his little bushy face, no, no signs of mutilation or muggery and the rest of the apartment's shipshape,
so a quiet death I'm sure. Painless, really, a blessing.
What I think I should do, Madz, is call the S.P.C.A. and
have them come and get him. But Madeline says no, she
knows from Finnegan before him they won't make house
calls. We'll have to take him to the S.P.C.A. ourselves.

Mammoth incredulity. *We? Ourselves?* Aghast, she was
thinking nix, I say, on this plural, but yes, says Madeline,
I can't face it alone and I want to say one last goodbye. So
please put him, gently put him, in that old Samsonite
suitcase under the bed and meet me at South Station at
7:49. Oh, deeply indebted, infinitely grateful in this my
hour of need.

At 7:40 Emma arrives at the station where a husky,
boozy, derelict man approaches her hastily, as if he had a
mission in mind. Fear.

"Hey, little lady, let me help you with that."

"Oh, no, thanks, it's—"

"It looks really heavy. Let me give you a hand."

And in a flash he has grabbed the handle and he is running like Bill Rogers around a corner and she is screaming:

"*Stop that man!* He's stolen my suitcase!"

An old, black woman waddles by and says:

"Times is hard, lady. Have mercy."

Now Madeline comes dragging up the platform with a tear-stained face and two shopping bags. One is a big, brown bag on which the retailer thought it pertinent to print "Big Brown Bag." The other is white and is covered with sprays of purple violets. And while Emma explains to Madeline, she thinks of Mel Tormé, the Velvet Fog, and while her mouth is making obligatory noises her head is humming a song called "Violets for Your Furs." She is overcome with a feeling that is all too familiar. That she isn't actually here on this platform with her aching arm slung around the weeping Madeline's shoulder. No. This thirty-five-year-old five-foot-five-inch woman with a maroon Indian gauze skirt lifting in the breeze is simply the shell that's sent out for public appearances. The shell is the emissary that the real, secret, Emma Rowena Riley contrives to present to maintain a pretense of sanity. As they get into a cab the humming continues in her head: I Bought You Violets for Your Furs and It Was Spring for a While, Remember? The sympathetic murmurs roll steadily off her lips but suddenly there is a swelling of mirth rising up in her throat. Oh, to have a picture of the boozer's face when he opens the suitcase!

They drive up Commonwealth, that stately street of shabby grandeur, and who knows when she'll see this street again, or whether there'll be anything comparable in New Haven? Glancing to the left at a cross street, she spies the outer reaches of M.I.T., crouching complacently by the Charles. Hordes of Emerson and B.U. kids are arriving over on Beacon Street in search of cunt and cock and higher education. It is all very pretty and full of hope and aspiration. Madeline has calmed her wrenching jerks and Bitsy's been dumped in Heaven knows what alley trashcan. And there is autumn in the air and madness in the world.

Two

In *Little Women* the family was so poor the sisters extracted, carefully rewound, and saved their basting threads for use again. In the Shea family we were so poor old Kevin tore a twelve-inch length of dental floss from its spool every Monday morning and that twelve-inch length was saved in the medicine cabinet to serve the teeth of the three of us for a week. It was especially disgusting after corn on the cob. We ate voluminous amounts of that each summer because we couldn't afford meat, and we grew the corn in our back yard. As a child the trick was to be the first to the floss. Otherwise, it still had bits of kernel on it from the user before. And nauseating as it is, that's how poor the Shea family was. I mustn't tell *that* little tale to the Professor in New Haven or he'll think:

Blue-bum Irish scum with one foot still in the cave.

And how to explain to the Professor and his wayward son the various other perversities of my life?

I am on my way to bid farewell to Kevin and Peg. I've tucked the exhausted Madeline into bed, but isn't it unfortunate that Madeline hadn't the grace to say goodbye and good luck in New Haven? No justice at all, which I've known since emerging from Peg's womb, but wouldn't it have been nice if Madeline had mustered the wherewithal to at least inquire:

"So how come you're moving to New Haven?"

"I have to get out of Boston."

"Ah. The divorce."

"Michael and Dan will be everywhere I am."

"So how come you're going to New Haven?"

"Well, I saw an ad in the *Globe*. It said:

'WOMAN WANTED. Live-in.
New Haven, Conn.
Perform household tasks.
Widowed professor and son.
Call collect, 203-865-7883.' "

"Emma, you've always been a Kelly Girl. This is a fucking *maid!*"

"So I called and I said how come you're advertising in Boston when you live in New Haven? I mean, are you so impossible that you've gone through the entire New Haven domestic work force like a dose of salts? And he said, well. If you really want to know, I grew up with an Irish nanny who was kind and generous and pleasant to be with. And now he's looking for someone just like that to put his house in order. So I said, listen, if you're looking for cheap Irish labor, you're about a hundred years too late."

"Good! Put those Yalie mothers in their place."

"Then he said I sounded somewhat unstable so I told him I was a Rock of Gibraltar among women, and I hung up. But then, Oh, Madz, despair. God, I've got to change my life. I lit a cigarette thinking, Jesus, my only salable skill in this world is typing and I'm sick to death of the steno pool, so what can I do? Then I looked down at the match cover and it said, *Earn more. Become a skilled electrician.* Despond followed, waves of hopelessness tidal in their dimension. So I called him back and accepted. Six hundred a month, Madz, and it's all cream. The son's twenty-three and sounds delinquent.''

Oh. Well. In *that* case, let me be the first to wish you health, happiness and prosperity in your new adventure and won't you take with you please this ancient emerald tiding? May the road rise up before you, and the wind always be at your back.

But Madeline didn't have the grace.

I'm going to tell old Kevin about this in a minute and I know what he'll say. He'll say:

"Oh, grace is a commodity in very short supply.''

And now I am in what is known as the neighborhood, always a very complicated place for a vulnerable soul to be. This is the neighborhood that provides Boston with most of its policemen, the neighborhood my father came to, off the boat, at ten years of age, my mother came to, off the boat, at thirteen. They both liked to say their exodus wasn't caused by any particular potato famine, just hunger in general. Most of the families on my street locate their roots in the Great Famine of 1847–48, so it has always been rather strange for me to proclaim that I am first-generation American, so lately, in the twentieth century. That status is reserved, in my neighborhood, for Puerto Ricans and Asians. Over a million Irish fled the old sod in 1847–48, and there is widespread belief that those who didn't get the point at the time, who didn't know enough to emigrate then, were unalterably dim, with wits as slow as snails.

One block from my house is St. Anne's, where I went to school until tenth grade. I was the only one in the class allowed to leave the premises and go home for lunch, because we couldn't afford the meal fee. In January of tenth grade Kevin went into the ring with the Mother Superior to argue about unpaid tuition. Filty Lucre, Kevin called it. And fortified with Dutch courage, having swilled a pint of Haig and Haig, he took it upon himself to inform the Mother Superior that in his considered opinion she needed a good screw to iron out her kinks. Five months of humiliation then, and eleventh grade found me taking the bus to Hillford High, a public center of learning where slacks and cursing and feeling-up and pot in the lockers went unnoticed. And people said, "I'm going to the lieberry." A girl named Annie Pringle was rumored to have given a blow job to Robert Sayre, and Emma Rowena Shea thought that was something you did with a snow plough, after a blizzard. Well. It all took some time to absorb and adjust to.

I pass the McNulty house.

When I was ten, a photographer from the *Globe* came out to take a picture of the famous McNulty corn, the tallest in Boston. And needing someone to stand among the stalks and give perspective to their height, Mrs. McNulty summoned me, and there followed two days of fame and unabashed celebrity because my name and face were unleashed on the newsstands. Word of it spread as far as Montreal, and Aunt Colleen, who'd married a Frenchman, called to ask me for my autograph.

That Saturday we went down to Firestone and Parson to look at some fine Australian opals, and I wondered if I should wear sunglasses and go incognito lest I cause embarrassment. But no, no one at the Ritz recognized me. Seeing my disappointment, Kevin said:

"Oh, Em, fame's a flash in a fickle pan. Something one shouldn't rely on."

The last roses of summer climb an Anchor fence in front of which stand Maggie Tilson and Betsy Sullivan. Old familiar flash feeling now of the displaced person, little Minnie Misfit. Wandering Infidel, The One Who Got Away. These two, Heavens, large again with child, graduated twelfth grade at St. Anne's, then punched the compulsory cash registers for two years at K-Mart, and then

married into the neighborhood. Not for Maggie and Betsy
to love and marry a flaming faggot faerie queen actor who
dropped out of Harvard junior year. Not for them to learn
to say Merde on opening nights before vomiting your guts
out from nerves in the Buskin Theatre crapper. No surprises or chances taken here in the circumference of these
lives: born on the first floor, raised on the second, married
and renting on the third, and not too long from now in
middle-age they'll descend again to the first floor when
their parents depart this earth.

Eight children between them, and it seems to me the
most banal exchanges of my life occur here on this street
where there's no frame of reference in which to form
sentences. Everything's fine, although Jamie's on the night
shift, but glad to have that in these hard times. Everybody's OK, all the old folks as well as could be expected
in these, their advancing years. And Maggie's first-born
son has grown taller than his dad and she laughs, and for a
moment plays the coquette as she says the boy's a great
lout of a man now, built like a brick shit-house, and can't
be spanked and sent to his room. Curious moment. Eerie
and freighted with the sexual. Best not probe into *that* too
deeply.

Oh, mercy. I must ward off the solace emanating from
their eyes. They think I am Our Lady of the Sorrows.
Surely they don't know, couldn't even conjecture details
of the ripples and wrinkles along my route, what Michael
called The Odyssey of Minnie Misfit. And yet they look so
informed, inscrutable, would I dare to call it sagacious or
would I more accurately call it smug? Yes. The claustrophobic security of the ones who never dared. Runs rampant in the world, that dead gray look of resignation. Not
lives of quiet desperation, but desperation mute. I tell you,
it's a bloody epidemic. They think St. Vincent Millay is
someone buried in a Vatican catafalque. They don't know
that juicy lady wrote:

Safe upon the solid rock the ugly houses stand,
Come and see my shining palace built upon the sand!

Oh, it does get to you though, when you dare t
with fecund females diligently fulfilling biologica??e
tives, brown rubber pacifiers on strings around the
postpartum pendant, the cross they bear, hunkering d
on cellulite hips from too many spuds, too much b
the corn. By the Anchor chain fence for a twilight ga
tucking in the clone-babes and hearing evening pr

Anger wells up, familiar old festering flash fee
rage. I must lie down on a couch and have it all ana.
someday, when my ship comes in. Rage against Kevin
having his brains up his ass and causing that crucial ri
the cut of the St. Anne's cord, and the catapult into the
world beyond the neighborhood. Not to mention ensuing
knowledge of, Saints preserve us, the cosmopolitan. Ignorance was bliss and a little learning is a dangerous thing,
but what a kick it was at twenty, meeting the wildly
idiosyncratic, highly erratic Michael Riley who was mad,
bad, and dangerous to know.

Our Lady of the Barren Womb climbs the peeling porch
stairs and bangs on the screen door.

"Ma? It's me."

There's a hole the size of a thumbnail in the screen and
Kevin's patched it, can you believe it, with a large corn
plaster from Dr. Scholl. Now to drag myself in and admit
defeat and provide a closing chapter to the Riley saga.
Thanks be to God they won't suggest a visit to the parish
priest for advice and consolation. Their last churchly act
was the exchanging of their vows, a tardy act at that, for
Kevin was forty-two and Peg was thirty-eight. When still
a toddler he took me on his knee and told me the church
offered only blarney and guilt, and both should be avoided
assiduously, like the plague.

Seventy-eight now, small, leathery and intense. He
scurries down the hall with a spring in his gait and tears in
his eyes.

"You're only thirty-five, Em. You've got a lot of
innings left."

walks like Alec Guinness playing Gulley Jimson in *Horse's Mouth*. His grimy old olive green cap is ...ed on the side of his head and his smells are strong, ...olent of the workshed. Varnish, turpentine, linseed oil, ...ethane, Butcher's Wax. He Jimsons along the hall that's ...vered with thirty-year-old cabbage rose wallpaper, and ...e passes the spot where a hole in the wall was mended messily with sheet rock tape. Four years ago he put his fist through this wall when he learned of Michael's bisexuality. When he did that Peg threw a skillet at him and screamed:

"You're a deranged black Irish son of a rutting bitch!"

His fury expended, he mopped the blood from the skillet wound and quietly muttered it was a damn good thing he hadn't hit a stud and busted his south paw. Semi-retired most of his life, totally retired these last ten years, his life revolves around meals, television, the local lending library, and baseball at Fenway Park. Fatigue is as foreign to him as a regular paycheck. He sleeps like a baby, dreams of pink, buxom ladies resembling the women in the old *Esquire* cartoons, awakes early, farts, belches, and then, shouting obscenities, stands at the back stoop with a slingshot and shoots navy beans at marauding dogs who overturn the garbage.

Patsy said: "My dad's a switching man on the telephones."

Meredith said: "My dad's on the road for True Value Hardwares."

Emma said: "My dad's a carpenter by trade."

A lousy carpenter for the most part, because he found no joy or imagination in the construction mania that surrounded Boston with tract housing. What he loved most was antique furniture. Winter weekends found him at museums and Historical Houses looking for adze marks and satinwood inlays. He loved to take an old, alligatored piece and strip it down and discover its burl and grain and decipher its provenance. He loved mahogany and walnut and cherry, but he thought modern pine common to the point of vulgarity—furniture foisted on the poor unknowing creatures who ordered by number from Sears' catalogue. He had never finished high school because he never attended classes. He went to school mainly to play hockey, but he couldn't contain himself there, either, and was kicked off the team at sixteen. The coach said that Kevin Shea left too much of other people's blood freezing on the ice.

He follows me into the kitchen where we'll all have a cup of tea. Peg looks up from the ironing board.

"I can tell you your solution in one little word."

"Yes?"

"Speedwriting."

Peg elaborates.

"Gone are the days when typing would provide the bread and butter. There's an office revolution going on, Em. I can tell from the commercials. You've got your Xerox and your Apple, and IBM's got machines that talk and remember. Wang's got word processing and typewriters that think. They can put the accumulated know-how of all mankind, I daresay since Eden, right on a silicon chip. So typists are obsolete. You screwed up bad, Em, when you didn't take shorthand."

"But, Ma, I told you. I've made my plans."

She finds a folded newspaper and hands it to me.

"There. Speedwriting. You can learn it in six weeks. It'll broaden your horizons. It'll rescue you from the Kelly Girl steno pool. It'll give you some *leverage*.

Sign up tomorrow and you know what you'll find? A class full of dumbos and dunces, because the world's full of dumbos and dunces, *present company*, meaning himself over there, excepted, of course. If it takes them six weeks to learn it, you can do it in four.''

There is always a sense of emergency about Peg, a need to outrun time's wingèd chariot. I look up at the wall. The faded, spattered, sepia-colored newspaper photo is still tacked there, with the headline ''The Corn Is Green.'' Under it is the ceramic head of a chef. The chef has a small hole in his mouth and inside of his head there is a ball of string which is threaded out through his puckered mouth. He looks idiotic, as if he is forever drooling a single piece of spaghetti, as if one good suck would restore him to normal.

Peg is not big on bodily contact. She doesn't leave the ironing board to greet me. She still takes in laundry at seventy-four. There are three families left, in Louisburg Square, who entrust to her their custom-made shirts and their Porthault sheets. I have no memory of her anywhere else. She is stuck forever in front of the washer and dryer and that's the image I'll recall in New Haven. There's a large laundry sink nearby where Peg washes by hand the Brahmin lingerie, the filmy bits of gossamer for which Maytag hasn't created an appropriate cycle. Beside the sink is a stack of brown paper sheets in which she wraps the finished product, then winds the package up with string from the drooling chef.

''These New Haven plans,'' Peg says, ''are stupid. Christ knows what you're in for with this professor and his pup.''

''I have to get out of Boston.''

''The scars are on your soul. New Haven won't relieve them. You've been a white collar worker, Em, with wall-to-wall carpeting and two legal coffee breaks twice a day.''

"Michael and Dan will be everywhere I am."

"A curse on them," Peg says. "A curse on all the earth's bum-fuckers."

"Oh, Margaret," Kevin says, "will you confess that, I wonder, when they administer last rites?"

Peg tells Kevin he can shove his last rites up his rectum. I find this conversation blatantly anal and I refuse to participate. My capacity for tuning out is my private inoculation against the foibles of the world. I think they're like the Sprats of the nursery rhyme. Kevin's a stringbean and Peg is rotund. He could eat no fat, she could eat no lean.

When I was twelve they took me on a circus visit down in Quincy, and I had nightmares for six months hence because we saw the freak show. A woman born without arms had copied the entire Bible, writing with a pen between her toes. The Bible was for sale at eight-fifty, and Peg said, Oh, we really ought to buy one. And Kevin said absolutely not, no matter which of the digits copied it, it's all bilgewater. And then we walked along the midway and paused at the fat lady's tent. The fat lady had married the star midget and there was a huge poster of the two of them in front of their tent, and a large sign that said:
   "Who put him up to it?"

Peg is snapping her fingers.

"She's doing it again," Peg says. "She's gone off in one of her trances."

If Kevin's the most unreliable of men, Peg is the most dependable of women. She is known in the neighborhood as a strong woman, a matriarch who held the family together with not much more than the string from the chef's head. I want her with me when God suddenly drops me in the jungles of Burma. She'll rub two twigs and build a fire and get me a meal and cajole the natives into showing us out, with our virtues more or less intact. About her is an air of the omnipotent, the supernatural. Her focus on mere survival is zealous, sometimes mindless, and this armor is so impenetrable it makes her enigmatic. It must be because she intuits peril around every corner of her life. And dreams at night of bill collectors, failing banks, broken treaties, incurable diseases, acts of God that no insurance policy covers, and worst of all, bum-fuckers who marry into the family. Her set of dentures rests in a glass by the laundry sink. Their absence from her mouth causes the planes of her face to be exaggerated. Cheekbones elevated, jaw sunken, and every now and then she gives her gums a good suck, reaffirming that the manmade intruders are elsewhere. The dentures look slightly magnified in the water. She got them five years ago, so now Kevin has his twelve-inch length of floss all to himself. She puts the iron down and goes to wrap four shirts.

"Sea Island cotton," she says. "The best."

She was, as Kevin said, a wonderful wartime ally, but her enemy never surrendered. She won a medal for the efficiency of her work at the riveting plant in 1943. Kevin married her a year after the war ended and he had assumed that her tendencies of urgency and emergency were wartime characteristics. He was wrong. It must have been the eyes that won him. Wondrous eyes, even now. Sometimes violet, sometimes periwinkle blue. Kevin said, years ago:

"Eyes to die for."

And I am, so it would seem, a chip off these two old blocks. Peg is snapping her fingers again.

"Ma, listen, I've been working part time for a dozen years earning a hundred dollars a week. If I work full time, even with speedwriting, I'll be making two hundred a week to start. Now. At eight hundred a month I'll take home seven hundred, and I have to buy duds, you know, to go to business. And Michael's left me with a five-hundred-dollar-a-month apartment, plus utilities and phone. I suppose I could share with some girl and cut my costs, and then I'd have the privilege of dealing with her bras in the shower and her boyfriends in the sack. All very feasible at twenty-five, maybe, but I feel too old for it."

"Oh, Em," says Kevin. "You've got a lot of innings left."

"You can move back here," Peg says, "and live rent free."

Now, no offense, really, I love you both dearly, especially since I've been away and have had the distance to see what makes you tick. But if I'm too old to deal with foreign bras in the shower, something deep within, possibly Darwinian, tells me I am too old to share the floss.

"Look. At Professor Goddard's I'll be given what he describes as a large, sunny room, my meals, my phone, and six hundred dollars a month. Don't you see? It'll be pure cream. And I won't have to buy duds. All I have to do is house-keep, which I've done free for Michael for fourteen years. This New Haven plan, really, is not stupid. Really, this New Haven plan is a paragon of logic."

Three

New Haven, Connecticut, on first impression requires two of Peg's maxims. It is homely as a mud fence and it's nothing to write home about. A squalid affair this train station, and I wonder why the town fathers allow it to stand an abandoned abomination boarded up, when it still shows vestiges of elegant, remembered salad days. I always feel sorry for the old people traveling alone, jostling luggage up and down stairs with arthritic limbs. A crying shame, really, when you think of all the foul weather they've seen, they ought to at least be accompanied. Put me in charge of U. S. S. S., United States Social Services, and I'd corral the vagrant youth of the nation, give them crew cuts, deodorant, a smattering of sensitivity training, and then place them at train stations, air and bus terminals, to assist the old folk up and down stairs. Actually suggested that once to an eleventh-grade teacher and he said, no, you couldn't afford to do that and have missiles too. It was the first and last suggestion I ever made at Hillford High.

It appears that arrivals and departures in New Haven occur not from the station itself but from a sort of shanty-shed built alongside it. There are two rows of plastic chairs bolted together against thievery and the floor is filthy, cracked linoleum, shit-brindle brown. Near the exit there is a dingy coffee counter from which emanates the effluvium of greasy hotdogs rotating on an electric wheel. Thus far, Michael, I say it is to puke. But I see a sign that says certain architects have got this thing under renovation. Feeling magnanimous, I forgive the town fathers.

It's a sharp, bright blue day, which is always to be appreciated when you consider the alternatives, and outside there's a whiff of industrial harbor. Across the street one sees the beige public housing where the black people live behind concrete blocks and little balconies with barbeques and tall, thin bags of charcoal. Slight disorientation in the head for a moment, wait a minute, where am I? A billboard says I am in New Haven, Gateway to New England.

God bless America for its advertisements of itself. I remember a sign in New Jersey that says, "Trenton Makes—The World Takes," and every October Kevin and I muse at the gall of the World Series that pits two American teams against each other and is of absolutely no interest to the rest of the world. This particular American vision resides in its own peculiar tunnel, and when Michael and I went to England that summer we couldn't help but display it: it's in our genes by now. The Brits found it arrogant, self-centered. And Michael said, Over here the impression U.S. citizens promulgate is singularly, self-centeredly, US.

Now a very accessible Italian cabbie, Joseph Gagliano, goes along Church Street past the spacious Green and he says the three churches are very famous. Behind them is the dark old famous freshman dorm, and behind that is a lot of Gothic architecture, every nook and cranny of which has been extolled in poem and song, and is very, very famous. But Joe, where I come from they say:

> Harvard was old Harvard
> When Yale was still a pup.

Onto Whitney Avenue which has residential possibilities here and there, but I think these big houses shelter not the single family, rather a maze of student apartments. Too many bicycles in the driveways. This Whitney is after Eli, of the cotton gin, and the cabbie says what a way to start in America, having *that* particular patent tucked up your sleeve. That's exactly what Kevin would say. And it's good to smile.

A left up Edwards Street and a right onto St. Ronan, which is the address I have pencilled on the paper in my lap. This Ronan Saint is unfamiliar, not one of the retinue we memorized so laboriously at St. Anne's. Oh, I think I'm in the midst of the patricians here, the folk who dress for dinner, pass wind when they fart, keep their elbows off the table, and when they curse they say Pshaw. The Goddard residence needs paint and the plantings have gone berserk at the foundations. It has a large, bare, uninviting porch across the front of it. Fix that soon. Bring a fine Irish hand to provide a smidgeon of the lace-curtain. Wicker rockers with chintz cushions, three or four hanging plants, and a swing like the one Kate Hepburn had in *Alice Adams*. But now Joe and I have this major decision. The front door or the back? At my instruction we follow the driveway to the back, and it seems the Professor antici-pated this because he bolts out the back door as we brake. It is nice to have one's instincts immediately confirmed.

Richard Goddard is not keen on eye contact. There is, in his greeting, the implication that I have gotten him be-tween appointments, pushing his Sunday out of whack. I'd anticipated a leisurely tour of the twelve-room house and he'd show me the linen closets and where you find the Hoover, and explain the garbage routine. Instead, we stand at the back of a darkened hall, directly below the stairs. I spy to my right, beyond the stairwell, a study. The walls are lined with serious, scholarly-looking books, and there is a small china cabinet that houses a collection of porce-lain bulldogs. To my immediate left is the kitchen, which looks not exactly *House Beautiful*, but praise be the Lord, newer than the house. Directly ahead at the end of the hall is the front door, which leads to the uninviting porch.

We pause here in the dark, and although I can't see his face, I can sense his size. His person takes up most of the hall, and I'm squashed against jackets and coats which hang on pegs behind me. Distinct vibrations here of merchandise sent by UPS from L. L. Bean.

There is, in certain meetings, an abject denial of social custom. And although there is madness in the world, and more than a little in my head where the frontal lobe has suffered of late severe disconnection of wiring and the neuropanel has blown one or two fuses—nevertheless—I have extended to this man a friendly shake of hand, a flash of pearly whites, an air of capability. Culled my experience and mustered my strength to send out for this public appearance The Emissary. Richard Goddard cannot do the same. Weariness in his voice, lethargy in his stance, and down at his feet his socks don't match. Unable to see him, I sense overwhelming defeat in the man, and this is unexpected and somewhat surprising since St. Ronan promised to be the street of Stiff Upper Lips. Defeat along with the size, which I might eventually call hulking because the voice comes down from a foot above me. He has food on his mind.

"I'm afraid I don't know what we'll do about dinner. I'm not prepared."

Well. I'm sure I'll be able to put something together. I see three walls of cupboards in there, and unless they're absolutely bare I'm pretty good at, one might even say ingenious at, combining little scraps of this and that. Like Jesus, if I may be so bold. Give me a loaf and two fishes and I have on occasion fed a multitude of starving actors. Not to mention the entire technical crew from the Buskin Theatre.

"But I'm wholly unprepared."

There is annoyance in his voice, which compels me to reassure and say there is no reason why you shouldn't be. You did, after all, hire me to do the marketing, run the kitchen, wash the laundry, make the beds, take the messages, and you hire in a stalwart weekly to do the heavy work, as you said on the telephone. So, if we can just be

very patient with each other for just this single night, I'm
sure I can forage about and deliver up something to please
the palate. I just need a moment perhaps to wash up and
have a little leak you know, not having dared to pee on the
Amtrak because Peg, the matriarch, holds to be true that
nothing less than the Syph is contracted on the toilet seats
of the Amtrak. And then, perchance, just a fleeting to open the
suitcase and closet the contents.

"Oh, yes, forgive me. I'll show you up to Nanny
Culligan's room."

On the landing I need a candle, like Olivia DeHavilland
playing Catharine Sloper in *The Heiress*. No light reflects
off all this dark mahogany, and if he tries to emphasize the
present cost of kilowatts I'll tell him this isn't frugal, it's
treacherous. A second-floor door opens, a flash of light
from a bedroom, and Wendell appears, black-lit, in a
nimbus. He says:

"Welcome to the mausoleum."

I think there's nothing to do but flash the pearly whites
again and ignore that. Rely on The Emissary to get me
through the sticky patches. Oh, Kevin, this is looking
ominous. Wendell's apparition disappears and we're in for
the same lack of illumination after we mount the steps to
Nanny Culligan's room on the third floor. Panting. Both of
us. I can tell he's a smoker from the laboring lungs.
Perhaps if I were to push this little button on the wall the
ceiling would open, ejecting a yellow plastic oxygen mask,
like that perilous time on Pan Am.

"I'm sure you'll find this quite comfortable. The
bathroom's just around the corner at the top of the
stairs. That door is the backstairs route to the kitchen.
The two other rooms up here are used for storage
now. We had five in help in the old days, but time
does cause erosion. One stole my father's ties for her
boyfriends and another forged his signature on checks.

Caught her tracing, once, at a sunny window. So it
dwindled down to Nanny, whom we kept until she
died at seventy-one. I'm sorry the stuffing is coming
out of this chair.''

Well, I'm sorry, too, but why can't we indulge in a little
jolt from Connecticut Light and Power so I may see my
new abode? I think what we've got here is the Blanche
DuBois syndrome. The man's spirit wants to live in shadow.

He sits in the chair that can't contain its innards, reclines, yes, in a kind of life-exhaustion, and me standing
with two coffees and a Diet Pepsi busting the bladder and
imminent hysteria if I don't light up a smoke. He tells me
he was born in this house. I think I'll just take it upon
myself to crouch a little, reach to the right, and, risking an
irreparable lesion in employer relations, flick on this little
lamp. Mercy, it's a twenty-five watter. It lights him from
the knees down. Sock of forest green, sock of burgundy.

He was born in this house in 1928, and in 1946 he left it
for college. Jonathan Edwards at Yale, approximately three
miles away. In 1950, his senior year, his father died and
he returned to the house to pursue his Master's and his
Ph.D., and to companion his mother and old Nanny
Culligan. In 1955, at twenty-seven, he married Marion
Hotchkiss and brought her to this house. In 1958, Nanny
Culligan died, and in 1959 his mother died, and in 1961,
Wendell was born. At Grace New Haven Hospital. A year
ago, in 1982, Marion died. Of natural causes. I beg your
pardon? Heavens, I should hope so.

"Mrs. Riley? You seem to be off in a trance."

"Oh, no, sir. I'm sorry."

"Well, it *is* a lot of dates. But I thought you'd be
interested in the chronology. I'll leave you to unpack."

Mr. Clark Thompson at Hillford High thought the same
when he informed me that Martin Luther was born in
1483, nailed his ninety-five theses on the Wittenberg Church

in 1517, was served with a papal bull of excommunication in 1521, and thereafter was condemned as a heretic at the Diet of Worms.

"Miss Shea," Mr. Thompson said. "You seem to be off in a trance. I thought you'd be interested in the chronology."

Well, Mr. Thompson, the truth is, the emissary I send out for these utterly ridiculous daily appearances at Hillford High observed in first grade, and was duly impressed by, the significance of the first six letters of the alphabet. There are in this life A's and F's. And the amount of respect one receives at the hands of the world is in direct proportion to one's performance on the report card. Therefore, I behave accordingly, I accept your data, record it sequentially, and commit it to the memory bank for all eternity. But if you were to assume that the real, secret, Emma Rowena Shea was interested in the aforementioned chronology the reply would be, in a word,

No.

A cinch to remember, though, 1521. The year of the bull and the worms.

He is gone. In my solitude I perceive, dimly, because all three lamps in the room contain twenty-five watters, that Nanny had padded hangers. This would have pleased Faye Dunaway playing Joan Crawford in *Mommie Dearest*. First thing in the morning I'll hie me to a store for light bulbs. He told me on the phone that Marion's old Volvo was at my disposal.

Sprays of wisteria on the wallpaper across the dormers, and two shelves of tattered *Reader's Digest*s. A nice piece of embroidered Irish linen in the dresser scarf, with lots of yellowed ivory objects on top of it. Mirror, comb, hairbrush, clothes brush, and, in a little crystal tray, nail file and scissors. Purple velvet pincushion containing pretty array of colored pearl hatpins. Antique blanket chest. Pewter frame containing 1928 picture of Nanny, forty and portly, holding the baby Professor after christening. Lo, a rosary in her chubby hand. Took it with her no doubt to the ceremony to ward off evil spirits in the infidel church. Old sachet of lavender in the top drawer.

And it's all quite fitting, really, the wisteria and lavender way up here in my spinster's aerie, because my heart is broken and my real, secret spirit is shattered. Oh, Lord, all I want is a room somewhere, far away from the cold night air, with one important chair. Which I'll mend up this evening, commendably, because I was, in my youth, all too well acquainted with the threadbare.

Four

I find, in the refrigerator, a package of sliced ham, six eggs, two blue rubber bands, three onions, a six-pack of Budweiser, fourteen packages of Celeste frozen pizza, a carton of sour cream, a half wheel of Vermont Cheddar, five twelve-ounce bags of Doritos Nacho Cheese Flavor Tortilla Chips, and a small white bottle of prescription eye medicine. The expiration date on the sour cream is August 27 and this is September 10. Nevertheless, we sit down to a gimcrack quiche. I apologize for it and promise something superb after I shop, but the two men offer cataclysms of compliments and dig in like pigs in swill.

We are gathered for dinner in the large dining room, and Professor Goddard has unaccountably held a chair for me and I sit, unaccountably, at the head of the table. There is, where my right foot touches the floor, a hole cut into the carpet. The knob of a bell protrudes. Wendell explains that it no longer works. In his father's youth, it was used to signal the kitchen at course-changing time. I look around the dining room smartly, having turned on the chandelier the better to see the pale, apple-green walls. And in this room in the not-too-distant past, someone has painted the woodwork a mushroom color in a soft, eggshell finish. But the baseboards are filthy and the windows are opaque with muck. There are four old Victorian plant stands stationed in each corner of the room, a dead Boston fern on each stand. The plants have molted little rings of dead leaves on the worn Chinese carpet.

And, finally, a chance to have a look at them. The Dad

36

is to my left. He is quite handsome, this elder Goddard, mid-fifties with nice eyes and full mouth. So important, the mouth, the shape of which speaks volumes. The full ones tend to come with generous natures, the thin ones tend to whine and frequently are afflicted with hardening of the emotional arteries. So I have observed. His hair is neatly barbered and is all white, too white for the unlined face. I think he is Jimmy Stewart with Spencer Tracy hair. I love it that he went and got a tie to wear to dinner. If I were Peg, I'd lean over and have a quick feel of the shirt-stuff. Is it lawn, or is it Sea Island cotton, I wonder. The best. This fellow resides, as Kevin would say, on Quality Street.

Professor Goddard now tells me that when the kitchen disposal goes on the blink all I have to do is push forcibly against one of the blades with a broom, upended into the cavity of the sink, and the handle will serve to dislodge whatever was lodged. Wendell tells me, with his eyes, that he is a compendium of tolerance for this sort of conversational aberration which places the working of the garbage disposal ahead of the normal niceties. In this moment of silence I wonder if I dare comment on the large bandage that reaches from Wendell's right eyebrow into his hairline. I also ponder whether Goddard the elder has even noticed this bandage because he has not once in these five minutes looked at Wendell above the chest. He seems to be mesmerized by Wendell's T-shirt. It says:

Perish, or publish T-shirts.

Best not to make an inquiry, or they'll think me a pushy Boston broad.

Wendell is to my right and he, too, is unable to raise his eyes above his father's torso. Over six feet, both of them, two long drinks of water. But Wendell's length, at twenty-three, is leaner, more linear, more elastic in action. He's sewn a big red flannel patch over a rip in the crotch of his jeans. It looks like a codpiece from Brueghel's days. He caught me looking at it and I blushed, but Heavens, it's a great red bulge and what's he doing, anyway, advertising his privates in primary color? If Wendell ever smiles I think he will have dimples. There's evidence in the cheeks of little lines of levity. And the full mouth is the identical twin of the Elder's. But what a hairy ape he is, thickly auburn on the top and carrot red in the beard. And quite a lot of it, like henna down, on his arms.

If something doesn't interrupt this silence, I'll break out in shingles. Perhaps I'll trance a bit now, keep mum, and test their aptitude for the awkward. I see a third Goddard, in oil, directly in front of me as I gaze past this table which seats twelve comfortably, through the front hall, into the living room. He looks sterner than the two beside me. The founding father, I think. Kevin would place him in early eighteenth century. There's something smacking of trade about this one, not a diploma but a balance sheet rolled up under the arm. I'll write Kev and tell him the founding father answered the clarion call of commerce.

Wendell's table manners are atrocious. He leaves his spoon in his coffee cup and when he drinks I fear he risks the loss of an eye. And when he licks his knife I fear a gash in his tongue. And when he wets his finger and runs it in a circle around the plate, to lift the crumbs, our four eyes avert and the Elder and I concentrate on the distant founding father. I wonder at the incongruity of the unrefined boy and the impeccable father. I wonder if Wendell has never been taught, or if this brazen display is a performance for me. To show me that he is above and beyond the call of common courtesy. This behavior proclaims loudly:

"*I pay no heed.*"

Fix that soon. Get in there with a heavy Irish hand and say, Lad, while you pay no heed onlookers experience waves of nausea and find themselves unable to look on any longer. And now I refer to the bandage. A small, humble cough as preface.

"Wendell, that looks rather serious. Have you seen a doctor?"

"Yes, yesterday. Eight stitches in all."

"Oh, dear. I'm sorry."

The Elder's lovely mouth turns grim now. He really shouldn't do that; it ages him ten years. He folds his napkin, meticulously, on the table.

"Wendell, would you like to explain?"

Wendell, stifling a yawn, replies,

"No, I don't think so."

"Well, Emma—I'll call you Emma if I may—the night before last, Wendell got hold of some cocaine. After that he drank a pint of vodka. As I understand it, he was afraid to come home in that condition. So he crawled up into a large Salvation Army container, located at a shopping mall out on Dixwell Avenue. He intended to spend the night there, and sleep it off. Then, shortly after dawn, some suburban woman drove up to the bin and threw, actually heaved, a large broken toaster down the chute. It descended at some velocity, leaving a gash in Wendell's head. It required a trip to the emergency room at Grace New Haven Hospital."

Wendell interrupts.

"The staff knows me well down there. They welcome me with open arms. Be forewarned, Emma. They have a hot-line to our number."

Traces of irony ran rampant through this story and I kept expecting smiles to burgeon. Underlining it all, however, was something singularly parental on the part of Richard Goddard. Some mixture of disapproval, despair and guilt. There was rebuke in the slight shaking of the head, but in the despair there was something more subtle. Chagrin, and a concern that I might blame the father, censure *him* for the son's cocaine, vodka, and stitches. At the same time, a

startling hint of inclination—willingness—to take the blame.
Mea culpa. Finally, looking directly at Wendell, he aban-
dons his attempt to conceal his utter disconsolation. His
eyes are forlorn, Wendell's are hostile, and I can not begin
to fathom the pages of their history. I feel only the rift, the
chasm, the unpardonability of the offenses they have apparently inflicted on each other. The Elder rises, turns his
fork over so that the tines face down on his plate, and his
mouth grows even tighter.

"Emma? May I see you in my study in an hour? I
promise you a happier experience than this."

He walks out of the dining room and turns right, into the
hall, headed for his study. Wendell looks decidedly glum,
and here we are with the terrible silence again. He brought
a book with him to the table, rather like a safety blanket,
and now he turns it over. It is John Berryman's *Homage to
Mistress Bradstreet*. He bites the knuckle on his index
finger and stares at the tablecloth.

"Do you know why he does that?"

"What?"

"Turns the fork tines down."

"No."

"That's what they did at the turn of the century, to
alert the servants that the plate could be cleared. He
can't break the habit. Also, the hospital is called Yale
New Haven. It hasn't been called Grace New Haven
for twenty years."

I'll remember that. Delete grace from the vocabulary. A
cinch for a fallen Catholic long gone from the fold.

"He's a physicist. Ever know one?"

"No, I don't think so."

He pushes *Mistress Bradstreet* aside and stretches in his chair.

"There are two kinds of physicists extant. Theoretical and experimental. Both are the scourge of the earth, but experimental is to be preferred. As luck would have it, old Dickie's theoretical."

Wendell doesn't talk like your average twenty-three-year-old.

"Basically, theoretical physicists decide early on that the best way to hold life at bay is to confine oneself to equations on paper. Experimental physicists have to actually mess around with the vagaries of laboratories and engineers and mechanisms and instrumentation. That is, *matter*. Theoretical physicists need only their brains, their desks, their paper, and their solitude. Have you noticed the four dead ferns?"

"Yes."

"My mother's been dead for a year and he can't bring himself to throw them out. You'd be mistaken if you think this is due to grief. Sorely mistaken. You see, there'd be, in throwing them out, a mandate to replace them. You'd have to measure the diameter of the stands and then go out to the nursery on Whitney and then, of course, you'd be encumbered with the responsibility of caring for something *live* in the house. Dreaded matter. And old Dickie never was any good at that."

He rises, and squashes his napkin into his water glass.

"Oh, Emma Riley, you walk in groves of mystery. I would like to know what has hurt you, and why you're so crusty, and why you're so young, and what disasters brought you to these troubled portals. But I hope you won't give me the chance. This is not a house that live things survive in. When you go to his study, tell him you've changed your mind.''

"Wendell, if you hate it so much here, why do you stay?''

"Economics. The usual reason that people are found in untenable places.''

He picks up his book and bends low, as if to bow out, but, Mercy, I think he's going to kiss me! He butts his lips against my ear and whispers:

"Don't ship with Ahab.''

Five

Two brandy snifters sit on a small black Chinese table alongside a bottle of Grand Marnier. The collection of porcelain bulldogs is, unfortunately, in direct view. I've always thought the bulldog somehow arrested in its evolution. It waits in a time warp on little stunted legs for another millennium to pass. They say cat faces attract because the eyes are so luminous and large, disproportionate, dominating the face. That must be why the bulldog face is so hideous. The repulsive little eyes are beady, for all of their hyperthyroid bulge, and the snout dominates the face. Truly, this dog would reside more naturally in a sty.

Row upon row of green, soft-backed journals before me. Decades of American Physical Society issue. And: *Fabulous Isotopes, Elementary Particles, Calculator Calculus, Basic Optics, The Laws of Physics, The Arhitecture of Molecules, The Evolution of Scientific Thought, The Theory of General Relativity.* I might have a gander at *Einstein's Universe* one day. It has a humane, universal look about it. But I think *Surprises in Theoretical Physics* would best be avoided. "Include me out," said Samuel Goldwyn.

Relaxed, here in the bookish sanctuary, tension gone from the neck, tie-knot loosened, collar askew displaying sexy Adam's apple, he pours a bit of the Marnier and says that his grandfather thought it took a lot of loving to make a house a home. His father said it took a lot of money to make a house a home. And now he has come to the somewhat confessional conclusion that it simply takes a woman to make a house a home.

I wonder if he'd let me cadge a cup of this stuff some-time to make Michael's pièce de résistance of desserts? You sauté crêpes, thin as razor blades, and then you roll them around strawberries and whipped cream enhanced with a tinge of kirsch, and then you pour Marnier over the whole works and set it afire. This is especially dramatic in darkened rooms, of which the Goddard house boasts an abundance. We will do this some evening when Wendell's offensive bandage has gone to the trash.

"Isn't this nice?" he says. "Just a hint of orange."

Does he think I don't know from Grand Marnier? Oh, dear. Familiar, irksome chip on my shoulder. My hus-band, after all, was a Harvard dropout, the sixth-generation scion of a family that went swiftly and profitably from livery stables to used car lots; a man whose family incul-cated at an early age the lasting theory that the best things in life are, in fact, very expensive. Having been exposed to taste and discernment over a fourteen-year period, I sit here the very embodiment, sir, of the process of osmosis.

"Well, Emma, do you think you want to try it?"

I'm prepared to make a six-month commitment to his employ—longer if I'm able to successfully straddle the apparent breach between the two men. If I don't mind his asking, he would like to know what brought me here.

"I needed to leave Boston. I needed some time to lick some wounds."

The dicey moment has arrived, the predictable predica-ment. What tack to take? Should I send out the protective emissary to explain the failed marriage? Should I adopt Michael's flippant, faggot facade and talk of fruits, pansys and nancys, assuring myself by doing so a safe encamp-ment on Professor Goddard's heterosexual turf? They are usually more comfortable with that approach. Just two straights sitting here in the autumnal twilight aligning ourselves in our righteousness against that dark and tawdry world, against the love that dares not speak its name. And there'll be all those lofty, genteel undercurrents, the kind that exist when well-bred WASPs gather to talk about the Jews. But he does seem remarkably accessible. Perhaps I will risk emitting, *stingily* emitting, certain elements of the truth.

"When I was nineteen years old I was working as a typist at Collison Chemical, in Boston. A friend took me to the first play I'd ever seen. It was in Cambridge, at the Buskin Theatre. It was *Camino Real*, by Tennessee Williams."

"Ah, yes. I noted his death a while ago. I read somewhere that he said, one time, 'Hell is yourself.' I thought that quite profound."

Oh, God, do I dare allow myself to think, for just this fleeting moment, that he's a kindred spirit with reservoirs of angst as deep as mine?

"Michael Riley was playing the character called Kilroy. He was very handsome and very talented and very masculine. He was a sophomore at Harvard at the time."

"Really?"

Sir, I observe that your face is the Dow. And my stock has climbed a point.

"I joined the Buskin as a property girl on the technical crew. A year later, we got married. We divorced this year because Michael finally lost his long battle against homosexuality."

"Oh? Oh, my."

"When I met him he'd only had one such encounter, at a boarding school in Rhode Island. But it was

latent, and the waging of the battle began to cost each
of us, dearly. He wanted a baby and I refused. He
became very sour and cynical. And I became a shrew.
And finally, the new artistic director, Daniel Graham,
fell in love with Michael. That was when I filed the
petition and withdrew.''

Quietly, sir, like Sandburg's fog. On little cat feet, reeling
back stoically on silent haunches.

''It must have been quite tawdry.''

''Yes. Quite.''

''How did he actually, I mean, *tell* you?''

''Well, it was a steamy June evening when the heat,
you know, was a hex. We'd finished a vichyssoise
and cold salmon with anchovy sauce, and I was scraping plates in the kitchen. He came in and leaned
against the counter and there was something very taut
in his manner. He avoided looking at me and he said,

> 'Strange fits of passion have I known
> And I will dare to tell.'

And then he told. And he cried. And we went to bed
and I just held his whimpering body all night long.''

''Is that Shelley? 'Strange fits of—' ''

''Wordsworth.''

''Ah, yes. Loved his sister.''

''Yes. Like Byron.''

Your facial Dow, sir, clambers in its ascendancy.

''Do you still love him?''

"I love the *idea* of him. And I'm trying not to love
the sadness that he's left in me. I think self-pity is
loving one's sadness."

"You say that you 'withdrew'?"

Yes, I did. With consummate grace, which, as my old dad
would tell you, is a commodity in very short supply. Lo, his
mouth turns old again. He is steeling himself for something.

"I guess that's what we really have to talk about.
May I assume that you continue, then, in a withdrawn
state?"

"Oh, if you mean do I live in a state of gloom, not at
all. I've mounted quite an offensive, you see, I mean,
just being here. Just—continuing, you know, is proof
of that."

I mean, sir, there was a tendency for a while to become
another statistic. To follow those ladies who simply sub-
merge themselves in the Charles.
He rises, goes to a window, and pulls a cord which
draws a drapery. He stands, preoccupied, fiddling with the
wooden knob.

"It's such a chore, isn't it? Fending off sadness. It
takes so much energy. I know from experience how
difficult it is, so you certainly have my sympathy. I
think you'll find quite an assortment of diversions in
New Haven. Do you like museums?"

"All but the natural history kind. When I was a kid
my dad hauled me around to see endless stuffed
Kodiaks and gnus. I do like looking at art, if it isn't
too modern."

"Well, we're not quite up to Boston in that regard.
But we do have the Yale Gallery, and the Center for
British Art. I'd be happy to introduce you to them."

"Thank you very much."

He returns to his chair, emitting a slight groan. He suddenly seems exercised.

"What we really have to talk about, I guess, are our
mutual expectations. I'm very bad at handling these
matters with the . . . help. My wife Marion was
worse, and it's always been left to me, and I just
don't have the tools. I mean, I hack and fray where I
should cleave. So I ask for your patience. The thing
is, you're a surprise. I hadn't bargained for such a
young woman. I must ask, will be looking for a
husband in New Haven?"

"No, sir. Not actively looking."

"Well, I'm glad to hear that. I'm afraid I'm sending
you rather mixed messages. The thing is, I do want
you to enjoy yourself, and you'll find me very lenient
about hours and all that. On the other hand, I'm very
anxious to promote as much of a family atmosphere
as I can. We've never had that in the house, which
you'll come to understand as time goes on. Wendell
needs it desperately and I'm very conscious that this,
right now, is my last chance with Wendell. Do you
see what I mean? My last chance with my son."

Actually, I don't see. The boy is twenty-three, their
pages are unfathomable, their offenses have been laid in
there like layers in an onion. If I'm being asked to eradicate the past, if some burden of compensation is now laid
on *me*, I ought to hie myself the hell out of here. I'm
distressed that he's transformed so quickly to The Boss.
I've been too open, tarried too long displaying too much of
my bleeding heart.

"So. I guess I'd like it understood that on no occasion are you to entertain men at this house."

The plural, sir? Heavens.

"And on no occasion are you to drink my liquor."

Dare I swallow this, or should I spew it out?

"Also, although uniforms certainly aren't required, I would appreciate it if you wouldn't wear excessive amounts of jewelry or perfume. And, of course, I expect you to confine your social life to Thursdays, your day off."

"Is there a curfew, on Thursdays?"

"Of course not. I mean, within reason."

I think, privately, we both regret the sudden swerve of this interview. He feels obliged to set his guidelines—experience, trial and error, have taught him that it's prudent to begin on the right footing. And I feel obliged to indicate that he's gauged me incorrectly. I am a woman of some substance, and these jewelry, perfume, and promiscuity warnings are a lot of crap that doesn't apply. I send him this indication by contemplating my ankles while my sensitivity emanates from every pore. I see, in an obscure corner behind my chair, a set of volumes quite unlike the others. They have been relegated to a shelf of oblivion, and are beyond the ken of the room. There must be some fond connection, some mental tie that prevents them from being boxed and removed to the attic. Huxley, Nin, William Blake. *The Young Shelley, Shelley and His Friends in Italy, Aspects of Shelley's Poetic Imagery. Desire and Restraint in Shelley, The Last Days of Percy Bysshe Shelley.*

"May I be excused?"

"Certainly. And thank you for your patience."

As I pass him he touches my arm, to stop me. I halt and look at him but he is looking down at his mismatched socks.

"Miss Riley. Emma."

His hand slides down to hold mine. We are both startled at the contact, the actual touching of flesh, and we quickly drop our hands to our sides, standing stiffly then, like stick-men.

"It occurs to me that all three of us are looking for a new departure. You're looking for a second chance in life and I'm looking for one with Wendell. His mother died a year ago, in July, right after he graduated from Yale. He took off for Berkeley immediately, without so much as a goodbye. He returned last spring without so much as a hello. He says he returned because he was broke, but I think he's looking for a second chance with me. In all honesty I have to admit I have no evidence of that. I have only the reality that he returned, that he's here. So if, as time goes on, you find any opportunity to promote a family atmosphere, I'd appreciate it very much."

I close the study door and there stands Wendell, gloating against the hall banister. He wears a look so self-satisfied, I'd like to smack him one upside his bandaged head.

"Wanna go for a beer?"

I don't answer. I'm anxious to mount the stairs and reach the safety of my aerie. He grabs me by the shoulder.

"I said—"

"I heard you. Are you crazy?"

"Probably. It's hereditary. Listen, I had the ear at the keyhole for a minute. Heard the stuff about excessive perfume. He's damn tricky, Dickie is. Lures you in on one pretense or another and then, zap. Goes for the jugular."

"He's the boss. It's his right to have rules and regulations. And, Wendell, I wish you wouldn't refer to him as Dickie in front of me. I believe in all that old stuff about honoring thy father and thy mother."

His mouth gapes and his eyes are incredulous.

"You can't be serious."

I hurry up the stairs, toward the darkened landing. It's hard enough to navigate this route sober, and the Marnier has addled the brain. As I reach the second floor, Wendell hollers up:

"Hey, you got any plans for next Thursday? I'd like to show you the town."

As I reach the third floor, he hollers up again:

"Hey, am I ever gonna meet this Michael guy? He sounds OK."

Six

A troubled night, because the boy is unmanageable. A Vesuvius of a person, this Wendell, severely severed from reality. Anger seething in the eyes and fury in the long, lean limbs. Somewhere along the line all this resentment might have been checked. But I am guilty here of perspective; the almighty "might." Still, there's something very appealing, naughty and rambunctious and puppylike. And a vast yearning in the blue eyes. I think not just for attention and approval, but also for something larger. An ambition to make a mark, to leap out of the passing parade, the humdrum chorus, and sing a glorious solo. If I'm wrong, there's no hope. If I'm wrong, he is none of the above. He is merely a pain in the ass.

I sit at the kitchen table attempting to eat a soft-boiled egg out of its shell. Not an egg cup in the place and I've never been able to enjoy my morning ova in a dish. Peg started me on this habit three decades ago; one egg every morning propped in a pretty china cup brought from Ireland. When I married she donated two of her egg cups to my sadly deficient trousseau. I should have brought one of them so as not to burn the fingers and have hot yolk caking on the cuticle of my thumb.

There's a bird feeder hanging outside the window, and several blue jays have gathered there, under the acrylic dome, looking for breakfast. But the feeder is as empty as the kitchen shelves. My concern at the moment is the dictum about excessive perfume. The only soap in the third-floor shower was an old, cracked bar of Yardley. The scent was sandalwood, and strong, and after the shower I used a deodorant that seemed innocuous enough in Boston, but now seems rife with narcissus. The combination might prove too much for the Professor. He'll take one whiff and think I'm:

Belle, from the Bordello.

He has already refused breakfast. When I passed his room he opened the door and said he'd skip it. I wonder if he is one of those who don't care about breakfast in particular or food in general. That class of people who take no cognizance of mealtimes, who take no pleasure in the victuals they consume, who consider the bounty they receive no more than a fuel injection—that rum lot has always been highly suspect to me. He jangles in, dangling keys which he hands to me, explaining these are house keys and the two silver ones are for Marion's old Volvo. When I ask just how old Marion's Volvo is, he talks at length about the engineering marvels executed in Swedish car factories. He's nervous: beads of sweat gather on his brow.

"You need an egg cup."

"Yes. It was stupid of me not to bring one from home."

"I went to bed last night very upset about our interview. You talked of your life most candidly and I'd have liked to do the same, but I was evasive. I skirted the truth because I wanted you to think well of me. The thing is, I've failed my son miserably."

He lays the sentence out like that, flat, without wrinkles or folds, without any texture in which to hide inner meanings. I wait for a connecting word to modify the blunt edge of the harsh fact. I failed my son, because. I failed my son, unknowingly. Due to circumstances beyond my control there were occasional lapses in the rearing of my son which cause me deep regret.

"My wife was mentally ill for years, seriously so at the end. I made the decision to keep her here because she was quite harmless, until the end. And, of course, because Wendell loved her. Most outsiders thought it was a bad decision; certainly the doctors thought so. It seemed to me at the time a humane decision, but at the time I couldn't, of course, calculate the fallout.

"There was no marriage, just a sort of housing arrangement. And I was never able to span the gap. I mean, I was never able to reach across this sort of *mental* divorce and touch Wendell. And as a child he had no real understanding of her strangeness, her illness. But he did intuit that we had divorced ourselves, mentally, that I buried myself in my work. So he resented me, and clammed up and didn't in fact *want* me to touch him. That was the impression he gave. What I wanted to say yesterday was that Marion's death was a relief. It's a cruel thing to say and I knew if I said it you wouldn't think well of me.

"At any rate, there's a dreadful rift between us, resulting in a very angry young man. We ignored each other too successfully for too many years. Now, with Marion gone, it seemed to me I might have a chance at spanning the gap. I thought a new woman in the house would provide not only order, but a buffer. You're a most appealing young lady, and I think you'll do just fine."

It is now his turn to feel overly exposed. He checks both his watch and the wall clock. He wants to terminate the subject.

"I'm sorry to say you're bound to find him a handful. If it becomes too difficult, let me know and I'll try to

assist. To my knowledge he has respect and regard
for only one person. Lydia, our cleaning lady. Now.''

He reaches into his shirt pocket and brings out a small
piece of paper. He refers to it, and I see that there is an
agenda.

"Now. In the last four years, Wendell has totalled
three cars. The insurance payments became astronom-
ical. For instance, just to make the point, the monthly
installments would very nicely cover your salary. So I
have had to deny him his own car. It's a reluctant
denial, but there you are.''

Here I am, and I sympathize. And if we were two
different people in a different geography, and your brow
furrowed thus deeply, I would give you a pat, and possibly
a hug. As it is, however, I am still smarting slightly from
last night's guidelines. I hope you note a small innuendo
of compassion in these, my silent thoughts.

"This leaves him, of course, housebound. He's got
the hang of the public transportation during the week,
but the weekends are a problem.''

The beads of sweat appear again; there's a flush of
blood across the face and a furtive glance at the agenda.
He's out of sequence with this mention the weekends; he
flounders a moment, needing to mend his fences.

"Now. Regarding the weekends. I have a lady friend
in New York. I go to see her most weekends. Her
name is Ariadne Marchant. She may call. Wendell
also has a lady friend, an artist at school, at Bennington. He frequently goes to visit her, on the weekends.
Her name is Monica Dunstan. So you see, you'll
nearly always have peace and quiet to look forward to
on the weekends.

"But as I was saying, the weekends are a problem,
regarding the Volvo. And Wendell's trysts at Ben-

nington. I've given him a set of keys but, unfortunately, when he does go, *you'll* be housebound. I don't know how to get around it. I just can't buy him another car.''

''I'll be fine. There's always, as you say, the public transportation.''

''Yes. Thank you so much.''

He puts the agenda back into his pocket; he gives me two hundred dollars in cash to replenish the larder, and then climbs into his Peugeot.

An unexpected wave rushing, spreading over and across me. Loneliness. What brought on this sinking feeling of abject disconnection? It's the kitchen. OPKs, Peg called them. Other People's Kitchens. This one will never be mine. These cups, saucers, plates and platters speak to me in a foreign tongue. I'll adjust to them, of course, with passing meals and seasons. And there's a certain challenge inherent in this brioche tin. Turn my hand to that one day. Whip up something golden, puffy, *aerated*. And this fluted copper mold. Get in some Knox gelatin and do something spectacularly *visual*. Don't cook, Michael said, *create*. It's a matter of acquaintance. It'll all be second nature, eventually. Knowing there are four of this and six of that, champagne glasses for twelve, a fine array of finger bowls, three cream pitchers with no matching sugar bowls. Tough on sugar bowls, this family. Tough on tureen lids, too. But the problem isn't OPKs. That's not what's causing the tug at the heartstrings. It's the china and utensils left behind. Stored in Peg's attic in Florida orange cartons lugged free from the supermarket on the same day that I lugged dead Bitsy. Egg cups covered with shamrocks, a lovely French soufflé dish Michael found on sale at Jordan Marsh, eight lemon-yellow glasses Peg collected at the movies long before my birth, and at least thirty pale green pressed-glass salad plates Peg collected out of soap boxes. She used a lot of soap and I recall her now in front of the large, deep sink, behind her ironing board. I recall the obsolete brands of my extreme youth. "Dreft" was one, and wasn't "Duz" the other? "A little Duz'll do it." Altogether, the dishes were *mine*. They made their entrance into my apartment, they were baptized in my sink, they found a home on my shelves. They confirmed for me my right to be there. Richard is off now, physicking. God, yes. Fending off sadness is such a chore!

I'm anxious to get to the store but I'd like to establish a daily pattern with Wendell. He is, however, daunting. He clearly places himself out-of-bounds in his room, and emerges at his own times, on his own terms. I resolve to knock on the door and say good morning. He opens it, four inches.

"I keep it double bolted. What do you want?"

"I just wanted to say good morning before I leave for the market."

"You can't come in here, ever. This room is not to be aired or cleaned. Even Lydia, whom I trust, is *verboten*."

"But it must need, now and then, a quick pass with the Hoover."

"It has no such need."

Dirty laundry is strewn everywhere, among books and papers. A pair of pale-blue jockey briefs hang on the bedside lampshade. And the old, gymnasium smell of sneakers wafts out to the landing.

"I write poetry in here. My mother thought my scribblings internalized, insipid stuff. I tell you that because my mother, when well, was my loyal ally. So you can understand why Dickie, that is, my honored father, is not allowed a glimpse."

He smiles, just in the nick of time. It redeems him.

"The crushing blow was delivered two months ago.
The last time Lydia vacuumed. She sat at lunch,
eating her Colombo banana-strawberry yogurt—you
must always have that in for Lydia, by the way—and
she said the graffiti on her alley wall had more balls
than anything she'd ever read in my room. Now, we
must take into account that even though Lydia doesn't
know much about art, she does know what she likes.
And she likes me. And I like her. And so, to preserve
our meaningful relationship, she no longer has access
to my work. You will find that I am an *acutely
sensitive* person, frequently given to tantrums."

"What is that? A warning, or a pledge?"

"A fact. Let's go out for a beer."

"No, Wendell."

"What are you doing Thursday?"

"Please, Wendell."

"I heard the third-floor plumbing when you showered. It's nice to wake up that way, thinking of a
naked lady in a stall."

"Mercy."

"Jesus Christ, I have to ask, where did you get those
eyes?"

"From my mother, Margaret."

"Can I meet her? I bet I'd like her, too. So listen,
what about Thursday?"

"Surely you realize, Wendell, that if we went for a
beer, if we went anywhere together on Thursday,
your father would fire me on the spot."

"No, he wouldn't. He's been wanting a keeper for me, forever. To relieve *him* of the responsibility."

"You're too old to need a keeper. And you must not persist with this. It embarrasses me, and I don't know how to respond, because I'm in your employ. Also, please stop touching me. I am thirty-five years old and this sort of flirting is ludicrous. Really. I never imagined this would happen."

"Neither did I. But am *I* responsible because you inherited Margaret's gorgeous peepers?"

I'd best nip this in the bud, authoritatively.

"Are you responsible for *anything*? Do you ever even *attempt* to behave responsibly?"

"That's it, kid."

His face turns livid. He slams his door and I hear the bolts turning.

"Wendell, please, this is infantile!"

He shouts, from the depths of his room.

"Listen, fuck-face, you wanna make judgments, walk a mile in my shoes sometime!"

I hear things being shuffled, moved, kicked and thrown.

"I'm getting the fuck out of this fucking mausoleum! I'm going to Vermont."

"To see Monica?"

"Right! Up to Bennington for my fucking bi-monthly Monica fuck!"

I bang on the door.

"Wendell? *Wendell?*"

"*What?*"

"You mustn't talk to me that way."

"Then don't fuck with me, lady! Stay offa my fucking back!"

The door flies open and he whips past me, carrying a duffel bag.

"Tell the Dick he'll see me when he sees me."

I stand, stunned, as I hear him flail out the back door. It is only when the motor starts that I realize he's taking Marion's old Volvo. I dash out the front door and stand in the middle of the driveway, whirling my limbs like a windmill.

"You can't *do* this! I've got to haul groceries!"

He screeches past, directly onto St. Ronan, without stopping. But in a brief flash I saw that he was crying. Dear God, I mustn't chance another reprimand with Wendell. I had no alternative because I'd let the thing advance too far. He had slid his hand up, under my skirt.

I went into the house and called a cab, and asked if that nice man, Joe Gagliano, was on duty. Joe agreed to sit outside the Whitneyville Food Center and wait with the meter off. He was also a font of previously hidden information.

"So. The Volvo's down again."

"How do you know about the Volvo?"

"Oh, I used to drive Mrs. Goddard to the New Haven Lawn Club when she was healthy and the car was

down. She wasn't healthy the last few years. Sad
lady. Very thin and very nervous.''

"Why didn't you tell me that you knew her?"

"Oh, I wanted you to start off straight."

"What do you know about the professor?"

"Never driven him. But his son says he's unknowable."

"That's not true. So you've driven Wendell, too?"

"Only when the Volvo's down."

I push a heavily laden cart around the market and notice
a strange agitation, deep within, surfacing. Who is Ariadne
Marchant when she's at home? And what kind of phony,
trumped-up name is Ariadne? Came across it only once
before, in Bernard Shaw's *Heartbreak House*. Questioning
Michael, he said all he knew about the original Ariadne
was that she had fooled around with a couple of establish-
ment Greeks, several thousand years B.C. I wanted to do
some sleuthing in that regard with Wendell, but now he's
gone up to Bennington for his fucking bi-monthly Monica
fuck. In the meantime I must buy Colombo banana-
strawberry yogurt for Lydia, who arrives tomorrow. Some
birdseed for the jays and finches. Some G.E. hundred-
watters to eradicate the dusky dim that stalks the Goddard
house at witching hour. And if I ever do get my hands on
the Volvo, I'll go out to the nursery and replace the four
dead dining-room ferns.

Ariadne. Such an interesting thing, this business of
names. An appellation at birth, a designation for life. I
never knew a Sally who could be taken truly seriously, but all Sheilas and Charlottes have been im-
mensely kind. My favorite names always begin with
M, although I'm presently having my doubts about
Marion. I knew a sweet Melissa once and a blonde

Miranda as pale and beauteous as any Botticelli. After
playing with one, I wanted Marionette. After wearing
it, Madras. And Kevin would say,

"I'd like you to meet my daughter, Madras Shea."

At nineteen I actually scrounged up fifty dollars to
legally change my name to Mona. But it was insuffi-
cient without Lisa and that was just silly—sillier than
Sally—so I reconsidered. I gave up all but one of
these flights of fancy when I married. *Mirabile dictu*
haunts me relentlessly. "Wonderful to relate." For
years, in class at roll call, I imagined Sister Helene
calling out:

"Miss Mirabile Dictu?"

And I would reply:

"Here!"

Monica Dunstan, Wendell's girl, seems possible. But
Ariadne is an aggrandized name. An appelation smacking
of advantage, or rank. Or as Michael, the sometime social-
ist would say, rank advantage.

Seven

"What? He took the Volvo to Bennington?"

"Yes, I'm afraid he did."

"On a *Monday?*"

"I'm afraid so."

"And you shopped with a taxi?"

"Yes."

"This is unconscionable."

"I'm afraid I'm to blame. I got angry with him."

"Do I smell baked ham?"

"Yes. And scalloped potatoes."

"Why did you get angry with him?"

"I felt I had cause. I felt his manner was a little too . . . familiar."

"I hope you mean verbally."

"Just a little . . . fresh, Dr. Goddard."

"Please, call me Richard."

"It was all about his room, and my suggestion that it be cleaned, and it went from there to talk of responsibility. I suggested that he was somewhat irresponsible, and that sent him into a rage."

"Good! You were absolutely right, and I think you handled the situation superbly. But he doesn't usually go all the way to Bennington."

"Well, he went to see Monica."

"Did he say why?"

"No."

Lying through my teeth, and not understanding why I'm protecting Wendell when his hand was on my thigh and the boy was practically rutting. And he was humming bits and pieces of that old song that starts, "Jeepers Creepers, where'd you get those peepers?" I shan't tell you, Richard, that when he left he was crying, and I thought I detected traces of the emotionally battered child.

"This looks sumptuous. What a joy to come home to a hot meal. You'll join me, of course?"

"Well . . ."

"Nonsense. I'm not going to eat alone in that dining room."

I've been assuming that, after the first night's display of democracy, I'd be consigned to the kitchen for meals. In reality, the kitchen is a very pleasant room, bright and comfortable and spacious, and there is a butler's pantry between the kitchen and the dining room. Already, I've come to think of the pantry as a little oasis of Baccarat and

Royal Doulton that separated me from the whims and wiles of my employers.

Again, I sit awkwardly where he places me, at the head of the table, and with just the two of us alone spontaneous talk is a problem. What I know about physics you could put in a thimble. The very word called to mind the old English "physick," still prominent in restored seventeenth-century Massachusetts apothecary shops. I thought, until I reached high school, that physick was a purgative, something that gave you cramps and sent you to the bathroom. Wendell, no doubt, would agree. Still, I venture:

"How was your day?"

Richard is chairman of the Physics Department at Yale. He says, without enthusiasm, that he is one-quarter physicist these days and three-quarters administrator. He has spent the entire morning on the phone to the Department of Defense, in Washington, hereafter referred to as D.O.D. He was trying to get research contracts to support two of his department's Ph.D. candidates. He went to lunch at Jonathan Edwards, his old college. Because his Director of Graduate Studies was ill that day, Richard had to pitch in and take the man's appointments. So he spent the afternoon trying to convince a Mr. Coomaraswamy, an Indian student who wanted to pursue a doctorate at Yale, that a 1978 Master's degree from Bombay would not facilitate his entrance into graduate school. The experience depressed him. The skimpy diploma was creased and soiled and was, Richard feared, forged. The man smelled of curry, spoke very little English, was utterly confused, and all the while a beautiful woman in a turquoise sari sat in the outer office with two howling infants. I listened attentively because I thought he simply sat in a quiet, darkened room with reams of paper and juggled equations around until they all jibed. Something like checking your subtraction by adding your answer to the number you were deducting in the first place. I wondered if the Coomaraswamys had friends in New Haven—if they had a place to sleep this night.

"Did knee call, by any chance?"

"I beg your pardon?"

"Miss Marchant. Ariadne."

Ah, so it's Knee. As in cap, or water on. An opportunity to sleuth.

"Not while I was here, but I spent two hours at the market. Does Miss Marchant work in New York?"

Knee doesn't really work. She had the good fortune to be born the daughter of Jason Marchant of Marchant, North Carolina. Jason sold his cotton mills to Burlington in 1960 for ten million. Richard looks at me, wanting a reaction, wanting me to share, somehow, the Marchants' good fortune.

"Goodness, what a nice piece of change."

"Yes, wasn't it? Knee had made a very bad marriage in 1958, to a sailor stationed at Newport News, Virginia. The whole family wanted to get rid of the scoundrel but, of course, with that Burlington sale, he asked for the moon."

Well, if she was approximately twenty when she married in 1958, I quickly calculate she must be forty-six at present. No spring chicken.

"Jason bought her out of the marriage. It's a mystery why she never married again. Of course, she's economically solid, and she's obsessed with her mobiles."

Knee has bought herself an art gallery in SoHo. It is there that she displays her handmade mobiles. She travels the world looking for exotic marine seashells on exotic beaches and then she comes home to Park Avenue and waxes them, and varnishes them, and combines them into what *Time* magazine called, in November 1981, the Singular Marchant Mobiles. They are the Thing To Have on the Upper East Side.

He says it's quite interesting, really, once you get into it. Basically, there are two kinds of seashells: univalve and bivalve. All the bivalve shells have two distinct sides with a valve on each. These would be our clams and mussels and scallops. Knee collects mostly univalve—three categories specifically: whelks, spindles, and conches. These are the cone-shaped shells with an open aperture displaying shades of pink inside. Univalves have more mass and are easier to wire, for mobiles. Knee is a well-adjusted, happy woman of forty-eight.

Ah. Married, then, at twenty-two, pushing fifty presently, rich. A curse, I say, on the world's well-adjusted. In case you have the remotest interest, Richard, I think I hate her.

"How long have you known her?"

A frown. A slow, deliberate folding of the napkin as if practicing origami.

"I will tell you this, because if I don't, Wendell surely will. I have known her since before my wife died."

"I see."

I see. But I know that this sort of sentence carries a sentence. So I have observed. It's dropped lightly; it is mere words in his mouth, but such words always carry a penalty. Is Marion suing for damages from the grave? Is she agitating through Wendell, her earthly medium?

"I don't go to see Knee every weekend. The fact is, the weekends have almost been intolerable when it's Wendell and me, alone. We stayed home together this weekend, to greet you. There's a sort of unspoken agreement that if he's not going to Bennington, I will go to New York. And vice versa."

Well, what does that mean? The two women serve as no more than escape hatches?

> "I don't know what to do about Wendell's room. The door is double-locked against intruders who might read his poetry. He never asks my opinion of it because he knows that I had a great love affair with Shelley in my youth. I guess he thinks my poetic inclinations out of touch. He always asked his mother what she thought. But poor Marion, bless her, had a mind stuck securely in 1910. She grew up on James Whitcomb Riley. Do you know him?"

> "No."

No, I don't, and I share his name, and I suffer inordinate frustration when faced with these glaring omissions, when forced to admit ignorance. You, of course, are oblivious to all this and you will forge ahead blithely. You don't know that we, the fanatically curious but informally educated, are forever lacerating ourselves with F's. It is very wearing and very hard on the psyche and it sometimes hinders one's otherwise ebullient zest for life. But how could you even intuit these thoughts when they have undergone, in me, a lifetime of concealment:

> "Well, there's 'Little Orphant Annie,' and another called 'The Raggedy Man,' and then there's my favorite."

He leans back in his chair and lights a mid-dinner cigarette, which causes me uncontrolled craving. He smiles broadly and begins, blithely.

> "When the frost is on the punkin, and the
>   fodder's in the shock,
> And you hear the kyouck and gobble of the
>   struttin' turkey cock,
> And the clackin' of the guineys, and the
>   cluckin' of the hens.

And the rooster's hallylooyer as he tiptoes
   on the fence,
Oh, it's then's the times a feller is a-feelin'
   at his best,
With the risin' sun to greet him from a night
   of peaceful rest,
As he leaves the house, bare-headed, and goes out
   to feed the stock,
When the frost is on the punkin, and the fodder's
   in the shock.''

Mary, Mother of God, he is very nearly irresistible when he's enjoying himself. And how he loves to do dialect, especially the rooster's "hallyloo*yer*." Mary, Queen of our hearts, Mother so pure, why does this man have that obstreperous son, that defiant boy who bleeds color from his face and is a thorn embedded so injuriously in his side?

"Do you mind if I ask, what are these verminlike things in the salad?"

"Bean sprouts."

"Ah, yes. I suppose they're good for you?"

Suddenly we hear a car coming up the driveway on the opposite side of the house. Richard moves quickly to the back door, and then returns to the dining room.

"It's Wendell. Stay right where you are and finish your dinner. I'll do the same. In all probability he'll go right upstairs without a word."

"May I have a cigarette?"

"Certainly. Go ahead."

Wendell comes in and moves along the hall to the staircase. He stations himself in the dining room archway. He has taken off his bandage and there is dry, crusted blood along the toaster-gash. Facing us, he slouches and there is remorse in every muscle.

"I owe Emma an apology."

Leaning forward, with a tentative gesture, I invite him to join us. Richard pulls at my arm and pushes me down into my chair. He says,

"Go ahead, Wendell."

"Well, I was very rude to Emma this morning, and I've felt lousy about it all day. I wondered, actually, if she'd still be here."

"She is, as you see. Apparently there are secret strengths hidden in her small frame. It's good of you to volunteer an apology and we appreciate it. You didn't go to Bennington?"

"No."

"Where did you go?"

"Away."

"I see. Emma had to take a taxi to shop."

"Yes. I'm very sorry. I'd really like to make this up to Emma. I wonder, Dad, if it's OK with you, if I gave her a tour of the town on Thursday? Unless she has other plans for her day off."

"I think that's very nice, Wendell. I'm sure it would help her to get her bearings."

"I just wanted, you know, your permission."

"Thank you, Wendell. You have it."

I have remained silent throughout this apology, puffing fervently on Richard's brown Sherman cigarette. My fate for Thursday is sealed and Richard does not seem aware that he's been manipulated.

Wendell declines dinner, having just consumed two Big Macs, fries, and a chocolate milkshake. Richard goes directly to his study while I load the dishwasher and scrape the baked-on honey from the ham pan. I take down all the kitchen curtains and all the chiffons in the dining room, and load them into the washer for the morning laundry. Later, when I go to my room, I find a note under the door.

> We have a date for Thursday, kiddo, sanctioned by the master Dick. I promise to be a good boy. Sweet dreams.

Kevin, these Goddardian vicissitudes are complicated but not, I hope, insoluble. I've got my hands full and I'm fending off those double demons of doubt and defeat. I don't mean to imply hopelessness; I'm not without resources. I have all kinds of verbal and mental cutlery in my drawer, but I wonder if I have the sword to cut through this Gordian knot? Richard was so pleased that Wendell and I would have a tour together. Richard thinks Wendell is sowing seeds to promote family atmosphere. Best not dwell on this or sleep will never come.

And so I pull up the covers, snuggle down, and detach. Richard sits two floors below amidst his atoms, molecules, and bulldogs. It's possible that he and I might, at some simultaneous moment during this night, reflect on the four benighted Coomaraswamys, and the way they crossed our path and haunted us on this September day.

Eight

Lydia arrives at nine, carrying a brown canvas Channel 13 tote bag, which one of her employers must have given her. She also carries two one-gallon plastic containers. Richard, over scrambled eggs taken in the kitchen, has warned me of Lydia's idiosyncracies.

She believes that the city of New Haven provides good drinking water to St. Ronan, and bad drinking water to Howard Avenue, where she lives. She fills the old milk containers with good, St. Ronan drinking water before her son picks her up at four o'clock. She never wears black and doesn't perform very well if anyone in the house wears black in her presence. When Marion died, Richard saw that Lydia's winter coat was thin at the elbows and he offered her Marion's eight-year-old full-length Persian lamb coat. She refused it, because it was black. Something to do with ancestral voodoo, Richard said. The bane of her existence is a man who lives on the first floor of her apartment house. He raises snakes, professing that their urine is an aphrodisiac for impotent men. The potion apparently enjoys brisk sales among older men in the New York garment industry. However, he sometimes lets the snakes loose in the downstairs hallway, and when that occurs Lydia will not descend. She stays home, snakebound, and loses wages. Richard and Lydia have mounted a campaign to have the man evicted. But, groaned Richard, you wouldn't believe the red tape or the exigencies of race relations. Much as the entire building would like to be rid of the snake man, the other black tenants think Richard's endeavors somehow racist.

Lydia has luminous green eyes, and Richard says she
has a better knowledge of world history than Will and
Ariel Durant. Her expertise in this field is awesome,
but her specialty is war. She knows, for instance, every
move made by Dwight Eisenhower during World War
II. She appears to be about sixty. Her greeting to me
is pleasant, but she quickly heads for the solvents and
detergents under the sink. She does not take well to
interference.

"Lydia, we're practically sticking to this kitchen floor.
I don't know when it was washed last, but I'd appreciate it if you'd start in here."

Lydia pulls herself up to her full height, which is a corpu-
lent five foot ten inches.
"I doan bends," she says.
It's not that she can't bend. Her back, her haunches, and
her limbs are limber as a polecat's. It's just that in her long
and arduous life she has set a certain standard for her
domestic work. Getting down on hands and knees is a
degree of servitude she will not tolerate.

"How old you bees, Mizz Riley?"

"Thirty-five."

"Well, I din bends for Mizz Goddard, who was fifty
and sickly, and I doan bends for you."

"I see. Would you consider washing the windows in
the dining room?"

"Ohyez," she says. "Dey ain seen de rag in quite
some time."

There's a sponge mop in the broom closet, but it won't
make a dent in the filth on this floor. I recall that Peg
never got down on all fours without a sponge-rubber pad
for her knees. I've got a bucket of Spic and Span, a brush,

and a paring knife to lift the spots of accumulated and hardened muck, and I feel the sweat of hard labor trickling between my breasts. Wendell comes in and halts at the butler's pantry. He carries his *Mistress Bradstreet*. He's washed the blood from his scar.

"Good morning. I see that you bends."

"Yes."

"I'd like two eggs over easy, a slab of that ham, and a muffin with marmalade."

"Wendell, in your own parlance, fat fucking chance. Get out of here and come back at lunch."

"What's for lunch?"

"Colombo banana-strawberry yogurt, all around."

"Sounds good to me. Listen, I don't know where you stand on race, but you should know that I'm in love with Lydia. So if it turns out that you're one of those Irish nigger-baiters, you'll have to answer to me."

Best to ignore the lad when he's like this. He pads across the wet floor and gets a glass of orange juice from the refrigerator.

"Are you familiar with Virginia Woolf?"

"I know only that she was familiar with Vita Sackville-West."

"Shit, everybody knows that."

"I also know that if you've got five hundred a year and a room of your own, you probably have the wherewithal to hire another woman to wash the floor of your room."

"Cranky today. Not surprising. That gleam on your chest is making you hot under the collar. Actually, somewhere in Virginia Woolf she refers to a shop girl. She calls her the girl behind the counter. She says she would rather have that girl's true history than the one hundred and fiftieth life of Napoleon, or the seventieth study of Keats' use of Miltonic inversion."

"So?"

"So, I would like to have, Emma, the history of the girl on our kitchen floor."

"Wendell, let's make a deal. I'll tell you my history if you'll let me vacuum your room."

"No deal."

He turns on his barefoot heel and goes out to the back yard. There he reclines on a yellow chaise longue and rests one arm under his head. His hair turns bright copper in the sun. He would say to me if I were there:

"Emma, peel me a grape."

The only wax in the place is the old paste kind. I recall that Peg had a gizmo called a buffer. It was a pole connected to a heavy metal weight. You put an old towel under the weight and pushed the weight around the fresh wax until it shone. While I'm waiting for the wax to dry, and trying to conjure some reasonable facsimile of the gizmo to prevent sheer elbow grease, the front door chimes out the first three notes of Brahms' Lullaby.

"I ain gettin' dat," calls Lydia, standing on a dining room chair.

I have a visitor! This person has come to see *me*. She is Grace Serio, who is the live-in next door at the Silvermans'.

"As long as you know me," she says, "don't ever say anything bad about the Jews."

Mercy, everyone I meet today seems to think I have connections with the Klan.

Grace is about my height, but lean and wiry. She is thirty-two and has long black hair done up in thick French braids. She has heard about me, and is surprised that I am white and young and, she says after the briefest scrutiny, civilized. She says I have no obligation to be her friend, but she knows we have at least one thing in common. Thursday is our day off. When she sees what I am doing she makes a fast retreat to the Silvermans', and hauls back an electric buffing machine that weighs more than she does. I can't offer her a cup of tea until the wax dries, so the two of us retire to the living room.

Grace's relationship with the Silverman family is one to warm the cockles of the heart. When she was pregnant and unwed ("some high school quarterback called Dominic") at eighteen, the Silvermans took her in and trained her as a housemaid. She didn't train as a cook because she had already learned Milanese cuisine from her mother, the best cook down in Wooster Square. Grace, too, has a third-floor aerie, which she shares with her thirteen-year-old son, Raymond.

"Guess where Raymond goes to school?"

"Where?"

"Foote."

The Foote School is a private preparatory school on nearby Loomis Place. It has always been a reserve for the children of Yale faculty and the New Haven well-to-do. Tuition and books amount to five thousand a year.

"Emma, do you mind if I ask what you earn?"

"Six hundred a month. What do you earn?"

"The same, only really I earn what they pay post-docs at Yale. Because the Silvermans are putting Raymond through school."

The sun rises on Raymond, who looks like a Roman god, and sets on the Silvermans, who have a daughter at Radcliffe and a son at Oberlin. Grace once rammed her knee into the balls of a heckler in a bar because he called Professor Silverman a kike. And she caused one thirteen-year-old Bradford Wakefield, at Foote, to be censured with a month of detentions because he called Raymond "a bastard Wop." It is interesting that whole months can pass without racial slurs falling on one's ears and then, bingo, here's a day plum full of pejoratives.

"Is Wendell around?"

"He's out back, sunning."

"I have to thank him. He helped Raymond write a paper on Galileo, and Raymond brought it home last night with an A. Wendell's cute, isn't he?"

"Yes, he is."

"He's just going through a bad phase."

A prolonged bad phase. I wonder if Grace has a man in her life.

"No. Sometimes there are men who have me in *their* lives. I begin it, and I call the shots, and I end it."

"How do you know when to end it?"

"When it gets like marriage. When the romance is gone and there's nothing left, you know, but *dailiness*."

"But don't you think about being old and alone?"

"Oh, I won't be alone. I'll live with Raymond when he graduates from Yale. And when he marries, he'll take care of me."

The best laid plans of mice, men and mothers.

Grace invites me to have dinner and do some dancing on Thursday night at the Club Vincent on Whalley Avenue. It's not really a pick-up place, the food is inexpensive, and the men know when to quit. Panic sets in at this suggestion; the very idea makes me squirm. I beg off, saying this Thursday is taken by the Goddards, who are taking me touring.

"The following Thursday, then. No excuses."

I nod, with agreement, and dread. It is amazing that, at thirty-five, after fourteen years of marriage, I consider my date at the Club Vincent with only one question in mind. What would Sister Helene think? Sister Helene said, in tenth grade, "If you'll look out of place in white gloves, it's not a place for a lady to be."

It takes only minutes to buff the floor with the Silvermans' machine, then I send out a call for lunch. Wendell comes in from the yard, singing:

"I don't want to grow up, I'm a Toys R Us kid."

Wendell, Grace, Lydia, and I sit down for yogurt and Bath Oliver biscuits. The biscuits are limp from the humid New Haven summer. Wendell—graciously, I think—holds a chair for Lydia and the two of them dominate the conversation.

"So, Lydia, what's up?"

"Nicholas, dat czar. He be on de series now."

"Oh, yeah."

"You watchin'?"

"Nope."

"Teddy Roosevelt mess up bad on dat one."

"Really? How so?"

"De czar, he be miscalculatin' de Japanese navy in nineteen-hunnert-five. Dat Jap navy dey be whuppin' de Russians bad. So de czar, what he do? He turn his eye west."

Wendell listens in deadly earnest. Lydia suddenly sounds like Uncle Remus masquerading as Alistair Cooke.

"To de White House. He be askin' de Prezdent for help. He say he got big domestic trouble and he doan get help daze goan be revolution. Teddy he say he doan want no part of de Russian expansion. He say dat in de diplomatic language but everybody know he mean no dice. So he support de Japs instead of de Russians and dey loses. De peasant dey revolt and dey kill de czar. An' dis Soviet Union we got now, dat be lyin' on Teddy Roosevelt doorstep, nowheres else I can see."

"Do you like the cast?"

"I do, I like dat boy-chile. You know de one? He be a bleeder."

The yogurt and biscuits did not satisfy Wendell. When Lydia left he came in from the yard and ate four slices of Portuguese bread. He spread a layer of butter on each and then a one-inch layer of strawberry jam. He set all the slices in the toaster oven and did not notice the acrid smell as the jam juice ran, burned, and smoked up the appliance. It's going to be a bitch to clean.

"Wendell, has Lydia had any schooling at all?"

"Very little. But she's a devout watcher of public television. She commits all the programs to memory. Dad gives her a membership to Channel Thirteen every year."

"That's nice of your dad."

He brings his fist down on the toaster, dents the top of it, and burns his hand.

"Look, I don't need you to tell me when he's nice. Once a year he goes to the phone and puts it on the plastic for Lydia. Big fucking deal."

What a brat.

"Tell me about Miss Marchant."

"She lives in New York."

"Yes."

"He doesn't see her often. I've asked him not to bring her here because this is still, as far as I'm concerned, my mother's turf."

"She must get lonely in that kind of arrangement."

"She has a lot of rich girlfriends. She meets them for lunch every day."

"Tell me about women like that."

"What's to tell?"

"Well, what do they *do*?"

"They diet and shop."

The jam did not reach the corners of the bread. He now takes them, sixteen in all, and dips them in peanut butter.

"I was there last May, at her apartment. It's a veritable rain forest of mobiles. All tall people have to bend their spines and socialize at an angle. She bores you to death with seashells. Rocks, cowrys, conches and limpets. If you ask a question, out of courtesy, you're in for an hour. Frankly, I don't know how the hell he makes love to her. When I visited we put the coats in her bedroom. There were a dozen goddamn mobiles suspended over the bed. You could strangle yourself, climbing in. But maybe it turns him on. Conches, for instance, are very vaginal. They have an inner lip, an outer lip, and a small canal leading to an aperture."

Really, I don't think he should talk to me this way.

"And inside, they're all pearly oranges and pinks and fuchsias. Maybe that's what he needs to get it up."

"Wendell, I wonder if you could, next time, place the bread on foil, so the jam won't drip."

As I was ironing the dining room chiffons, Ariadne Marchant herself called. She sounded well-adjusted.

"Is this Emma Riley?"

"Yes."

"This is Knee Marchant, Richard's friend. I'd like you to call me Knee, if you will. Do you have a moment?"

"Certainly."

"I can't tell you how pleased I am that Richard's found you. I think your very presence will calm them both down. I can hear it already, in Richard's voice."

"Well, thank you."

"Would you ask him to call me when he gets home? I'd like to know if he's coming into the city this weekend."

"I'll give him the message."

"I'd like to meet you sometime. Perhaps, if you can keep Wendell calmed down, it might be possible for me to visit."

Mary, Mother of God.

"That would be nice."

"The trees will be changing soon. Perhaps I'll come up to see the fall color."

"That would be nice."

"I'll look forward to it."

I wonder, when she comes, if Richard will put her at the head of the table and me below the salt. I wonder what I'll cook to get the kudos. Filch the Marnier maybe: do the strawberry crêpes. Beef Wellington always gets the kudos, but the pastry casing is such a hassle.

Wendell passes through and stops to read my neatly written message. He laughs.

"You don't spell it 'Knee,' Emma. You spell it 'Nee.' "

"Oh, I'm sorry! I thought it had a K."

"As in 'water-on'?"

"Yes, or 'cap.' "

"Yeah. Or, more fittingly, 'jerk.' "

Nine

Anomalous set of signs this daybreak, stealthy and secretive. I bustle around the kitchen while Richard hangs about in the hall. He seems to be waiting for something to transpire and he has twice poked his head around the door, glanced at my activity, and quickly withdrawn to the hall. The minute I slip my egg into the boiling water he enters, carrying a small, square, gift-wrapped box.

"A present," he announces. "How long do you boil that egg?"

"Five minutes."

"Then you must open this immediately."

I don't know how to react, and consummate grace eludes me. I don't want to tear into it and I try to pick the Scotch tape away daintily. Inside is an English bone china egg cup, made by Aynsley. Its whiteness is translucent and there's a spray of deep purple hand-painted violets on the side. He is rather full of himself over this gift and I'm moved to kiss him on the cheek but I resist this inappropriate urge. I extend my hand and we are both quite uncomfortable with the similarly inappropriate handshake.

"I had a hell of a time finding it. Macy's had nothing and I ended up at Sykes-Libby, a jeweler."

"Thank you so much. Really, it's very thoughtful of you."

"Well, I just didn't want you to go on burning your fingers."

At breakfast he watches me intently as I delve down into the properly vertical shell. And he has further surprises. He's taken the morning off. I'm to dress for a visit to the Yale Center for British Art and lunch at Mory's.

"Do you know about the tables down at Mory's? The place where Louie dwells?"

And then he smiles, his eyes twinkle, and he bleats:

"Baa, Baa, Baa?"

I do know about the poor little lambs and I've known about the bulldogs for quite some time, too. And it seems to me these Yalies are more than a little hung up on quadruped mammals. Best not probe into *that* too deeply.

Dowagers of St. Ronan, do you see me here in this car? I am Her Ladyship, Lady LaTeDa: carriage trade. And when I eats me morning ova I does it out of Aynsley. And Aynsley don't come cheap. Nor do these Peugeot 604s. Twenty grand, conservatively. Tell me, Dowagers, do you have any *sense* at all of the distance between here and Dorchester? I'm light-years away from the floss, the laundry sink, the vainglorious denizens of the Buskin. A lifetime away from heartbreak and the love that dares not speak its name. Far removed from my humble origins but not, alas, out of touch with original sin, which is close at hand even in this august vicinity. Is it his height or his generous mouth or his reservoirs of angst? Why is he bothering to introduce me to a museum?

"You're a delightful surprise," he says. "You're an *entity*. I really hadn't bargained for that."

Oh, Mary, all the world's askew and I know it. If only there were prevention in knowledge. But Heaven help me, these present impulses are vastly preferable to the orderly pain of the recent past. I know these impulses to be askew, awry, amok and amiss, yet I plunge headlong, not for want of wisdom, but for want of recreational relief from a life too thoroughly examined these last few months. Let's hear it for the unexamined life and the lapses it may engender. Thumbs down, I say, on an ounce of prevention. If I come to tears, I'll simply be back on familiar ground.

As we glide down Whitney, onto Temple, I know why there's both lapse and folly in my reaction to Ariadne Marchant. It is not rational. It is highly neurotic. But as George Hearn sang in *La Cage aux Folles*, I am what I am. Bit of plagiarism there, from Popeye the sailor man's earlier, sweet-potato motto: I yam what I yam. I seem to be transferring to that New York lady all of the latent fears I harbored two years ago when Daniel Graham darkened my door. Ariadne is out there somewhere threatening my status quo. Representing interference, intimidation, impending disaster in the cocoon I propose to weave around my New Haven household. Not rational. Nor is the fact that I'm transferring to Richard other old baggage, dashed and disappointed paternal hopes of my childhood. Richard Goddard has been, through the thick and the thin of his mysterious marriage, a good and constant provider. He's never faltered in the bringing home of the bacon. He is not like Kevin, who, when faced with jobs—or even errands—he didn't relish was wont to throw up his hands and exclaim:

"Fuck this. I'm going to a ballgame."

Dear God. If Richard's looking for Nanny, am I looking for Daddy?

I wonder what sort of progression this is, or if it's progress at all. Possibly it's regression, relapse instead of advance. The qualities of consistency and dependability that presently appeal did not figure at all in my youthful attraction to the wildly diversified Michael. Whatever is

cooking here hinges on the portrait of the mercantile an-
cestor and has something to do with continuity. There is
durability, if not stability, in the Goddard bloodlines. What
is it that I'm feeling so strongly here in this car in this
close proximity to this man? It's a strange, alien sense of
inheritance, of dynasty, of Goddard's biblically begetting
Goddards for three solid centuries. And when Richard took
my arm and guided me onto this chamois leather seat,
there was quickening in the heart. I felt linked to something that had endured in the past and would persist in the
future. Perhaps because Kevin and Peg bore no sons to
carry the name and continue the line. Perhaps because
Michael and I bore no sons. Whatever the reason, the man
is emitting some sort of generational guarantee: intimations
of the continuous and perpetual. And the quickening is
there again when he takes my arm and guides me up High
Street to Chapel.

Downtown New Haven appears to exist solely because
of Yale University. Historically it must have had some
other reason for being; possibly the initial attraction to the
initial Goddard was the spacious harbor. *Trade*. It's too
big for a college town, there are vestiges of industry in the
drab old brick factories, but there is no apparent sense of
independent, secular city.

The museum is new. It was completed in 1977 with
funds provided by Paul Mellon, Class of 1929. It, too,
purports to nothing secular. It houses Mellon's single-
culture collection of British paintings, drawings, prints,
rare books, and sculpture. I can tell at a glance that one
hour in here will have me screaming for something *pre*:
Madonnas on triptychs by one of the Fra's. Or *post*, and
patriotic: Andrew Wyeth in Maine, Georgia O'Keeffe in
New Mexico, Reginald Marsh in Harlem.

"Our time's a little limited because I have to get to
the office. But you can come back and dawdle here
whenever you feel like it. Now, there's quite a lot of
Turner and Constable. Or would you like to look at
some of Benjamin Marshall's wonderful horses?"

Quadruped again. I don't think so.

"Why don't you show me what *you* like?"

He has, as I intuited, a penchant for the generational.
We move to gaze upon distinctly pudding-faced eighteenth-
century assemblages in works by Johann Zoffany, Arthur
Devis, and Thomas Gainsborough.

There is The Drummond Family, three elegantly attired
generations of them posing with two horses in front of an
old, gnarled tree. Richard says you know they're in Mid-
dlesex because the low buildings on the horizon are Har-
row. The Swaine Family of Laverington Hall, Isle of Ely,
Cambridgeshire, are fishing with their children by a pond.
The Gore Family is posed in their music room and Richard
says that thing being played is a violinchello. The Gravenor
Family is in the woods of their estate. They have no
personality and no activity and are rigidly inert. Gainsborough earned his commission on this lot; he must have been
at a loss to pose them. I think they didn't know what to do
with their hands. He gave the father and mother hats to
hold, wildflowers to the two anemic daughters.

All of the women in these pictures are satin-clad and
their blood does not seem to circulate above their necks.
The men have bulging bellies under buttoned waist-coats.
Too much ptarmigan, thought she, grousingly. They all
of them have phlegmatic eyes that have looked but not
seen. They are the most insipid, eviscerated, diluted
bunch I have ever encountered on canvas. Worse even
than the Spanish royal family, who were at least Latin
and dissipated. I think the little children in these pictures
grew up to go out to Inja with their memsahibs and get
all pukkaed up in pith helmets. And I think these folks
had their clothes cleaned, their food prepared, their houses
swept, and their bums wiped by people whose faces were
less pudding and more Mick.

"You don't find them attractive, do you?"

"I'm afraid not."

"Neither do I."

"Why do you like them?"

"I don't know, really."

He lifts his right arm and rests it on my right shoulder. He is musing on the pictures and I don't know if he's aware of the gesture's innate familiarity. My sense of propriety tells me that if he isn't aware, he should be.

"I guess I like them because they convey a kind of unity. A certain family solidarity."

We meander around this museum and the hand does not leave my shoulder. There's nothing flirtatious in his manner, no blarney in his palaver, nothing ulterior in his eyes. Still, something instinctual is happening. It is when we come upon a huge portrait of a woman that we are jolted and we both realize that we have been too receptive to each other. The woman has, unaccountably, one breast exposed. The picture is flagrant among the other, decorous paintings. The bare breast sits there pointedly suspended on top of the neckline on the woman's tangerine gown. It's a proud, impudent breast with a cheeky little nipple. Her effect on us is astounding, and Richard's hand falls abruptly. It is as if this picture, so fraught with the sexual, commands us to declare our intentions. "You can not," the woman admonishes, "look at me with indifference. You must take stands, draw lines, rise and be counted." When I ask who she is, he is silent and disturbed. He nods his head. He doesn't know.

Separating, I walk to the little placard and report. She is Diana Kirke, mistress of Aubrey de Vere, the Earl of Oxford. She married the Earl in 1673, becoming the Countess of Oxford. He is listening, and I am reading, but we have both been brought up short. The lady has confirmed that there is, between us, the possibility of something untoward. As we leave the museum we give each other a wide berth. Has this happened because I've lived for a year without one iota of affection? Is my distress such a malady that I carry it on me visibly, beckoningly? Richard, too, is asking questions of himself. On the way to the car he offers a partial explanation.

"I've felt an affiliation with you since the day you arrived. I think we've both been crippled by failed marriages."

Michael and I went to New York for a weekend once, and spent two whole days standing on line at the half-price theatre ticket booth so that we could afford to dine at Sardi's. The walls at Sardi's were decked with photographs of the living talented. The walls at Mory's are decked with photographs of the dead athletic. And the tables down at Mory's must be where the country's losing battle with graffiti first began. Every inch of every table top is gouged and carved with the initials of old male Blues. A little sign at the entrance says that gentlemen will not be admitted without jacket and tie after five-thirty. One can only wonder at one hundred and thirty-five years of gentlemen whipping penknives out of their proper attire and defacing the furniture. And I hadn't quite expected the nautical aspect, the long oars running along the tops of the walls. These are the preserved prizes from races won by Yale at New London, with speeds dutifully engraved thereon. While we wait for our food, Richard takes me upstairs to the Cup Room, which is full of trophies in glass cases. I wonder if he expects me to be impressed, but his own amusement lets me off the hook.

"Sometimes I think Yale isn't about education at all," he says. "It's about winning."

We sit down to clam chowder and salad.

"Does Wendell have any plans to work?"

"Oh, he does work. He works very hard on his poems. But you mean employment."

"Yes. Don't poets usually go to graduate school so that they can teach and support themselves?"

"Usually they do. But, unfortunately, the usual does not apply to Wendell. I don't think he'll do much of anything in life until he resolves his feelings about his mother and me."

There is hubbub and noise around us, clinking and clanking, phones ringing, waiters running. The feeling of fall at the university, assembling of professors, dissemination of summer travel stories. A whole group that went separately to visit I Tatti, Berenson's villa, expressing amazement that they didn't bump into each other. And animated conversation about the new crop; the upcoming year. Richard watches me watch, and leans forward.

"You know, I'm reading a lot these days about the new man, the modern, sensitive man. Talking to you, I'm very aware of your age and I feel called upon to show you that I know about these new requirements. I guess it's a kind of middle-aged vanity. I don't want you to think me some old misogynist. On the other hand, there's always the threat of looking like a sissy. And in addition to that, there's an effort to adhere to the old rules of employer-employee relations. And there's something about you that requires, really demands, frankness. So you see, just talking to you is full of traps."

"Should we go?"

He laughs.

"No! Goodness, no. I'm enjoying myself. I guess I just needed a preamble to get to my point.

"You probably find this situation between Wendell and me pretty discouraging. So I'd like you to understand why I'm determined to grapple with it. I can't recall a time when my house was empty. For fifty-five years I came home and there was always someone there. If not my parents then Nanny and the other help, and for a while in my teens Nanny's niece stayed with us. Even in my marriage, what I came home to was sad and unsatisfactory, but there was life in the house. When Wendell left I was alone for the first time. I wandered around the rooms so full of my family's past and I kept asking myself, what did it all amount to? Marion was dead, Wendell was in Berkeley; at work there are young men waiting for my retirement. For a variety of reasons I never pursued what I really wanted in life. And there I was alone, looking over this expanse of half a century, and I felt desperately estranged. When Wendell came home I was happy to have him. He didn't even talk to me the first month back but even so, things seemed to account for something. I'd never have hired a housekeeper, just for me. I'd have struggled along with Lydia. It took Wendell's return for me to see that we had to have a woman. And here you are. We have Wendell to thank for that. Let's drink a toast to Wendell.''

We raise our glasses and drink to the boy who is scribbling at home behind his bolted door, in the rubble of his filthy room. I have not been this happy in two or three years. I'd like to just stay here, in this venerable, if somewhat mawkish Mory place.

''You know a lot about theatre, don't you? Because of your husband. We have two good ones here, the Yale Rep and Long Wharf. Would you like to go sometime?''

''No, thank you, I don't think so. I might know some of the actors. If I did, I'd have to go back, after.''

''Go back?''

"Backstage. And explain. And talk about Michael. Really, I don't need to be entertained. I'll be quite content at the house."

Because I, too, feel an affiliation with you, Richard. Because of your height, your generous mouth, your reservoirs of angst, your endurance. Because you make me feel something continuous and perpetual and *linked*. Because I, too, have looked back over the expanse of my life and found myself unlinked and unable to account for anything, and have been desperately estranged and have felt for months not like an entity, but a piece of refuse that someone dropped at the curb. Discarded litter blowing randomly around a vacant lot. Null and void, passé, a relic loving my sadness, longing to be rescued from a slough of self-pity. So yes, let's lift the glass again to Wendell.

Ten

I am telling too much. Because I've had too much wine. All that wine at lunch barely had a chance to wear off when Richard brought home this California Glencannon white, for dinner. Imbibing twice a day is not wise; it blurs the boundaries of my status, dilutes the subordinate in my soul. And I'm not out socially here, I'm at my place of employ with all of its restrictions. With two glasses under my belt, and Richard pouring a third, Wendell has asked me to tell them about Michael. The windows are clean, the chiffons billow beautifully in the breeze, I can see the kitchen floor shimmering and there's a relative thaw between father and son. I'm not overly aromatic, fellows, there's no cheap jewelry, just a little slurring around the sibilants. I ask for your forbearance.

In a nutshell, Michael was my education. To be with Michael was to embark upon a journey because his mind was so eclectic. He read everything: *The New Republic, Variety, The Manchester Guardian, Rolling Stone, Architectural Digest, Screw*. He read Doonesbury. He even read match covers and billboards in their entirety. Give him any two lines of Shakespeare and he gave you the play. And he waited with gleeful anticipation for every written word that issued from the pen of Gore Vidal.

Michael built a rock garden at our place in New Hampshire, alyssum, impatiens, salvia, viola, and knew all the Latin names for all the plants. Michael played the clarinet. His rendition of "Trust in Me" broke your heart. Michael was a man of parts, exuberantly funny, but also ineffably sad. I guess you could say that he fended off his sadness by devouring published reports of human activity, and then he meted it out again with irony, wit, and quite frequently spleen. But I always forgave him for that.

When Michael wasn't cast in plays at the Buskin, he sometimes traveled to the Alley Theatre in Houston, the Guthrie in Minneapolis, the Mark Taper in Los Angeles, the Seattle Rep. The absences made our hearts grow fond, and they renewed our appreciation of each other. We bought a small old saltbox house on four acres in New Hampshire. When we were financially stable, and Michael didn't have to perform in summer stock, we spent our summers there. He carved a sign that said "Last Resort," and nailed it on our door. One wonderful spring we spent April in London and lived on pub lunches so that we could see everything in the West End and at the National. Michael stole me a rose from Hampton Court and a piece of stone from Canterbury Cathedral. Our lives were very active, but it came to pass, you see, that all of this activity was an avoidance of the Lower Depths. He was, how to put it, charismatic with other men. About twice a year he would flirt with and come dangerously close to what he called his Lower Depths.

And then he would sit in the dark in a rocking chair and listen to Vivaldi, and sink into a coma of depression and degradation. And murmur:

"Now are the four seasons of my discontent."

Everything was dirty for him then, everything was soiled. He'd shower and wash his hair three times a day, blow his nose incessantly, brush his teeth every half hour, change his shirt every hour. I stayed close to him during this cleansing process, and got in provisions of shampoo, Kleenex, toothpaste, laundry detergent. He never asked for a separation, but he never resolved anything, either.

I remember one night he turned off the Vivaldi and put on the radio. They played a hit song, recorded by the Bee Gees. We listened to those balding Australians singing in their eunuch tones. We thought of John Travolta, svelte, eurythmic, scaling new heights of Saturday night fever. When it was over, Michael's face turned anguished. He murmured, in the half light:

"That's what the whole, execrable business is all about. It's all about stayin' alive."

He said it as if the alternative—death—had a sudden appeal. It was only then that I realized there is a time when one must step back, graciously, on quiet little cat feet. It is when life itself is in question. It is when pride and ego and rivalry become meaningless, and all one sees in the face of one's love is misery.

Not too long ago, the Buskin's subscription audience began to lag, and the board hired a new artistic director. Daniel was my age, thirty-five, and very handsome. And he and Michael discovered they were going through the same thing; they both had an inordinate fear of aging. They would get drunk and rage against time. They stayed out of the sun to prevent wrinkling, they quoted Dylan Thomas and vowed not to go gentle into that good night. And then, together, they descended into the Lower Depths.

Daniel came with a U-Haul on a Sunday morning, and I had nowhere to hide. I stood in my shabby robe on our shag rug and watched from the front window of our apartment. It was the most public, most declarative moment of my life. The people across the street were washing their windows. The husband was up on a ladder, washing the outside, and his wife was washing the inside. I thought,

"How lovely that is. He is her mirror image."

Their flannel rags, fragments of waived winter pajamas, moved in unison as Michael and Daniel loaded the truck. And all the while I stood behind a tapestrylike width that we'd bought from a weaver in Newton. Michael called it our "arras."

"Jesus Christ, an *arras!* Hurry up, *conceal* something!"

I had tried to buy curtains for that window, but he made me take them back:

> "Priscillas? These curtains are actually called *Priscillas?* I say no, emphatically, to this singular, exceptionally singular Priscilla. No, categorically, to these plural Priscillas."

And then, squashing them back into the box:

> "Down, wenches, down!"

I watched as they put the largest piece, Michael's five-drawer dresser, on the U-Haul. They stopped and wrapped an old blanket around the stereo. It was an old blanket, but it was mine. It was an old Hudson's Bay blanket, a wedding gift from Aunt Colleen, who married a Frenchman and moved to Montreal and had nine sons in a row.

> (Kevin said, "A baseball team.")

I guess Michael had a right to that blanket, but it hurt me to see Daniel throwing it over the stereo because, do you see? Daniel had no particular *history* with that blanket. He didn't know that the day before Aunt Colleen bought it her oldest son graduated from McGill, the first college graduate in several centuries of family. A week after she bought it the same son died in an automobile accident, and Peg had to go to Montreal and cook for the Héberts because Aunt Colleen had a nervous breakdown and spent two months in a mental hospital.

When Michael stood before me for our last confrontation I was nauseous and there were floaters in my vision. I felt turbulent rumblings in my belly and I wondered if I'd have diarrhea right there on the shag, in front of the arras. He kissed me goodbye, tenderly, on the mouth, and said softly,

> "Thanks for the memories."

My mind was in the medicine cabinet, looking for Kaopectate. And as he hurried out to the waiting truck I felt something running down my leg. The following day my mother said to my father,

"And when that pervert left, you know what she did? She shat on the floor."

I bolted myself in for a week. I wouldn't answer my mother's calls. My father came and hammered on my door and yelled:

"Are yuh *daid*, Emma?"

I told my father to bugger off, and he replied,

"Poor choice of words, Em, in the circumstances."

That's when I saw your ad. Woman Wanted. It seemed anachronistic in the eighties. But *I* have always seemed, if I may say so, somewhat anachronistic in this life. I thought the ad flagrantly anatomical. It didn't call for a mature person or a responsible person or an experienced person. It was a blatant call for a female domestic, a sort of paid wife, sans charge cards. And I thought, well, there'll be no packing it in at five here, no evening hours and weekends in which to indulge in a six-pack and hoist the finger to the boss. No freedom to pad around the house barefoot in bra and panties with tits and stomach hanging out. On the other hand, there'd be no blood connection, so I could stay on the periphery. A kind of satellite to your lives. A reversion to the Historical She. I thought there was something essential, almost primal in that, linking up with all the past Historical Shes who feather-dusted cobwebs, mended little holes, ironed little wrinkles, and mitred the sheets at the corners of the beds. Nurtured the rubber plants and nursed to health the occasional wounded bird found limp from fearful flapping on the lawn.

Another glass? Oh, by all means, yes, thank you, it's awfully good, this stuff is.

And I, Emma Rowena Riley, promise to be the Supreme Keeper of that crucial household drawer that contains Band-Aids, nine-volt batteries, rubber bands, postal tape, Krazy Glue, thumbtacks and Marvel Lubricating Oil. Promise to garner to myself a treasury of lids to fit any array of containers, to keep a cache of candle stubs to unstick occluded zippers, and also to allow a flickering advancement on those stormy nights when the hurricane threatens and the power goes off. Promise to provide a sumptuous repast for the returning Titans at the end of their day.

I prayed, Oh, Mary, Queen of my heart, please let them be humane in return. Hail, Betty Crocker, mythic mother of Minneapolis, let me trust implicitly in the veracity of your jingle that nothin' gets the lovin' like something from the oven.

Richard hands me a handkerchief. I must be crying.

But I must tell you what happened a couple of days after I accepted your job. I got a call from a friend, more of an acquaintance, really, who wanted me to feed her dog while she was in New York, on a buying trip. She had this Sealyham terrier called Bitsy who was given to massive, mephitic shit-fits whenever there happened to be horsemeat in his food.

I am sobbing uncontrollably, and Richard is guiding me up the stairs to my room. I'm blubbering.

"See the light, Richard? See how it dispells the gloom? Thomas Alva Edison did not intend for us to use twenty-five watters, Richard. No. Contrary to the habits of this house, Thomas intended the big ones. More profit that way."

Wendell stays behind and lingers by his room, on the second-floor landing. Richard has his arm around me; my head is on Richard's shoulder and Wendell doesn't like it. Well, brat, that's your problem.

"Oh, Richard, you've got to call Nee. There'll be hell to pay if you don't. She wants to know if you're going in, Friday."

"I'm not."

"Richard, I've met the maid next door."

"Oh, yes. Amazing Grace."

"Don't say anything bad about the Italians, Richard."

"I didn't intend to. She's an amazing woman. And the nice thing is, the Silvermans know it, and appreciate it."

"Don't say anything bad about the Jews, Richard."

"I didn't intend to."

"Richard, may I pose a question? Is there any connection, I mean, any archaic linguistic connection between the Jew in jeweler and the fact that so many are named Silver and Gold and Ruby and Pearl and Diamond?"

"I don't know. All the names were altered when they arrived at Ellis Island."

"While we're on this subject, Richard, I just want to get this off my chest. There's a theory in some quarters that Jews manage and manipulate the world's financial markets. Have you ever been to Newport?"

"No. Shouldn't you go to sleep now?"

"Newport contained the rankest collection of crooks and scofflaws and robber barons the country's ever seen. Astors, Berwinds, Thaws, Vanderbilts, Van Rensselaers. Then there was Carnegie, Rockefeller, Frick, Gould, Morgan, but I think they summered somewhere else. In California there was Huntington Hartford and Leland Stanford and then Hearst and then Getty. In Texas, Hunt and a whole slew of

others. Christians all. Given to philanthropy at the
end. Camels. Trying to get through the eye of the
needle.''

"You really are a surprise. Now I must say goodnight, Emma.''

"I just wanted to get that off my chest, Richard, a
week from tomorrow I'm going with Grace to a place
called Club Vincent on Whalley Avenue. I see you do
not regard this as *de rigueur*. But I have to do this,
Richard, in the name of neighborhood relations. And
I don't want any shit from you and Wendell when I
go. Is that understood?''

"Yes.''

"Will I be fired in the morning?''

"No.''

"Good. Wendell and I have a date tomorrow morning.''

"He'll take you to Grove Street Cemetery.''

"How do you know that?''

"Oh, I just know. Wendell is long on excuses.''

He plumps my pillow and as I succumb to the bed he
pulls up the quilt. After the door is closed I wonder if
anybody ever helped old Nanny Culligan retire when she
was too much on the sauce. And maybe Ariadne will
prove to be overweight, titless, and walleyed.
Slumber is such a lovely, soothing, kindly word.

Eleven

Grove Street Cemetery is in the heart of New Haven, surrounded by the buildings of Yale. There is a massive Egyptian Revival portal at its entrance and a wrought-iron fence along its front perimeter. For the first hundred and sixty years of New Haven's history the dead were buried under the New Haven Green. But after the plague of yellow fever in 1794, there were so many graves that the Green was deemed morbid and unsightly. Michael and I used to visit the Mount Auburn Cemetery in Cambridge, so I am not a neophyte in this business of visitation upon the antiquated dead. However, Wendell needs to have the last word. Mount Auburn dates from 1831 and Grove Street from 1796.

The day is, as the weather-casters say, partly cloudy. Kevin used to rail at the manner in which the media consistently sought to give us the dark side of the weather. Old Kev refers to toss-up days like this as mostly sunny.

The leaves have begun to fall on the graves of Dwights, Daggetts, Danas, Flaggs, Osbornes, Prouts, Porters, Shermans, and Woolseys. Lyman Beecher is here, the father of Harriet Beecher Stowe, as is the widow of Samuel F. B. Morse, of the Code. Eli Whitney of the cotton gin is here, as is Eli Whitney Blake, inventor of the stone crusher, as is his brother, Philos, inventor of the corkscrew. Noah Webster of the dictionary is here and Charles Goodyear of vulcanized rubber is here. Wendell says it was Mr. Goodyear's vulcanized rubber that led to the first condom patents in the 1840s. I do wish he wouldn't talk to me that

101

way. Both Denison Olmstead and Elias Loomis, first observers of Halley's comet, in 1835, are here. Alexander Twining, inventor and first producer of artificial ice, is here. And Theophilus Eaton deserves special homage. He was not only the first Governor of New Haven colony, he was also the stepfather of David Yale. David was the father of Elihu, who founded Yale College.

The women were mostly Historical Shes. They married these eminent men and bore their children. Louise was lovely and beloved. But nearby Mehetable was just plain laid to rest in 1788. Across the path, a weather-ravaged stone says, simply, "A Mother's Grave, 1847."

They all seem to be here, all the country's seedling scholars, engravers, diarists, clergymen, statesmen, educators, inventors, industrialists, merchants, and philanthropists. All the Jacobs, Algernons, Isaacs, Ebenezers, Nathaniels, Aarons, and there is even one Yehudi. As we approach the two Goddard obelisks, I see that Wendell's mother is here. The grass on her grave is newer and greener.

Marion was a Hotchkiss. Her grandmother on one side was a Morse, on the other side a Stiles. Her great-aunts married Brewsters, Townshends, and Sheffields. Richard's mother was a Lyman, and Richard's great-uncles married Dwights, Daggetts, and Danas. There are three yellow chrysanthemums valiantly trying to bloom on top of Wendell's grandfather, but they are being choked by creeping ivy. Wendell applies this symbol to himself. He says these three hundred years of repressed Puritan morality have impacted his roots, cut off his air and stunted his growth.

Oh, my. I am overcome with a sense of déjà vu. Eliot Fry and Howie Evarts, two of Michael's old Harvard friends, were indigent lads paralyzed by their prestigious pasts. And Miltie Greenberg, who played all the "foreigners" at the Buskin, was wont to get drunk and drape himself over our refrigerator and say that the root of *his* problem was an aunt who was gassed at Auschwitz. And then there is Kevin Shea, who was orphaned at eight, and who sired me, and who has for seventy-odd years lamented his victimization by The Emerald Isle, The Church,

The Trade Unions, The Fuel Company, The Electric Company, his mother, my mother, various employment applications and tests, and companies that sell you things to assemble at home and then don't provide the proper screws in the little plastic bags.

"Wendell, it's a bit of a stretch, and I don't buy it."

It's just, you see, that I'll be thirty-six at Christmas. Strands of gray are beginning to glint in my hair; one of my molars is shot and if I don't get a crown I'll lose it. I won't tell you this, Wendell, because vanity, like hope, springs eternal. But I have detected a liver spot on my right hand and my toenails have gone brittle this last year. My biological clock is winding down and there are escalating intimations of my mortality. There will occur, one day, a gorgeous autumn such as this that won't include me in its scheme. I will not be here to see the vibrant sumac swaying on its branch, and I am fucking bored, Wendell, with the roots of people's problems. I am weary of the time spent in examination and analysis of their assorted crutches, the infinite and sundry justifications for their lousy behavior, the insipid excuses for physical, mental, and emotional infirmity. Let's hear it for the unexamined life.

"You think I'm copping out, right?"

Well. I don't want to risk another tirade, a kicking down of venerable headstones and bashing in of eroded sandstone obelisks, but,

Yes.

We amble down a few steps to Marion's grave. Wendell's head drops and his lean, long fingers spread across his face. When I reach for his hand, he grasps mine tightly.

"There's so much here that doesn't meet the eye."

He gestures to me to stay where I am, then moves around the rectangular grave slowly, as if he needs to distance himself.

"Did he tell you how she died? Did he use the hackneyed words?"

"He said she died of natural causes."

"Natural causes, yes. Did he tell you *where* she died?"

"I assumed at the house."

"She died at Silver Hill Sanatorium in Wallingford. It's a ritzy asylum for alcoholics, madwomen, child molesters, folk like that. Come on. I don't want to tell my sordid tale on consecrated ground. I'm taking you to lunch at Fitzwilly's."

We find the Volvo across the street, at Woolsey Hall, and proceed the half-mile to the restaurant. The place was a firehouse in the eighteen-hundreds; there are warm brick walls and huge hanging plants billowing down their greenery. We order.

"Let me tell you the truth about my dad. He, too, wanted to be a poet. His family said no and he capitulated. At twenty he fell in love with old Nanny Culligan's niece. She was poor, and Catholic, and his family said no, and he capitulated. His mother suggested my mother. He had reservations, and rightfully so. She was a walking tragedy. But he capitulated.

"They had an argument when I was six. I went to the bathroom at midnight, and heard them hollering. I think it was their last communication. He said he couldn't stand it any longer, it was a non-marriage. She said whatever it was, it was all she could offer. She said she wanted a bargain of celibacy—if he couldn't make such a bargain, she wanted a divorce.

The last thing I heard was his question. He said, 'Oh, for God's sake, what about Wendell?' Well, he accepted the bargain, and the marriage ceased. I was consigned to a kind of nether-land. Their disaffection was palpable in the house. When I returned from school, I felt I was traveling into a void. For several years I wanted to run and grab him and ask, 'Hey, what about Wendell?' But I never did. And I am, as you've probably noticed, the worse for wear.

"He stayed at work most nights until eight or nine, and he went to the office on Saturdays and Sundays. She retreated to her room. I visited her for half an hour every night after dinner. I became her ambassador from the real world. When I went to college, I lived at Jonathan Edwards. I made a point of getting home at least twice a week for that important half-hour. Her loneliness was awesome, and I guess it was during my freshman year that the doorbell rang, and she let in a woman. A Jehovah Witness lady carrying one of those *Watchtower*s. Rae-Ann Wilks became her bosom buddy. By the time I was a sophomore, Rae-Ann and I, and occasionally Lydia, were the only people Mother ever talked to. She got very strange. Lydia told me it was early menopause, but I put it down to the Bible-thumping she did with Rae-Ann every other day. Sometimes a week would go by without either of us catching a glimpse of Dad.

"Then, all of a sudden, he changed the rules. All of a sudden he discovered sexual congress. He met Nee Marchant during my junior year and he started spending the weekends in New York. Quite honestly, I assumed he was diddling, but I didn't see that it made much difference. Mother was living in such an ether, I thought, Jesus, he could fuck two-in-hand on the roof and she wouldn't notice. One morning during spring break I stopped at her room to say a quick good morning. She was wearing a chenille robe, she had her hair up in big pink rollers, and she was

painting her toenails. That image will haunt me until
my dying day because it was, to say the least, unusual.
And I didn't question it. If I had, she'd still be alive."

Once again, his eyes fill with tears, which he wipes with
his blue and white linen napkin.

"Wendell, let's get out of here."

"No, no. We haven't had dessert."

We both of us gaze across the parking lot, at students
entering the Yale Co-op, and Cutler's Record Shop. Wendell's knuckles turn white as he clenches the napkin.

"I didn't question it. I went over to the gym, for a
swim. Well, she walked, barefoot, in the curlers and
the robe, with the scarlet toenails, over to the lab. She
walked past Dad's secretary, into his office, and she
said, 'Richard, you've taken a woman in New York.
You've broken the bargain.'

"I was there when he brought her home. He announced, without any warning, that he was having
her committed. I was astonished, and he was ada-
mant. I said, look, she's never done this before—this
whole, outlandish business is because of your New
York fuck. I said, for Chrissake, stay home on the
weekends, just for a while, and maybe we'll all go
back to normal. He laughed. God, what a hollow,
mirthless laugh. 'Normal,' he kept repeating. 'Normal.' He said he'd capitulated all his life and he just
did not have one more in him.

"They hauled her out of the house, screaming like a
banshee. At Silver Hill, they wouldn't let her see
Rae-Ann. She never did recognize Dad again, and
when she recognized me, she asked for Rae-Ann.
Three months later she died. Of natural causes. She

had eighty-five thousand dollars, all of which she left to the Jehovah's Witnesses.

"The funeral was set for one o'clock. He left me alone in the house. He stayed in New York and fucked Nee until the eleven o'clock train, which got him to New Haven at twelve-fifty. He was late for the service. And the minute they lowered the coffin into the hole, he caught the three o'clock back to New York. The minister offered to come home with me, but I declined. I rode home alone, in the big, black limousine, and I didn't hear from him for forty-eight hours. He doesn't even *remember* any of this! Whaddya make of them apples?"

"Wendell, surely you have some compassion. There were so many extenuating circumstances. There was so much sadness in the man's life."

He refuses to hear me. He summons the waitress and orders a slab of carrot cake. I think of something I read this morning over my egg in its Aynsley cup. John Belushi, before he died, said, "No one can know how painful it is to be me."

"There's a cemetery outside of Leningrad containing the half-million who died during the Siege. There's a big statue at the gate with a plaque that says: 'Forgive nothing, forget nothing.' That's my credo. I'll never forgive him for incarcerating my mother. He might as well have murdered her. It's a score I intend to settle."

Mary, this is the stuff Hamlets are made of. There's a fierce vindictiveness in Wendell; the boy is in big trouble. The boy may even be Bad Seed.

"I took off for Berkeley. I stayed high, fucking wasted, all the time. I slept with anything female that had pot to share. I even dealt the stuff for a while. I borrowed money from everybody and spent most of my time dodging the lenders. Even out there, in a town full of miscreants, it took them six months to catch on to me. I think because I looked Eastern and honorable. When they did catch on, three burly guys kicked the shit out of me and left me bleeding under a bench. I called Dad. I said, 'I want to come home and write poetry.' He said, 'Bucko, the door is open. Let me help you.' I told him it was too late. I didn't want his help.''

"But of course, you did."

"I didn't."

"Why else were you calling?"

"I wanted a room, a bed, an occasional shower. That's all I wanted."

"I think he'd like to see your poems, Wendell."

"He'll see them if and when they're ever published. Look, we're sharing the ancestral roof and we're sharing a bucket of bad blood. You want me to forgive and forget and make him my fucking mentor. I can't *do* that, Emma! And if you think you can come in like Mary Poppins and kiss these twenty-three years all better, your head is squarely up your ass. Let's go."

He pushes his plate away with such force it slides across the small table and crashes into mine. We leave the restaurant reverberating from his invective. The car would be claustrophobic, and I suggest we walk to the next stop on our tour, the Beineke Rare Book Library. Eventually, Wendell adopts a certain objectivity.

"The interesting thing is, he rarely sees Nee Marchant now. He brought her with us to the Vineyard after the funeral. I nearly needed a straitjacket. I couldn't believe the *gall* of it! I think she was a fixation for him, at first. He was like a diabetic kid in a candy shop. He was so obstinate about it, I thought, Jesus, he's discovered his cock and his spine all at once. I said that to Monica when I met her, and she replied, 'Isn't it too bad that the two are inseparable in men.' Monica is not usually that clever.''

"Are you in love with Monica?''

"I love no one but Lydia. You, however, are a close second. You would find me most susceptible, if you dared.''

"Oh, Wendell, *can it*.''

In a flash, he reaches into the inner pocket of his corduroy jacket and hands me a sealed envelope. It's a gesture that must be done hastily, or not at all. A sort of tide in the affairs of Wendell and me, which must be taken at its flood. I accept it, gingerly. The envelope is expensive vellum, taken from Richard's study. Richard's name is engraved on the back of it.

"Couple of samples,'' he says, lightly. "For you to look at sometime. But not now.''

"Oh, God, Wendell, not *me*.''

"Why not? They'll either reach you, or they won't. That's all a poem can ever do, with anybody.''

I take the envelope and zipper it into my bag. I dread reading them; I dread the weighty responsibility. As we walk through the beautiful wrought-iron scrolls and leaves of the Porter Gate, he leans over and pats my shoulder bag, tenderly.

"No rush. Anytime. Of course, you realize that this is an act of trust. I have made you the custodian of my private thoughts."

"Wendell, why aren't you submitting your poems to magazines?"

He blanches.

"I beg your pardon?"

"I said, why aren't—"

"Jesus fucking Christ at Gethsemane!"

Bolting from the sidewalk, he holds his hand to his chest as if my question was an arrow to his heart. He lopes around the grass spasmodically, attracting the attention of both passersby and pigeons. He waves his arm around the expanse of the courtyard.

"Do you have *any* idea what's out there? Rampant rejection! Half the population's writing poems! Muhammad Ali is writing poems!"

"You're making a public spectacle! Get back here on this sidewalk!"

Huffing and puffing, biting his lower lip, shaking his head in incredulity at my stupidity, he sidles back beside me.

"*Thousands* of people out there are submitting their efforts to five or six harried editors who publish little magazines. Stacks and stacks of poems enter the mails every day. They send 'em back, unread. Or, they read four lines and something's wrong that day. They're constipated, they've got a turd stuck crossways, and back go the poems. If you put a blockade on poets, you'd have to fire half the employees at the U.S. Postal Service."

"What are you saying? You're going to be a closet writer all your life?"

"I have just attempted to impress upon you a lifetime of total, calculated rejection. I am *saying* that I am scared diarrhetically shitless."

"Wendell, you'll just have to enter the mails along with the rest of them."

"Listen, bitch, *critics* are out there! I don't mean your living-room carpers, I mean public fucking *scolds*. Guys who get paid to slap you on your sensitive wrists. To *cavil*. They're out there waiting to ambush the poor courageous bastard who dares to molt his skin and expose his soul. And their numbers are legion."

Déjà vu. Michael on the critics. How they blame the actors for the direction, how they loathe a strong concept and lament the lack of one. How you can, if you know your reviewers, predict each review before it's written. How art is a battleground: artists are warriors and critics are civilians. But Wendell hasn't even picked up a spear. He's got the jargon, but he hasn't earned it. Fix that right now.

"Wendell, tell me if I'm wrong. I think there is, in the act of writing poetry, a desire to have one's voice heard. Nobody's hearing your voice except, perhaps, the roaches which I suspect reside in your bedroom. As long as your rhymes are confined there, your voice is mute. So sooner or later you have to join the gang in the mailbox."

"Rhymes? For Chrissake, nobody *rhymes* anymore! And what the hell do you know about going bare-assed in public?"

"I was married to an actor who faced audiences nightly. Who went out, valiantly, and, to quote, 'cowed the beast.' "

"You know what you are? You're naive. Please, consider this subject *dropped*. Hey, look, there's the sun."

The library was a 1963 gift to Yale from the Beineke family, who made their fortune in S&H Green Stamps. Because it houses rare books and manuscripts, it is climate-controlled, and there are no windows above ground. The walls are thin panes of translucent white Vermont marble. There is something remote and aloof about this library; it's too rich for my proletarian blood. But in the sunken concrete courtyard surrounding the building there are three marble sculptures by Noguchi, and I feel an immediate response to one of them. The first is a squatting pyramid, representing Earth, the second a circle, representing Sun, and the appealing, beckoning third is a cube. This cube, says my guide, represents Chance.

"Why are you so turned on by this cube?"

It's difficult to articulate quickly, but:

"I just love the concept! I mean, that he didn't do the moon or the oceans or things representing, you know, science or literature. That he did the earth and the sun and then took into consideration the real mystery of our lives. Chance! Gamble. Haphazard happenstance. I'll have to write my dad about this. Kevin's big on a sort of lottery philosophy. Unaccountable things in the stars, in the cards, in the dice. Old Kev believes the whole voyage from cradle to grave is manned by a God who stands at the helm of a giant Irish sweepstakes. You go in. I'm happy to stay out here for a while."

"No, no. This is Yale's jewel box. You must see it."

The Widener, at Harvard, makes you feel that, if you can read, you are a welcome explorer among its hospitable shelves and stacks. But the Beineke makes no effort at the egalitarian. Everything in it is hermetically sealed; nearly everything in it is irreplaceable. Mrs. Stephen Harkness, donor of the Harkness Memorial Quadrangle at Yale, was also the donor of the Beineke's Gutenberg Bible. Printed in 1455, it is one of five extant in the United States. In the center of the building is a sealed glass core that houses the 1742 Yale Collection as well as innumerable other rarities, some tattered, some tooled and glittering gilt. In the manuscript vault, in the basement, are the works and letters of Eugene O'Neill, Thornton Wilder, Gertrude Stein, Robert Louis Stevenson, Alfred Steiglitz, Georgia O'Keeffe: a literary and luminary cast of thousands. Ezra Pound has his own room. Weldell asks, with some concern,

"What's the matter?"

"Oh, I just wish I could share this with Michael."

"Can't, kiddo. And won't. Ever, now. So why lacerate the heart?"

Good question, but I think it comes from one of the most determined laceraters I've ever met.

This library is a kind of intensive care unit for ancient books and bindings, and the present scholars who forage in the past. But light fades books, humidity rots them, heat warps them, arid air unsticks them. So the building is dark and antiseptic and is opposed to the foibles of a general public. Precaution pervades the rarified air. Even here, however, chance dared to play a role. My guide tells this story with relish.

"About six years ago, the Beineke received a shipment of old manuscripts from Europe. Shortly thereafter, the staff began to notice little bits of powder in the books. It turns out that those books came in with deathwatch beetles who were boring their way through the glue. And having carnal knowledge of each other at a rapid rate. All of a sudden the little devils were everywhere, nibbling away at one priceless volume after another. So, the library bought a blast freezer and blast-froze everything in the building. Nothing comes in, nowadays, that isn't frozen before it's catalogued.''

Did Isamu Noguchi prophesy this, I wonder, with his cube in the courtyard?

I fall into the car, exhausted. Did I say, when in my cups, that I'd live on the periphery of their lives, here in New Haven? This boy is so handsome, so young, so ripe and rife with a rage to live. Yet he means to do harm to Richard. A cold shudder passes down my spine, and I feel caught in something conspiratorial. There's a cruel streak that seeks retaliation. Is it his mother's death he wishes to avenge, or his own lifetime of neglect?

I want the little couch in Nanny's room, and a steaming cup of Irish Breakfast tea. And I'll stay there, secluded, because I don't know how to handle dinner on my day off. I guess I'll just skip it. If I cook for myself I'll feel guilty, not cooking for them. As we enter the back door at five o'clock, the Volvo appears to have ruptured something. Wendell says not to worry, it's just dieseling.

He stands in the kitchen doorway watching me, arms folded, as I fetch my teabag. While the bag steeps, he hunkers up and puts an arm around my shoulder.

"You would be, Emma, in the words of Cole Porter, Oh, so easy to love.''

"Wendell, this must stop.''

"He was an old Blue, you know, class of 'thirteen.''

"Actually, I knew.''

"Really? How did you know?''

"I'm very tired, Wendell. I want to go to my room and be quiet. Thank you for the day.''

His voice wafts up behind me as I limp up the stairs.

"So worth the yearning for. So swell to keep every home fire burning for."

Just about a year ago we had a birthday party for Michael. Everybody was nicely into the sauce and some of the younger ones were high on hash. Michael and Daniel and Eliot Fry and Howie Evarts started playing a game called "Did." It's a game where a sheet of paper is passed around and each person must add lines to the theme. It works best at two in the morning when pizza crusts abound, a distraught ingenue is crying in the bathroom, and molten wax from melted candles has congealed on the tables. "Did" goes something like this:

> Montgomery Clift in the buff, did
> Jean Genet in the rough, did.

> Marcel Proust in the sack, did
> Somerset Maugham in a hack, did.

> Monty Woolley of Yale, did
> Oscar Wilde in a gaol, did.

And there were variations.

> In the Florida keys, Tennessee did
> Down on his knees, André Gide did.

> Waslaw Nijinsky mincingly did
> Leonardo da Vinci wincingly did.

> Noel Coward mind-boggedly did
> Cole Porter bull-doggedly did.

And that night, Michael's was the final entry on the page.

> But dear old Christopher Isher-would
> Only if Auden said he could.

This memory is emetic. It causes me to stop into the third-floor bathroom and lose my Fitzwilly's lunch.

Nine o'clock finds me in bed deeply concerned about Goddards, père et fils. I am trying to read one of Nanny's old *Reader's Digest*s. An April 1938 article called "Twenty Months in Alcatraz," by Brian Conway, #293. Another Hibernian gone wrong. The shades are drawn tightly and I read with a flashlight, under the covers. I do this because, if Amazing Grace glances across from her third floor to mine, I don't want her to know that I'm home. My concentration falters, Conway's words blur on the page, and I close my eyes. In that foggy canyon somewhere between sleep and consciousness, Marion rises from her Grove Street plot, wearing the yellow chenille robe that still hangs in her closet. She floats over the roofs of the city like a Chagallian spirit; she wafts through the walls of Nanny's room. She speaks to me in a well-modulated New England voice. She asks:

"Do you think you can be of use here?"

I don't know. I think you have left, in your wake, the saddest, loneliest men I have ever met.

Twelve

"**I** gather you haven't read them yet."

Wendell catches me in Richard's bedroom. I'm attempting to change the bedsheets and I'm astounded at the condition of the linens in this house. The ones I'm removing from the bed must be thirty years old. They are so thin in the middle you can see right through them. The ones I intended to replace them with are worse. Long, ragged rips up the middle. And one hundred percent cotton. No polyester here, so they'll have to be ironed. These must have come down from Richard's, or Marion's, mother.

"No, Wendell, I haven't. Your father could give you a much better critique than I."

"I don't want a critique. I want your gut reaction."

"Well, your friend Monica, then. Ask her for her gut reaction."

"I've *got* that, for fuck's sake! She worships the paper I write on. She *fawns*, which is no help at all. Look, this is no big deal. Why are you making such a big deal? Just read the damn things. Any time. No rush."

"OK, I will. May I get into your room to change your sheets?"

"No."

"I don't get it. You won't let me in, in case I read your poetry. But you've handed me poems to read. What are you growing in there? Marijuana? Poppies? What?"

"Mold. I'll take the sheets off the bed and bring them to you."

Peg has a remedy for sheets like this. You cut them in two and flip them, taking the outside borders and sewing them together. That way the worn parts are switched to the sides of the bed, and the strong parts are in the middle. You do then have an irritating seam up the middle, but the life of the sheets is doubled. Peg also has a theory that (1) sheets don't get as dirty in the winter because people are cleaner in the winter, and (2) in all seasons the top sheet never gets as dirty as the bottom one. This led to a procedure whereby, when she changed the sheets, she changed only one. Put the top one down on the bottom, the fresh one on top. Michael refused to sleep in such half-soiled beds. I can't remember if they did these things in *Little Women*, but I imagine they did. I'll write home tonight. I'd rather call, but they both are unable to converse long distance. Kevin says,

"God save me from Ma Bell. Talk is supposed to be cheap. In fact, it's supposed to be free. Free speech is in the Constitution. Ma Bell is unconstitutional."

Waiting for Wendell's sheets, wanting to peruse and even, yes, snoop. Heavy mahogany Empire furniture here, with a V up the middle of all the drawers. Kevin taught me this was crotch-grain. On top of the dresser a hand mirror with long wooden handle and matching clothes brush. Cherry, I think. In a glass cabinet, tarnished sterling silver cups in front of four pewter drinking mugs, all engraved with *Lux et Veritas*. In the closet a surprise pair of black patent opera shoes, and four cashmere scarves

from the Hebrides via Brooks Brothers. If I'm here in the
spring when the ferns unfurl and the lilacs bloom I'll store
these in mothballs. On a shelf, an empty Asprey box. By
Appointment to Her Majesty. One Countess Mara tie, one
Hermès-Paris that Michael would kill for, and a dozen
from the Yale Co-op. All the shirts from Gant and Sero.
Studiously conservative. All the underwear also from the
Co-op. Isn't a cooperative store a paradox at a university
that declared, a half century ago:

> You may not bring your valet with you when you
> come to Yale.

Breathtaking, suddenly, this glimpse over the right shoulder, through the front window, across the porch roof, to a
maple in flame. Galvanized, for a moment, by this voluminous tree, its fiery breadth visible only here, in Richard's room. And the bed. The years alone in the bed, with
Marion quartered, cloistered, on the other side of the
bathroom. Their separate realms—disjunction, disfunction,
disassociation, with the bathroom up the middle like a
fissure. He said they all ignored each other successfully.
What could be successful in such ignorance? Bookshelves
in Marion's room containing the complete works of James
Whitcomb Riley, a thin volume of Elizabeth Barrett Brown-
ing's *Sonnets from the Portuguese*, paperback editions of
Victoria Holt, and three Bibles. Peg came to me on my
wedding night and delivered herself of these thoughts:

> "If there's trouble in bed, there's trouble everywhere.
> What happens in bed is the mucilage that holds it all
> together. This house is falling down around us. The
> city's falling down around the house. And in the
> middle of it all, your old dad's my mooring. And I'm
> his. See?"

Oh, my Pegeen with eyes to die for. I didn't then, but I do
now.
     Wendell's sheets, when he brings them, are in the same
tattered condition. I ask him if there's a sewing machine in

the house. There is, in one of the unused maid's rooms on
the third floor. I take four more sets from the linen closet
and head upstairs as Wendell returns to his room. Before
he bolts his door he says,

"Hey, listen, no rush, OK? Any time."

I set about threading the machine. It's a treadle, circa
1910. That must have been just about the time that Paris
Singer squandered his sewing machine inheritance on Isadora
Duncan. The profit from this treadle might have purchased
a Grecian gown for one of her recitals. An odd connection,
here in the mausoleum.

I must read the poems before the day is out. But in the
blessed name of God, my hands are sweating, my pump-
ing ankles throb, and my thoughts have turned once again
toward mooring. Cut adrift six months ago, I was con-
vinced I'd find a life-preserving buoyancy in floating free.
But more and more I find Richard Goddard unerringly
substantial. More and more he is revealed as a sort of
super-steward, caring for his mother and Nanny after his
father's death, providing for the frail Marion, tolerating
the mercurial Wendell, and watching through it all over
this deteriorating house. When the mail arrives, the little
windowed envelopes containing property taxes, automobile insurances, household insurances, bills from plumb-
ers, carpenters, glaziers—all are destined for Richard's
desk. He is the Keeper of the Accounts, he is where the
buck originates and where the buck stops. He is the um-
brella under which Wendell and I function. I've heard him
on the phone, playing guru to colleagues and students,
advising, informing, negotiating, mediating. And something deep within me stirs, and no longer wants to float
free. It wants his approval, protection, paternalism.

At breakfast this morning he said,

"You have extraordinary eyes."

"Thank you. Here," I said, proffering his toast. "I
give you this day your daily bread, with fiber."

"And your wit," he said, "is lambent."

He reiterated that he didn't intend to go to Park Avenue this weekend. It was an electric moment. The eyes latched and there was, in that connection, the unspoken hope that Wendell would travel to Bennington. I felt concern for him.

"Richard, this grudge that Wendell bears is quite serious. Are you aware of it?"

"Indeed I am. He has a vendetta in store for me."

"What form do you think it will take?"

Surprisingly, he smiles, unaffected by the gravity of my question.

"I think he will, someday, be a great poet. He has the mark. I think he won't ever compromise; he'll hew to his art at all costs. He'll take what he needs from people and then leave them by the wayside. And when I'm old, he'll go to Stockholm to accept the Nobel Prize. With bulbs flashing all around him he'll say, 'There is one person I wish to thank. My father. Everything he stands for is anathema to me. I totally ignored the role model he provided, and to this do I owe this great honor.' "

Damn it, man, this is serious.

"He told me about Silver Hill, and Rae-Ann Wilks."

"Yes, I thought he would. There are a lot of skeletons and a lot of dirty linen, but one fact remains. I stayed in my marriage because of Wendell. He will say I was here in name only, and that, regrettably, is true. He won't say, because he can't know, how desperate the alternative would have been. Had I divorced, Marion would have gotten custody. She wouldn't have married again, and she couldn't support herself. He would have grown up on limited means, isolated from the real world, a nursemaid in constant attendance to a woman who simply couldn't function. I've heard him say that he was Marion's ambassador from the real world. That's sad, and imperfect, but most of life is. I did provide him with some semblance of a real world, some of the time. It's not much but it is, for me, a small comfort in a lifetime of discomfiture.''

I followed Richard out to the Peugeot and it was there that he introduced me to our neighbor, Professor Silverman. I took a long, probing look, because he and Richard are the same age. But Silverman's seriously overweight. His heavy jowls make his face a moon when he smiles. Peg said,

"Chicken fat'll kill the Jews, olive oil the Greeks, suet the Brits, but the Irish'll flourish forever on Good Queen Spud."

I thought Silverman jolly, and sufficiently satisfied with his life. There is contentment in his walk; he's placid and pacific and I think he bears malice toward none. As Lotte Lenya sang in Harold Prince's *Cabaret*,

"You learn to settle for what you get."

Professor Silverman bought that, hook, line, and sinker.

Wendell thinks that Richard did, too, resulting in a life of sham. But Wendell, Richard didn't. Hasn't. I see something stifled in the spirit; the baser emotions are clamped in a steel trap. There's still questing in the eyes, and festering ferment in the head. He wants to cut it loose, I think, but can't. Shackled too long to moderation and temperance, abstaining too long from the primal scream. Oh, Richard, let me help you rout it out! Share with me your wildest dreams, your secret fantasies, your classified thoughts. My lips are sealed; I won't tell a soul. As Oedipus said at Colonus:

"Mum's the word."

Otherwise, Richard, when they stash you away in your appointed plot at Grove Street Cemetery, the epitaph on the obelisk will say: HE WAS SCARED DIARRHETICALLY SHITLESS.

Michael Riley, have you heard? Your old lady's gone south into Brontë country. You laugh. Ah, ha, you say, she's searching for the holy grail in Rochester's crotch. It's just, however, ritual at this point. (There are so few *choices*, Michael, when men and women are confined at one address.) And darling man, it's good to know one's instincts have survived. Good to know one's signs are still vital. Good to feel sex rear its head again. I'm talking now of that historical spectacle, the female receptacle. I reacted once again this morning with bedroom eyes and husky muskiness in the throat. I trotted about this particular cave, dropping spoor. I abandoned, for a fleeting flash, my emissary. I was true and real. How I'd love to live like that each moment of the day. How I'd love to, once and for all, *murther* the emissary. Hemlock in the ear, an asp at the neck, a dagger under the pillow. But I wonder, Michael, who would I *be* without her? What is the residue that would be left behind? A hermit? A misanthrope? A blithering blob that slithers about the world in unkempt, smelly suspension? How does one exist without artifice and wiles? The minute I'm able to fully countenance my real, true countenance, I'll banish the false fiend. I can't, as yet, and so we must companion each other and wait for further revelations.

I hear Wendell coming up the stairs. Sweet Jesus, let me seam these sheets in peace. He goes across the hall and slides something under my bedroom door. I pray it's not more Cole Porter. Night and Day I am the one.

Wendell, Monica is the one! Worshipping and fawning, nymphlike, no doubt, at twenty. Unrestricted by Catholic caveats. A nimble contortionist, free of barriers in the brain, barriers in the vaginal canal. Unobstructed by visions of buttonhooks prying loose the living fetus in back-alley butcher shops. Free of the absolute certainty of purgatory, eternally. How I always envied them, the Protestant, savvy girls at Hillford High. They found my St. Anne's thinking medieval. To this do I trace the anachronism of my life.

Piles of sheets, sliced up the middle and nicely rotated. I think this will guarantee approval from Richard. He'll say where did you learn to be so ingenious? At my mother's knee.

Inside Nanny's room, I stoop to read the neatly lettered card:

> *Wendell Wharton Goddard*
> *Requests the pleasure of your company*
> *Sunday morning at ten o'clock*
> *At the boob-tube in the upstairs sitting room*
> *To watch the Reverend Jerry Falwell*
> *Exhort, from Lynchburg, Virginia,*
> *Our feckless nation, steeped in crime and vice.*
> R.S.V.P.

This means he will not travel to Bennington this weekend.

Thirteen

The poems:

☐　　　☐　　　☐

My father, who had never loved my mother,
Laid her to rest in most indecent haste.
Her voice still resonating through our lives,
He peeled his mourning suit to play the suitor
With a woman, at our cottage, on the Vineyard.

They drove through Buzzard's Bay
Stopping for lunch at Sally's Clam Cafe
Where my mother, who had never loved my father
Took me to celebrate my twentieth
Ceremoniously ordering my first, public drink.

When they arrived, my father held the Leica
Photographing the interloping woman
Posed hip-high in day lilies.
My mother planted them in '70
Saying they were, unlike her, indestructible.

On the beach one day the woman posed again
Palm thrust forward
Displaying the radial ribbing
And undulated edges of a scallop shell.
She wore a hat, tied against the wind
A straw hat bought at Provinctown
By my father, for my mother.

The radiant sun was scorching hot, he said.
He *said* no insult was intended.

    ☐   ☐   ☐

Strutting down Telegraph
California girls in May
Nipples bobbing, clogs clacking
Oleander in their hair
They stop for abalone earrings
Haggling with a vendor at the curb.

I like them best at Strawberry Canyon
Around the pool in early day
In a gauze of fog
Crept past the Golden Gate
Trespassing in the hills.

Through filtered morning mist
Perfection. Bodies blur
Each sagging breast is vague
Bulging hips obscure
Forgiving fog has air-brushed every flaw
Shrouded each appendix scar.

    ☐   ☐   ☐

I have felt so alone with this charge. I have felt, for the first time, like calling Michael, soliciting his opinion. There's this kid here, Michael, and he's trusted me with these poems, and I haven't got the wherewithal. Help. I wait twenty-four hours, considering and rehearsing, editing and embellishing my reactions. I find Wendell in the back yard, on the yellow chaise longue. I carry the poems with me. His body turns rigid the minute he sees them in my hand.

"I like them very much."

"Do you? Why?"

I'm prepared.

"Because of what they convey. Because of what each conveys about you. In the first one you try, all through

the poem, to distance yourself from the pain of this
. . . interloping woman. It gathers momentum and
then, in the last line there is a howl. At the injustice
of her visit. Do you have a title for it?''

''Got it now. I'll call it 'Interloping Woman.' And
the other one?''

''Well, I think it shows more of your light side, and
less of your dark. We see how badly you want all the
girls to be beautiful, and I guess, by extension, the
world. So the forgiving fog isn't elemental, really. It
belongs to you. It is you, waving a magic wand over
the scene, to make the picture perfect.''

''You didn't take me seriously, did you, when I said
you'd be easy to love?''

''Wendell, do you have a title for the second one?''

''You're evading me.''

''Yes. Please allow me that, for both our sakes.''

''The title will be 'Forgiving Fog.' If you had just
one word to describe the poems, both of them, what
word would you choose?''

Mercy. I've been on a roll so far, but I fear it's skidding to
a halt.

''Let me think about that.''

''Don't think. React.''

''Coastal.''

''Pardon?''

''I'd call them coastal poems. I mean, Buzzard's Bay
and Berkeley. I feel the aura of the two places. The

Vineyard is formal, and Yankee, and Berkeley is loose, and laid back.''

He vaults from the chaise.

"Jesus Christ, a *blind* man would see *that!*''

"I'm sorry! Obviously, you have a word in mind, and I didn't hit on it.''

"*Hit* on it? You're not even in the fucking ball park! Christ, anything would be better than *coastal*. Poignant, pithy, searing, cathartic, Jesus, *anything* but coastal! You just don't take me seriously.''

"Oh, for Heaven's sake, of course I do!''

"You don't! You treat me like a juvenile. You find the work purile.''

"I don't know what purile means.''

"Fuck, you don't! If I were thirty, would you take my feelings seriously?''

"What are we talking about here? Your feelings, or these damn coastal poems?''

He grabs my arm, violently, and whirls me around.

"Listen, you are causing me frigging *torment!*''

Throws me on the lounge, and marches into the house.

In Richard's study I find Webster, and attempt to look up "purile." As Annie Sullivan said, in *The Miracle Worker*, "You have to know how to spell it before you can look up how to spell it." Ah. Yes. P U E. Puerile.

Childish. Silly, Akin to Greek *pais*.
Boy. Puerilism in adults: a symp-
tom of mental disorder.

That definition will get no argument from me.

I begin making a cheese soufflé for supper. I have four
eggs in a bowl, and as I start to beat them, Wendell hurls
into the kitchen. His face is crimson. He throws *Mistress
Bradstreet* across the room where it bangs against the
door of the dryer. I hear its spine crack as it hits the floor.

"Don't think I don't know what's going on! I've seen
him pawing you!"

"How dare you screech in here screaming at me! For
God's sake, my heart's in my mouth. I haven't been
pawed in months. What in hell are you talking about?"

"I saw him, at the car, when he said goodbye. He
had his hands all over you."

Quickly, this turns to nightmare. His mouth is buried in
my hair and he's repeating my name. Mustering force, I push
against his chest and he pins my wrists behind my back.
Merciful heavens, he's erect against my pelvis. His teeth
dig into my neck.

"Wendell! Jesus! You're *violent*."

With one hand free, I lunge for the eggbeater. I wave it
at him, spattering him with drops of liquid egg. Then I
shake it at him, spewing egg mixture into his eyes and all
over the kitchen.

"I swear to God, I really do think you have a mental
disorder!"

He falls against the counter, wiping his face, wailing:

"What do I have to do to make you take me seriously?"

"Grow up, Wendell Wharton! Grow up and smarten up. Now, listen to me, I think you're behaving this way because you want me to go to your father. You want me to tattle. You want a big brouhaha. Well, I won't give you the satisfaction. I give you a warning, instead. This is it, kid. You lay a hand on me one more time and I'll quit. Depart without explanation. Exit. Leave *you* to tell your father what a bad boy you've been.

"And furthermore, it's essential that you start taking *me* seriously! I have just come out of a disastrous marriage. It has shaken me down to my toes. It has aged me. And it's given me some insight into adult unhappiness. So I understand why your father vegetated for years. And I understand why he went to Nee Marchant."

He approaches me again, all contrition, arms outstretched.

"Please help me."

"Get away! Get out of here! Take the Volvo, for God's sake, and go up to Bennington. Go get your bi-monthly Monica fuck! *Promise me* you'll go."

"I can't," he whispers. "I can't leave you alone with *him*."

He backs away and glances at me, then turns and looks at me, amazed at what he sees. I have the eggbeater in one hand, a paring knife in the other, and one eye is peeled on a rolling pin. He shakes his head in disbelief.

"Good Christ," he says. "There's rape in the air."

He appears to be disoriented. He forces himself to look, methodically, from stove to refrigerator to washing machine, needing confirmation that he's in the kitchen. Swaying, he loses his bearings and reaches for the back of a chair. Is it a ruse? My instinct is to drop my weapons, run, and shore him up. He falls into the chair, breathing heavily, hyperventilating. When the crimson leaves his face he looks wan and jaundiced. He is, for a moment, without artifice.

"I've told this to a dozen psychiatrists, let me try it out on you. I have seizures. Sometimes they're euphoric and sublime, sometimes they erupt in behavior I don't understand. Like this . . . attack on you, just now. It's not multiple personality and it's not split personality, but it is some kind of omniscient madness. I remove myself from myself, stand back and witness this person doing irrational things. I'm astounded at what I see in me. And I'm astounded at what I see around me. My vision of things is abnormal, visionary, holographic, X-ray. I *sense* peoples' souls and psyches. They stand before me revealed, unwittingly. I'm prescient. I'm Svengali, Rasputin, Machiavelli and Peck's bad boy all rolled into one big conundrum.

"I can't contain it all. And I'm fucking furious at the imbalance of my nature. Wordsworth said poets begin in gladness and end in madness. I got half of the formula. I was born at the end. My mother was crazy Miss Havisham and my father's a robot. I am fucking *pissed* that I've been swindled out of the former. There's not been one iota of gladness to temper the madness.

"The shrinks fall into two categories. One group says they've got a cache of chemicals that will align all this and make me just like the boy next door. The other group listens, and pauses, and shrugs, and says, 'Poets are like that.' "

Gently now, he takes the utensils from my clenched hands and places them on the counter. He is calm, but he is not the boy next door, and I don't think he ever will be. I have my own prescient moment. My God, I see this boy's life bounding ahead of him in terms marine: stormy seas, tossing ships, turbulent winds, tortuous encounters. I see no peace or happiness or tranquility. If there is any logic, any sense, it will only appear on the papers that house his poems.

He puts his hands on my shoulders.

"Forgive me. And thank you for reading the poems. And thank you for liking Lydia, and ordering the house, and being so good-natured. Thank you, also, for your fairness regarding Dad. One has to appreciate fairness, wherever one finds it."

He leaves me and goes to fetch the battered *Mistress Bradstreet*.

"It's important, really, it's paramount that you stay. I give you my solemn promise this won't happen again."

There are three loose pages. He offers the book an apology,

"Sorry, old lady. A seizure."

As he leaves the kitchen, he turns and smiles. It is a sweet, open, dimpled smile, yet tinged with melancholy.

"It's a good thing people are more resilient than books."

I am fond of him.

Fourteen

Sunday morning and sad old songs linger in my head. Caused by Wendell, Richard, the season, life. The leaves of brown come tumbling down when an early autumn stalks the land and chills the breeze, and the days grow short when you reach September.

What will you do today, Michael? Rise at noon, exercise a half hour to wake up the old cardiovascular, sit down to Daniel's blueberry pancakes. Afternoon then, at the Buskin putting gels in the lights, storing away the samovar until the next Chekhov or Gorky, tracking down a crystal unicorn for Laura to fetch from the glass menagerie. Perhaps a light supper at the Cambridge flat. B.L.T.s. Then to grind the Colombian beans from that place down at Quincy Market. Goddamn things cost a dime apiece, but worth it. White sugar is bad for you Daniel says now, instead of me. Best use the raw brown. Sipping the brew then, while watching Mike and Harry and Ed and Morley, and sweet old Andy Rooney with his numerous gripes and protests.

I need a breather. I need to be alone in the house, to indulge my mood. To iron Bondex denim patches on Wendell's jeans, roam and ramble at my leisure, sample the vistas of the various rooms from chairs of various epochs. Glue the flapping rubber tubing down around the refrigerator door; improve the insulation. Spray bleach on the shower curtains' charcoal streaks, kill the mildew. And while immersing in Marion's bathtub, the only tub in the place, amidst the froth of Marion's Vitabath, have a deep think about Richard's appeal and Wendell's dilemma. And soak there for upwards of two hours, a reclining body of thought.

Instead, I'm in the upstairs sitting room at 9:55 A.M. At 9:57 Wendell comes in.

"What the fuck did you do to my sheets? There's a big sharp welt up the middle."

At 9:59 Richard strolls in, saying,

"For God's sake, Emma, if we need new sheets, say so. I'm being flayed to death."

You can take the girl out of the poverty, but you can't take the poverty out of the girl. I said that to Michael once and it angered him. He said it was an un-American thought, the sort of thinking that keeps the downtrodden down, the underdog under. He said that's what entrenches the debilitating structure of classes in England and in black ghettos across America. They are their own worst enemy. Shuffling, rolling eyes, frying the gut of the pig. Michael said that's why Sammy Davis wrote a book called, *Yes, I Can!*. With an affirmative exclamation point. Don't look back, he said. Expunge the past. But, Michael, if I do that, who the hell will I *be*? With an existential question mark.

We manage a little levity while watching Jerry Falwell. Richard wanders in and out, performing Sunday morning ablutions. He observes that he should have sent Wendell to Liberty College, instead of Yale. Engender the fear of God, he says, and forget about light and truth. Wendell clearly waits all week for this interlude with Jerry Falwell. It is for him a condensed hour of hateful homilies.

"Did you hear *that?* Did you *hear* what that asshole said? This is scandalous; it shouldn't be allowed. Jesus Christ, this guy oughtta be lynched! Where the hell is the moral minority? Where the hell is the FCC? And wouldja look at that audience? Lapping it up like hogs at a trough. Can you *believe* this is on

television for little kids to see? Little, innocent children all across the country are sitting with their bowls
of Apple Jacks watching this horseshit.''

He stands up and cups his hands, apparently addressing the
youth of the nation.

"Little, innocent children, hear me! *Get a second
opinion!*''

I do not share his hilarity. He stops and searches my face.

"You're not responding.''

He calls.

"Dad! Emma's in a funk.''

Richard rushes in.

"Look at her. Our live-in's got the blues.''

"What's the matter? Is it the sheets? Did we hurt
your feelings?''

This is embarrassing.

"No, no, it's not the sheets. Rainy days and Sundays
get me down.''

"Homesick,'' says Wendell.

"Well, we can't have that, can we?'' says Richard.
"Come downstairs. I'd like to show you some things.''

Richard sits me in his study and trots out memorabilia
that is dear to him. He thinks this will rouse me from my
Bean-Town reverie, and he's right eventually. First there
is a watercolor of their house at Edgartown. Gray shingles,
rambling roses, a deacon's bench, a wheelbarrow full of

petunias. An ancient, fragile map of New Haven County.
Then a prized first edition of *Boswell's London Journal*.
Encouraged, he pulls a photo album from a shelf and
shows me a small black-and-white picture of Wendell,
thirty-six hours old. The babe is so ugly I have to grin:
Wendell's little hands have been folded over his chest,
corpselike. His nose is listing toward his left ear, and he
has forceps marks on his temples.

Wendell hurries in with his own booty. A baseball
autographed by Reggie Jackson, a boyhood butterfly collection that is all vibrant orange and iridescent. A card he
made in first grade, for his mother. There is a Crayola
candle on the front of it and inside it says,

    hapy birthday mama from your SON.

I think they are like puppies, bringing forth their favorite bones. I think they're like me at fifteen, offering up
three hundred pictures from my Elvis Presley collection for
Aunt Colleen to admire when she came from Montreal.
They are also like Kevin, who continues to carry a wad of
string around just in case the new water-meter man hasn't
seen a cat's cradle. I try very hard to fathom the sentiments surrounding the mounting pile. Peg always said that
was my strong suit, fathoming the sentiments. Yes, Kevin
said, she's very good at that, but why does it always make
her cry? Premenstrual tension, said Peg. No, said Kev,
she came out of the womb ineffably sad. And when she
opened her eyes she saw madness in the world.

"Well, if she did," said Peg, "it's your fault."

The two men are being so kind, it is difficult not to
react. They have rallied to my side and, in doing so, have
unified themselves to some degree. Their old, rankling
history does not surface on this day. Perhaps if I were
gloomy more often, they would rise to the occasion more
often. The squeaky wheel gets the oil. But that is Wendell's song—the tenet, I think, that he lives by. He is,
however, a perfect gentleman today. His seizure, or al-

leged seizure, is a thing of the past. He does not understand that his unbalanced nature causes a dichotomy in the
reaction of those around him. So armored am I against his
wiles, his artifice, his performance, that I don't know how
to function when he sheds that carapace and reveals himself. And the sad thing is that Richard, after years of
constant exposure to Wendell's inconstancy, is oblivious
to the changes. Thus, when Wendell says he has to visit
Grace, to assist Raymond with a paper on solar energy,
Richard remains armored and doesn't reply. I, the novi-
tiate, make a stab.

"It's so good of you to give time to that boy, Wendell."

"Well," he says, and stops.

Mischief crosses his face. I'll bet he's got some smart
retort about boys who don't have fathers; fatherless boys
flocking together. But, no.

"Well," he repeats. "Thank you."

And before he leaves, he asks,

"How can I help the little lady today? May I set the
table?"

"That would be great. Thank you."

Richard is wearing a blue checked shirt under a navy
blue V-neck sweater. I wonder if he knows how well all
that blue complements his silver hair. He wanders into the
kitchen as I prepare to roast a chicken, and watches me
toss a stuffing of prunes, figs, and dried apricots.

"This is so good, Emma. Sunday, at home, with a
bird in the oven."

He tastes the stuffing and his left hand drapes around me
to rest on my hip. I am quite undone at the warmth of his

hand through my skirt. Jesus, Mary and Joseph, be still my palpitating heart.

"Try not to brood on your ex-husband. You're making such a contribution here, and surely this day is proof of it. You are the household catalyst."

It *is* good, and relaxed and enjoyable here in the Goddard mausoleum. It's good to have one's sulks attended to, good to see the prodigal pitching in, good to have a man beside you, sampling food and licking his fingers. Richard sits at the table and opens his Sunday New York *Times*—what Michael used to call The Sabbath Behemoth. He browses for a moment and then rises to get a cup of coffee.

"I wish you could stay here forever."

Mercy, is there an appropriate reply? What does he imply? Does *he* mean to stay here forever? Does he not intend to wed-up and bed-down with the seashell lady when the prodigal departs? Does he think he and I could exist here forever in some sort of platonic pact? Or is it just that God's in His Heaven, all's well with the world, when Wendell isn't agitating and there's a bird in the oven? I don't wish to dampen the day with intrusive inquiries. I drop a little spoor, instead.

"It might be difficult, over a period of time, to prolong the platonic."

(There are so few *choices*, Michael, etc.)

He looks stunned and strangely apologetic.

"Am I that obvious?"

"I don't know. It depends. I can't quite fathom the sentiments around your wanting me to stay. But there is . . . an affiliation."

He rises from the table and moves to the counter, beside me. For a moment he's silent, thinking, watching me shred cabbage for cole slaw.

"It's your eyes," he says. "And your wit is trenchant."

"Thank you."

"Emma, I'm fifty-five. And you've been badly hurt."

"Yes. We've somehow gotten all accelerated. I don't know if what you just said was a passing thought or a leading statement. I don't know what your commitment is to Miss Marchant."

"Neither do I. That's what prevented me from going this weekend. It's all very murky."

He returns to the table where he idly shuffles around the sections of the paper.

"I know that Wendell will never accept Nee. And Wendell's what I'm all about right now. Making amends with Wendell. Nee finds it all very boring. In a way it's wrong to continue with her, but I feel indebted. She saw me through the decision to commit Marion. She was a sounding board—she never urged it. She saw me through the funeral. I was a basket case when I met her and she saw me through it all."

I'm now going to be boldly intrusive. I'm going to ask a leading question.

"Is there passion?"

He looks away, ambling toward the butler's pantry.

"There's sex. Companionship. There's always been an . . . affiliation. But there's never been that . . . acceleration. To use our words."

Our words.

He moves back to the table, sits, finds the "Connecticut" section.

"I don't know. I just don't know. I'll have to work it out."

He reads for a moment and I wonder if we have terminated the subject. Immediately, the article annoys him.

"Damn! They're talking about striking again. The maintenance people at Yale. God, I hope it can be avoided. The last time it happened the students had to be farmed out to faculty living rooms."

"Richard?"

"Yes?"

"Wendell gave me two of his poems to read."

His mouth gapes. He falls against the back of his chair and removes his reading glasses.

"I don't believe it! Did you like them?"

"Very much."

"What were they like?"

"Well, he placed one at the Vineyard, and the other in Berkeley."

"Was the Vineyard one about Marion?"

"Yes. I don't think I should discuss them, really. Not yet. It'd be a betrayal of his trust. But I think we might make a concerted effort to get him to start submitting. I mean, he's never going to get to Stockholm, is he, if he doesn't join the gang in the U.S.

mails? So if you hear me making noises to that effect,
I'd appreciate your support.''

"You can count on it.''

We want, I think, to embrace each other. We don't,
because his indebtedness to Nee still hangs in the air. We
just smile at each other. We're in a kind of conspiratorial
cahoots, and there is mutual gladdening in our hearts.

Wendell Wharton, you're not the only one to get half of
the formula. You're not the only one pissed off at the
swindle. So few of us begin in gladness. It's not a given;
it's very hard to come by. But sometimes, after neglected
childhoods, disastrous marriages, premature deaths, even
after flaming faggot faerie queens marry into the family,
God or Whomever thrusts a little shiny fragment of gladness across your path.

Our words.

Oh, lambent, trenchant, happy entity am I.

My gladness held through the following day, and on
Tuesday Lydia arrived once again. There was a chill in the
house and I, unthinkingly, wore a black cardigan sweater.

"You takes dat off,'' she said, "and I stays. You
doan, den I goes.''

At noon, Wendell borrowed the Volvo, mysteriously.
He returned with a single rose swathed in green florist's
paper. He gave it to Lydia and kissed her, lightly, on the
lips. He said that he buys this rose weekly, from autumn to
spring, to help Lydia get through the winter. It was
endearing—his gesture, her reaction. In that moment, Wendell was gallant and Lydia was young. In that moment
their disparate cultures, colors, ages, fell away, leaving
behind a naked kernel, an essence of humanity. Still, the
moment made me feel inadequate to the task of this boy.
There was something aberrant in the kiss. What a bubbling
cauldron of complexities he is. What a witch's brew of
contradictions.

He sat, tucked up yogalike on the floor outside of the

downstairs bathroom. He listened attentively to Lydia while she scoured Vanish around the toilet bowl with a big blue brush. It was something about a German submarine that blew up the *Lusitania*. It was, again, an amalgam of Uncle Remus and Alistair Cooke.

"It's dem life boats, see? Daze none on de boat. 'Cuz dem bosses on de boat dey guilty of criminal neglect. History show twelve hundred souls meets dey death in de deep, and dat heinous act be lyin' on de door-step of British mismanagement, nowheres else I can see."

As she was preparing to leave, Wendell took her into the hall and whispered to her. I was folding laundry in the kitchen and I heard.

"Lydia, I finally showed someone my poems."

"Praise de Lawd! Who you show?"

"Emma."

"What she say?"

"Good things."

"Good things? Anybody who say *good* things, you got to *treat* good. You hear me, boy?"

"Yes, Lydia, I do. And I will."

She trundled off at four with her jugs of good St. Ronan drinking water. As night moved in the house grew chilly again and I went for my black cardigan. But when I got to Nanny's room I took a blue one, instead, out of deference to Lydia.

Fifteen

In my autograph book, in sixth grade, Maureen Cleary wrote:

> Little dot of powder
> Little dab of paint
> Makes us into something
> That we really ain't.

Amazing Grace and Minnie Misfit are together again for the very first time.

The Club Vincent is not for talking, it is for fun. Vehement, vigorous fun. Grace and I are eating spaghetti that suffers from oregano overkill. All You Can Eat For $4.99. There's a man at one end of the bar with a handful of peanuts. He rotates his hand three or four times and then chucks a peanut into the air as he cocks back his head. I'd estimate, from the nuts on the floor, a fifty percent success rate. At the other end of the bar there's another man rolling peanuts nervously in his palm. A sort of Neapolitan Captain Queeg. And there's one in the middle of the bar who appears to have his genitals in a twist. Repeatedly, and surreptitiously he thinks, he rearranges himself with his right hand. It's a gentle gesture, rather like plumping a tiny pillow.

This crowd is thirty to fifty and determinedly red-blooded. Opposite Grace and me, two young men attempt to converse over the blaring music of The Police:

"So she asks me, do I go to Yale? I say, yeah, Tuesdays and Thursdays when I bring them their milk."

A visit to the Club Vincent is not unlike a visit to the old neighborhood. Everybody here says wou-unt and cou-unt and shou-unt. And Cat'lic. Born one of them, why do I harbor these feelings of abject despair when faced with them head-on? It's not that I want to sit around discussing The Theory of Spectra and Atomic Constitution. I just ache for them to have some cognizance of other modes, other socioeconomic strata. Hey you, Salvatore, some parmesan please, and while you're at it, just a minute measure of perception, sir, into other voices, other rooms. But the hand that rocked the cradle punched the clock. Michael told me it was Thomas Gray who said that ignorance was bliss. I say up your Elegy, Tom. Ignorance is slow suffocation in a house whose windows are hermetically sealed. Grace says,

"Thank God the Silvermans got Raymond out of this."

"But, Grace, didn't they get you out, too?"

What I am really asking is what are we two classy broads doing in this gussied-up pizza parlor? Why are we sitting in this room rimmed with wrought-iron trellises which host a veritable forest of paraffin creeping ivy?

"No," she says. "You don't get out when you're Italian and pregnant at seventeen."

She says it is most clearly brought home to her at PTA meetings at the Foote School. She is unable to ask the correct questions about the curriculum. She just hasn't got the right vocabulary. She is most useful, she says, when they have bake sales to raise money. She contributes wondrous pastries, tortes, Florentine Corn Meal Cake, and something called Panforte di Siena. She takes her copper pot and sets up a booth and makes zabaglione right before their eyes. Her culinary efforts accounted for twenty-five percent of the new word processing machine at the school and forty percent of the funds needed to send the kids on a field trip to the Metropolitan Museum in New York. The ultimate compliment and the ultimate degradation occurred last year when one of the Foote mothers called and asked Grace if she would consider catering a private party.

"See? Mostly I shine in the kitchen."

She has strong, intuitive feelings about policy at Foote, and sometimes she sits in her room and rehearses what she wants to say at meetings. But the intuitive doesn't carry the day when you're in a classroom full of tired parents and teachers at eight o'clock at night. She makes her points passionately, persuasively, like an orator on a soap box or an evangelist in a pulpit or a politician at a rally. Her audience looks askance. They find something suspect in her arguments. They don't want emotion at the end of their professional day. They have been born and bred to thrive on restraint and understatement.

"No matter how much I rehearse, I always come off like an emotional WOP. But Raymond," she says, "won't. He'll be very calm and logical."

This conversation is depressing the hell out of me. But, hark, Vincent himself draws nigh. He is a velvet man, exuding softness and consideration. He is, I'm afraid, the victim of the madonna/whore syndrome where ladies are concerned. He's about five-nine, burly, with kind doe-eyes and no discernible neck. He asks Grace where she's been hiding me. He holds his ears against The Police and says that when he wins the lottery he's bringing in Julio Iglesias to sing *his* kind of music. Then he orders us another bottle of Chianti, on the house. I think I could like Vincent, especially if he'd take off his ring. It is large, boasting ten diamonds in a "V". The likes of this ring were never seen at Firestone and Parson. But, Lord, he is warm as a zephyr and he doesn't force himself. His talk is small at first and then, when Grace goes off to dance, he doesn't bulldoze. A waiter brings him a wine glass, and he quite definitely settles in for an overture.

Sweet smile, good teeth, Robert DeNiro mouth, a shade too much lotion on the face. Something French and pungent. Something Pour Hommes. He's been busy all day getting his sailboat out of the water, arranging for its winter berth. Forty, divorced, no children, nice gray belt purchased last summer in Florence. He went to Italy to have a look at Michelangelo's four unfinished "Captives" in the Accademia. I say, said the dwarf, things are looking up. Would you like to know my secret, Vinnie? Would you like me to tender my key? Engage me in the head and you've got me. My ex-husband was the best head engager in greater metropolitan Boston. Vincent says Michelangelo called our bodies our "earthly prisons." He is looking at my breasts, which are demurely swathed in layers of fabric, according to tenets laid down like concrete at St. Anne's during pubescence. And a good thing, too. It's a bit of a generalization, but generally speaking they are not moved to speak of the Accademia when the mammary glands are exposed.

Vinnie Basilicato (like in Basilica) left high school in New Haven and went to Las Vegas (Lost Wages), where he worked as a croupier for ten years. He married a showgirl from Lake Tahoe, Rose Santacqua (like in Holy Water), but lost her after three years to a movie mogul from MGM. He returned to New Haven at thirty and bought his club for cash-on-the-line. He's been the banker of his family since, lending mortgage money to two of his brothers and three of his sisters. He has a part interest in a funeral parlor in Hamden and he plans to visit Peru in January and have a look at Machu Picchu. He would love to take me home.

"Oh, thank you, but I couldn't. I came with Grace, you see."

And Sister Helene said it was holy writ, as imperative as the Tenth Commandment, that you depart the premises

with the one with whom you came. Otherwise Divine
Doom and Disgrace visited upon you like a scourge. Even
Dolly Parton addressed this loyalty I speak of:

"But just remember who's taking you home and in
who's arms you're gonna be. So, darling, save the
last dance for me."

Amazing Grace and Minnie Misfit visit the powder room
at the Club Vincent.

"Oh, *go* with him! He's nice. He's got a Jag."

"Listen, Gracie, he's got a part interest in a *funeral
parlor*."

"So? He's the money man in the operation, not the
mortician. He never touches the stiffs. He never
embalms."

"Yes, but isn't that business all Mafia?"

"I've known him ten years. He's clean. He's got a
big boat, sleeps six."

"Well, I think he's Mafia. Did you get a load of that
ring?"

"Emma, he's a catch. Go home with him. He's got a
ten-room split-level in Woodbridge. Please. Really."

And so, at 2 A.M., after closing the club, Vinnie and I
drive up St. Ronan. At my request he stops his white
Jaguar at the front curb. I feel like Minnie the Moll in this
jalopy, Vin, although I've noted and appreciated the lovely
walnut burl on the dash. But I mustn't dally here because
this is the street of the stiff upper lip. When they curse on
St. Ronan they say Pshaw and when they flush they don't
flush turds. No. They flush B.M., feces, defecation, ex-
crement, and waste. Stools occasionally, but never, ever,

shit. And then, you can be sure, it doesn't stink. In truth, Vin, rumors are making the rounds that some of them never *do*, in fact. Yes, I'd have to agree. That must be why some of them look that way.

I detect lights on in the house and I'm much disturbed by that. Alas, he wants to talk. About modern man's alienation from man. Breakdown of tradition and religious values. Divorce rate. Japanese taking over the world. Robots taking over Detroit. The arms race and a quick computation of shovels needed to dig our sorely burned and radiated selves out of the rubble. And Bonzo (sic), in the White House. And his need to find a good woman to hold onto in the midst of general global chaos.

We don't, as a rule, leave the porch light on. As a rule, the house is dark at 2 A.M. But Richard's bedroom light is on; he stands behind his curtain, an apparition. I see Wendell pacing in the front hall. And suddenly, when Vincent kisses me goodnight, Wendell goes berserk at the light switch. The porch light is flicked on and off roughly five times before Vincent pulls away.

"What is that?" he asks. "Some kind of maritime code?"

Normally everybody uses the back door, since that is where we park the cars. But as I leave the Jaguar, I see the two men standing boldly at the front door, a humiliating reception committee. I am truant and there will be an altercation. Vinnie nobly inquires if I'd like him to come in and take care of them. Oh, Heavens. No, I don't think so.

Richard wears pale blue pajamas. Wendell is bare-chested, wearing the bottoms of thermal underwear. They hit me with a barrage. They were worried out of their minds; they thought me dead on the highway. Didn't I, for Chrissake, have a dime to call in and report?

"Report? I beg your pardon. *Report?*"

Yes, damn it, inform us of your whereabouts. Wendell is so exercised, his hair is standing on end.

"I was about to call the frigging fuzz! And who the hell is that greaser in the Jaguar?"

"Vincent Basilicato. As in St. Peter's."

"Christ! From Vincent's, on Whalley?"

"The same."

"He's Cosa Nostra! He's the fucking kiss of death. If New Haven had a family, he'd be the consigliere."

"Well Grace says he's clean."

"I will not *have* it!" says Richard. "I will not have the Cosa Nostra at my curb. I will not have my housekeeper mauled publicly by some old roué."

"*Roué?* Oh, come off it, Richard. Don't pull that turn-of-the-century crap with me! Am I fired?"

"No. Are you on the pill?"

"Just where the hell do you get off, prowling the hall, flipping your digits all over the light switch, asking that I report in, for God's sake? What am I, a slave? You got a piece of paper somewhere, a document of *indenture?* Am I in *bondage?*"

"My father *asked* if you were on the pill!"

"Oh, Wendell, I was on the pill before you were even *sperm!* Now, listen to me, you two, and this is final. I have not had one moment away from you since I left Boston. I was promised peace and quiet on the weekends, and it is essential, do you hear me, that this weekend you leave me alone. Go to Bennington, go to Park Avenue, I don't care where you go. But I *deserve*, I think, two full days solo. Is that clear?"

They nod their agreement, grudgingly. Richard tries to take my hand, and I slap his.

"Don't be angry."

"I *am* angry. I am furious. Good night."

The three of us mount the stairs. Richard followed by Wendell followed by me. Two are barefoot, so the silence is broken only by one of my sixty-dollar Capezios on the stairs. Sixty dollars originally, but fought for tooth and nail in the fray of Filene's basement when slashed to twenty. I couldn't manage to seize two of the same size, and had to settle for a seven and an eight. I must have lost the wad of Kleenex I had in the eight, while doing some dancing. It has been my experience that a bargain is nearly always accompanied by a modicum of inconvenience.

Good night. But I have an ultimatum. You don't get your asses swiftly out of here tomorrow, I invite Basilicato in. With his henchmen, the Sons of Garibaldi. They descend en masse on St. Ronan, garrotes in hand. They rub you out. They give you concrete shoes and drop you in New Haven harbor.

Sixteen

The house is quite vast when empty. The back yard is out of the question, due to dreary precipitation. It's most comfortable to retreat to the kitchen.

I used Krazy Glue to fasten the loose rubber tubing around the refrigerator door. I didn't heed the direction that it takes only one drop. And when I bonded my index finger to my thumb, I began to cry. I am dull and listless and they've only been gone twenty-four hours. A good weep would solve it. One of those wracking, pillow-soaking, bleating blubbers would do the trick.

They left, in unison, out the back door. Wendell announced,

"I'm going to change my life this weekend."

Richard whispered,

"I shall miss you."

This morning New Haven's rather tacky little morning paper, the *Journal Courier*, carried an article describing communication among trees. Scientists now say that trees send airborne chemical messages to other trees. They warn each other in this way of attacks by insects and various other pests. They change the content of their leaves.

Richard and I are evolving into two rustling oaks with regard to Wendell's machinations. We don't know each other well, so our communications are activated by instinct. We convey chemical messages to each other which have resulted in a pledge of partnership. But the pledge is undefined; there is an anomaly at the heart of it. There are times when I feel that Richard and I are unified because we are the same adult species, and Wendell is the household mutant. And there are times when I feel we are unified simply because we are inclined toward each other. At his parting, he clung to my hand and his eyes spoke volumes. But his tongue suppressed the words. And I suppressed the most ardent urge to embrace him. His face was free of care and strain; he had shed all reserve and caution, dropping it to the floor like flayed skin. I did not want him to go, and I believe he wanted to stay. All of this was conveyed chemically, in the space and time of a heartbeat or two. These airborne, weighty messages are unmistakable but they leave me in limbo.

Like a bird set free of its cage, I don't know where to light. All the rooms are unwelcoming. Vincent Basilicato called and I was rude. None of the usual lame excuses, not washing my hair, down with the flu, cramped by the menses, just not available to him, ever. I'm really sorry because I found you most attractive but I'm going through changes, you know, a little crazy in the head just now with Job and Life and Anomalous Chemical Messages. Well be sure and let me know when you get it all together. Oh, you'll be the first advised if, in fact, such a metamorphosis occurs this side of the grave. In the meantime I am experiencing a kind of internal anarchy that has led to inexplicable suffering.

I gave a semblance of the same excuse to Grace when she called. She understood immediately. We Cat'lics, fallen as we are, never lose our frame of reference. A spike, hammered by one man through another man's flesh, is an indelible image in the formative years. Guaranteed to haunt you through your life.

I try to sit in the upstairs sitting room and finish *Twenty Months in Alcatraz*. I'd like to get done with Brian Conway and move on to something cheerier: *Cherry Blossom Time in Washington*, by Eleanor Roosevelt. I am stuck in 1938. Richard would have been ten years old when this *Reader's*

Digest arrived for Nanny. I saw his childhood roller skates in the attic when I seamed the sheets. I go back to the attic and sit with the skates in my lap. When he fell and bashed his knees and needed the antisepsis of the gentian violet, I wonder if he ran to his mother or to Nanny? It was probably Nanny who had to rabbit-ear this page and lay the book aside and run and make a sterile bandage for the bawling boy. Lay him down then, prop up the legs on a couple of pillows. Elevation will quell the throbbing in the purple knees. There, lad, easy now. Oh, my lamb, don't fret. Oh, my hurting baby, Nanny's here with a nice cold piece of soft terry to lay across your brow. How about a bright little song to take your mind off the fall?

> Oh, the days o' the Kerry dancing
> Oh, the ring o' the piper's tune.
> Oh, for one of those hours of gladness
> Gone, alas, like our youth, too soon.

Fidgeting, I go down to Richard's study. There are six picture albums on the shelves, covering approximately fifty years. The young Richard, in 1948, proudly wearing his letter "Y" across his chest. Wendell, only five years ago, smirking, displaying the same letter. Richard, Marion, and Wendell in caps and gowns. Richard at a lectern, addressing a meeting of the American Physical Society. Marion was given to wearing Confirmation dresses. Ruffles and ribbons, dimity and voile. All together, there is a certain overbred look to them, reminiscent of dogs I've seen on TV at the Westchester Dog Show, incestuously bred over too many years. Canine Hapsburgs. And there's a picture of Marion posing beside her spanking new Volvo, in 1971. Wendell, at ten, is behind her on a new bike. I am fathoming the sentiments around these photos; yes, Kevin, sorrowfully. What has all this Goddard history amounted to? An ad in a Boston newspaper. A maid-cum-factotum sent in by nature to fill the vacuums left around the pictures, to fill the black holes left around the lives. I need a drink. In the kitchen I help myself to a stiff double Scotch. Technically, this probably isn't included in board and room, and Richard did say I wasn't to drink his liquor. But too many messages have transpired between us since then. I no longer think he's Professor Prick and he no longer fears an inveterate sponger.

The eleven o'clock news watched in the study presents an Economy Watch. The housing market is recovering from eighteen percent interest rates. I have a vague interest in this because of my New Hampshire acreage. Perhaps I should sell the place and get the taxes off my back. It's comforting, though, to have a snug little plot tucked away for a rainy day. A roof and a stove and a bed and a toilet, a deed of ownership in my name. Blueberries and goose-berries and raspberries to put up, as they say, in little rubber-ringed Mason jars. Comforting to have something that didn't dissolve, along with the marriage.

Vinnie, listen. When the superpowers push the buttons and the missiles with nuclear warheads volley across the Atlantic, let's you and me jump in the Jag and wheel ourselves up Interstate 91 to My Property. You bring the pasta and I'll bring uncontaminated water in plastic jugs, like Lydia. And we'll hide deep in the old dry well. I've still got a few eggs left, Vin, trickling down monthly if left unhindered. We could copulate there at the bottom of the well and send forth legions of our own Mick/Wop issue to regenerate the earth. When the dust settles. Because I do have, as I think you do too, amidst the foment of internal anarchy and outward global chaos, a genuine reverence for life.

As I straggle up to bed, I am afraid. I have premonitions about the black holes surrounding Richard and Wendell. There are extraordinary forces at work in the chemistry of the three of us. I would like to explain this to Kevin and Peg, but they are wont to scoff at premonitions. I recall traveling with them to Montreal to see Aunt Colleen. I was four and the official at the Customs Gate scared me. I rolled off the back seat, hid on the floor, and covered myself with a blanket.

"What do you have to declare?" inquired the officer.

"We've got a bottle of bourbon and a carton of Camels we just bought at the Duty-Free," replied Kev.

"And what's that wriggling in the back?"

"Oh, that's our daughter. She's scared."

"Little girl? Why are you scared?"

"Because," said she, "I'm alive."

They had a good laugh over that, the three adults. A good, middle-aged guffaw.

"She'll grow out of it," said the officer.

Wrong. It persists. It hasn't subsided, it has escalated. And I am not surprised at three in the morning to hear noises below in the house. All the signs have been there since the day I arrived. It is Richard. Why do I pretend, then, that it might be a prowler, a burglar, a rapist, a murderer? I know it's not. Why do I engage in a fantasy that it is one of Lydia's people, crept over the Prospect Hill from the slum: large, dark, and demoniacal, switchblade in hand? I know that it's Richard. Why do I latch onto one of Nanny's old hatpins, her scissors and a nail file, thinking I'll stick the bastard to death, when I know there is no protection and none is required?

He opens the door and looks at my fists, clenching the tiny implements. I have no voice, my knees have turned gelatinous, and as I buckle he lifts me and showers me with kisses. And tugs at my earlobe with his lips and gushes words:

"I love you, don't say I can't or I mustn't because I do, I do, I know it in my bones."

Sweet Jesus, he wrangled out of Nee Marchant's embrace at midnight, fought off the jungle of mobiles, conches, cowrys, and limpets and blurted out his declaration. What he wanted was at home, on St. Ronan. Seventy miles an hour then up I-95, certain this was right, preordained, all the signs were there. On the breasts now, hungry, and while my hands clutch his thick thatch of hair I think of Wendell, and the unforgiving light of dawn when all explanations will seem vapid and hollow. I think of Noguchi's Sun, Earth, and Chance. I feel the old exhilaration in my loins, the old primal signal from the brain commanding the canal to make ready, make liquid, lubricate and warm the nest. He says,

"Live with me forever. Never, ever leave me."

The words are as rash and impetuous as passion itself and I am silent. God, I don't want to be. I want to use all the language I once used with Michael, the imploring, pleading, entreating, beseeching, desperately obscene language of the sexual supplicant. Perhaps I can explain in the morning. It is fear, you see, bordering on phobia. Not hesitant and timorous, not reluctant and tremulous, no. It is sheer terror that grinds back my words and locks them in my throat. I have a prodigious need to keep this contract indefinite, to withhold the sole and exclusive rights of always, and underlying all of this is the anomaly at the heart of the matter. Is my fear caused by Michael or is it caused by Wendell? Is it because I know from my past the mechanics of Gracie's *dailiness?* Of domestic wear and tear, of snubs and slurs and slights that leave you unresponsive to Cupid's dart? Is it because it is unholy, evil and base when the words expire and neglect and decline set in with a vengeance, and the contract is dissolved and the proceeds are divided? Or is it because extraordinary forces are at work and I do not understand the great, gaping, enigmatic black hole that is Wendell?

"You're so quiet."

"Forgive me. I'm sorry. I'm scared."

"Why? Oh, Emma, *why?*"

Because I'm alive. But I don't say that. I quote from *Holiday Inn*, 1942. As Bing Crosby trilled so sweetly to Marjorie Reynolds:

"Be careful, it's my heart."

Seventeen

Awake before Richard, I am thankful for a sunny Sunday. The influence of rain is quite different, floor to floor. One sees it splashing off shrubbery on the first floor, one hears it running in the gutters on the second floor, and here on the third it fairly drubs the roof and can't be ignored. The dawn now enters golden, gilding the lilies on the old Chinese rug, glinting metallic rainbow shades of blue and red where it catches the corner of Nanny's crystal dresser tray.

We are "sleeping spoons." My bottom is curled into the hollow of Richard's lap; his knees are bent to fit the bend of mine. And although morning itself is discordant to lovers, confirming the duality of separate spheres, the bodies themselves rest in physical, concave accord.

There are signs of Richard's passion in the sunrise. His jacket, slung on my commendably mended chair, his trousers rumpled in a heap, his socks bunched and thrown under the window, his watch on the floor. And beside it, his shorts, as he stepped out of them. They look, from my horizontal vantage point, like a figure 8, lying on its side. And the garnish on this scene is an occasional waft of sex from the sheets.

"What are you thinking?" he asks.

"I'm thinking about Goldilocks. What did Goldilocks say?"

"I don't know. What did Goldilocks say?"

"Goldilocks said: 'Somebody's been fucking in my bed.' "

And he laughs, stretches the lanky body, giggles again and asks if I know the songs of Dinah Washington. No, I don't think so. But I'm a walking compendium of golden oldies; to what specifically do you refer? He sings in a raspy, morning, nicotine-obstructed voice.

> What a diff'rence a day makes
> Twenty-four little hours
> Brought the sun and the flowers
> Where there used to be rain.

And then he smiles again. I've never seen this smile before. It is full of glee and the difference, I think, is me. Oh, it is this smile that will be my stranglehold. This mirth is the emblem he will carry out into the world. World, do you see this brand new Goddardian visage? It has my imprint: I'm the engraver. This smile was struck in the mint of Emma Rowena Riley.

At breakfast, he says he used to go to Harlem in his youth. Back in what he calls his "Shelley" days, you could have a jaunt on 125th and hear all the great black entertainers. Count Basie, Jimmie Lunceford, and the Duke. Billie Holiday and Ella Fitzgerald. It was the time of Juke Box Saturday Nights, and Rum and Coca-Colas. Everybody whistled M'airzy Doats and Elmer's Tune, and there was nothing like a dame. His mother saved her old silk stockings because Uncle Sam needed them in the manufacture of gunpowder bags. Cook saved bacon grease in coffee cans and returned it to the butcher. Uncle Sam needed it in the manufacture of ammunition. Then, sudden silence. He has slumped into a deep reverie, an introspection so deep I feel I should excuse myself and leave him to molder by himself. He reaches over and grasps my hand.

"I suffered a severe depression when I was twenty. I wanted to be a poet. Professor Dudley, at Yale, had introduced me to Percy Bysshe Shelley. I felt, in reading his poems, a total communication. I felt an affiliation and an insight that were almost mystical. But these discoveries tore me apart emotionally. Half of me craved order in my life, and half of me wanted to live intensely, like Shelley, on the razor's edge. I was intrigued with his radicalism, his atheism, his abundance of women and children. I loved reading about his harried excursions to far-flung villas and palazzos. I was, in all candor, not unlike Wendell today. But Wendell isn't torn. Wendell *loathes* order.

"Well, my family became very concerned. They made concerted efforts to convince me that a malcontented, peripatetic life would burn me out by thirty. As it did Shelley. I'll never forget my father's reaction to my poems. He said, 'These observations are finely tuned and metered, but don't you see that poets live lives of false pretense?' He said he thought that poets, in their work, assaulted the gore and grime of life, but, in reality, they lived in their clean imaginations and dirtied their hands with nothing but ink. For some reason, I understood that back then. I acquiesced and went on to a life of false pretense. It took two years, but I finally succumbed. Squelched that burning part of me. Snuffed it out and turned to the safe harbor of Physics. Certainty, security, three squares a day."

The pain of this resolution must have been massive because even now, as he relates it, his eyes fill with tears. I rise to go to him, but he raises his palm above the table to stop me.

"Marion's family had a house at Edgartown, just down the beach from ours. Somehow we fell into spending summers together. She never dated; she was still a virgin at twenty-five. I felt such pity for her. I kept thinking I shouldn't submit again. I felt that, in allowing the ease of the situation, I was somehow disqualifying myself from some important race. But I did nothing to stop it. The summers were so lazy; week after week of loafing—it just happened. She wasn't so much frigid as asexual. She simply didn't have the need. And regardless of what Wendell says, she was an unfeeling woman, without warmth. She didn't like to touch or make physical connections. I remember seeing other mothers constantly nuzzling their babies, and thinking, 'Why doesn't Marion nuzzle Wendell?' She transported him from crib to bath as if she were carrying a hot casserole. She was a non-wife, a non-mother, a non-lover, and eventually she became a non-person in my life. A fixture that required only minor civilities, mundane pleasantries.

"The irony is, I thought Wendell would provide cement for the marriage. But he was divisive from the beginning. He *sensed* that there was, in me, something adulterated. He sensed that burning part that I'd squelched. All he saw was the conventional, constricted part. By the time he was ten, there was disappointment in his eyes when he looked at me. As if he couldn't forgive me for some basic deceit in my character. I thought I'd made no more than ordinary compromises, but his view of me confirmed them, heightened them. The other irony is that he's inherited my burning part wholly and intact. If I'm lenient now it's because I'm trying to let him burn, even if it leads to conflagration."

We take our coffee into the living room.

"I must tell you, I've considered suicide frequently over the last fifteen years. Shelley, at twenty-nine, was exhausted and disillusioned by the world, and he wrote to his friend Trelawney, in England. He asked for a lethal dose of prussic acid. He said he wasn't suicidal, he just wished to hold in his hand 'that golden key to perpetual rest.' "

Flash now of Michael's suicide talk. Those days when he forfeited his energy for stayin' alive. He used the parlance of the theatre. There was always a point during technical rehearsals when a climax occurred but it wasn't a scene change, or an act change. And the fatigued crew, designers, electricians, actors, and director didn't know what to do. Invariably, the director would suggest going to black. Michael's death-wish was less romantic than Richard's. He didn't want to hold a golden key; he simply wanted to lose all voltage and go to black.

"Emma, I know this is right. You and me. My longing for the key stopped abruptly the day you came. My yearning for release somehow evaporated. If you can care for Wendell and me, if you can cut through this mire we've made of our lives, you'll have saved me."

In Nanny's bed, at noon, the second lovemaking is deep and long and rapturous. It is not cataclysmic, like last night; it is informed with the further, mellow dimension that occurs when confessions have been made, old sorrows laid bare. My spinster's aerie is completely transformed; there is nothing wistful in the mauve wisteria across the dormers now, and the day, as well as my life, has an axis to rotate around. I'm deeply touched by Richard's strangely abdicated life. There's a ring of familiarity to it, perhaps because Kevin and Peg bore me in middle age and I grew up among their peers. More than half of life was seen in hindsight, and the inevitable modifications and compromises made along the way continued to nag and nettle. Did Richard know that the picture he would paint had already been hung, so to speak, in the gallery of my past?

What is obvious, as I assemble it, is the parallel between the squelched part of Richard and the present, smouldering Wendell. It's a transference of natures and I think it will lead Wendell more assuredly to conflagration than to acceptance speeches in Stockholm. And I detected something perverse when Richard spoke of letting Wendell burn. The words were a stimulus and Richard was, for a moment, a voyeur. When he calls Wendell a handful, there is the same hint of excitement and danger. He yearns to goad his son into the limelight, and Wendell yearns to be there, but both are in a deadlock, stuck at an impasse.

"Are you thinking of Wendell?"

"Yes."

"Well, we'll tell him the minute he returns. We must tell him that you'll move down, permanently, with me."

"To the second floor? Are you sure?"

"Absolutely. We'll start it off right. Boldly, without misgivings. We can tell him together or I can tell him. Whatever you prefer."

"Together, I think."

"Good! Oh, my God, dare I say it? I'm *happy!*"

The twenty-four-carat smile returns. I am happy, too. I'll be the resident instrument promoting GOOD. What are Historical Shes if not conciliators? I can, if I'm very agile, practice a kind of shuttle diplomacy between one and the other, knitting up raveled sleeves of care. I am, in fact, rather giddy at the prospect of it.

As Richard helps me clear the breakfast table and load the dishwasher, the phone rings. He goes to the study and I go to the adjoining living room to listen to the lingo.

Talk like this was never heard around the Buskin. There's a lot of beta, for instance. Sometimes it's beta as in gamma; sometimes it's beta as in ray, particle, or receptor. But often it's Bethe as in the man, Hans. And Bohr is not as in ho-hum or yawn, but as in two related Danes, Aage and Niels. There's much reference to quantum mechanics, magnetic moments, hydrogen spectrums, positrons, and vectors. There's Van Vleck and Wernher von Braun and a

name I'd never wish on anyone, Polykarp Kusch. Pauli,
Rabi, and Fermi come up with regularity and always there
is agreement that the Dirac equations are beautiful, beautiful.

Richard is just putting down the receiver when we hear
the slamming of car doors at the curb. Rushing to the front
door, we see the parked Volvo. Wendell has returned but
has not parked out back, as is customary. He has a girl
with him and the back seat of the car is crammed with
luggage. He looks morose as he walks, with Monica,
lugging his long, baleful body up the pavement to the
steps. Richard exclaims,

"What the deuce?"

He opens the door and the two of us stand on the cold,
barren porch as Wendell and Monica ascend the stairs.

"Well, hello, Monica. Good to see you."

In unison, as if choreographed, they hold up their left
hands, displaying two rings of the Woolworth variety.
Monica smiles valiantly. Wendell's explanation is a
lamentation.

"We got married."

Eighteen

The feces has hit the fan, as they say on St. Ronan.

The changes in the airborne messages between Richard and me are quite remarkable. As bad as this news is, we have consummated our union, and it is this pooling of resources that gives muscle to our reaction. Richard relays to me that he can handle the situation as long as I'm there to shore him up. I relay that I am calm, reliable, dependable in crisis.

Monica has left school and Monica is moving in. This pretty girl with frazzled blond hair and ankle socks in penny loafers is, at twenty, Mrs. Wendell Wharton Goddard. The vows were exchanged at the farmhouse of a Justice of the Peace on Route 7, Vermont, at nine o'clock last night. The honeymoon was spent at the Bide-a-Wee Motel in Brattleboro. Monica is the only one among us who does not appear to be stunned. Wendell says he wants to unload the car right away because he is exhausted and wants to go to bed. There is no sexual or even civil inference in this statement, and Monica is left to put the best face on it. She looks at us sheepishly and says,

"I think Wendell's caught a bug."

And a virulent virus it is. It looks to me like yellow jaundice; I have never seen him so sallow. Richard asks him, gently:

"What made you decide, so suddenly?"

Wendell exhales deeply and shrugs. Monica sees through Richard's question.

"I'm not pregnant. We just got sick of it. All the arrangements and the appointments and the phone calls and the gas. We were never alone, in the dorm, and we really couldn't afford the motels."

The young bride waits for assistance, or corroboration, from the young groom. The young groom looks nauseous. She continues.

"And I'm flunking out, anyway. I've been telling my parents for a year, there's *no reason* for me to be there. Talent can't be taught."

She looks at Wendell, thinking this last will rouse him from his stupor. His cheeks puff out and his lean body appears to be bloated. He looks like the expanding, ballooning man on the indigestion commercial. She prattles on.

"All I want to do is paint, paint, paint. I *know* the rudiments. I can paint anywhere. All I need is good light. I can paint here, on the third floor, if we put a bubble in the roof."

I grimace, Richard gulps, and Wendell repeats:

"She needs a bubble in the roof."

"Poor Wendell. I think he's caught a bug. And all *he* wants to do is write! We'll get part-time jobs as soon as we can. We certainly don't expect you to feed us as well as house us. And there won't be any mess, Emma. I promise to take charge of Wendell's room."

This is the meanest cut for Wendell. He is in a daze, almost catatonic.

"No one," he says, "goes into my room."

Richard and I look askance. Did it not strike him, until now, that Monica would share his inner sanctum? With trepidation, signified by much clearing of the throat, Richard ventures the terrible word.

"Look, kids, it just may be that this is a mistake. It may be that we all need a good night's rest and a good, honest evaluation in the morning."

Wendell erupts in high dudgeon.

"Listen, Dick, what the hell do you know about honesty? I proposed to the woman, I called her father, I bought the rings, I took the vows, I've got a god-damned *certificate*, for Chrissake! How dare you call this marriage a mistake?"

"Wendell, forgive me, but I must ask. Were you on drugs?"

Wendell begins kicking the side of a wing-back chair.

"I really object to that question! Monica, you should, too! He's insinuating that we were not in full control of our faculties."

"Well," says Monica, "the truth is, Wendell was feeling poorly. It's this bug, you see. But Wendell, your father has a right to ask a few questions."

The phone rings. It is Mr. Dunstan, in Bloomfield Hills, Michigan. Monica goes to the phone. And while Richard and Monica assure her parents that we are all surprised, but *on top* of it, Wendell makes for the front door. I follow.

"Wendell? Are you in love with this girl?"

"I gotta unload the car."

"Look at me. Do you love this girl?"

"Oh, for fuck's sake, does it matter?"

Does it matter, he asks. I am dazed, and somewhat fazed myself, just now. I could, I suppose, get on my high horse where, at that altitude, one always appears uppity. I wasn't hired, you see, to cook and clean for Mrs. Wendell Wharton Goodard. Nowhere in the fine print of memory does that clause occur. And dear Lord Jesus, what if *she* cooks? Two of us in there, cooperatively spoiling the broth. By the look of her though, she doesn't. No ridicule meant, but at that age it's mostly Campbell's soup and tuna fish. The age of the phone call home, collect:

"Mom? Remember that Mulligan stew I hated? How do you make it?"

Monica is on the phone, rallying full force. Twenty hours a week at minimum wage multiplied by something I miss won't get you, if I may say so, a pot to pee in. And if it does, guess who'll have to clean it out? E.R.R. Oh, what is this cascade of panic plummeting in my breast? I am no stranger to these sensations; these flaws and frailties are ancient in my character. They are the ones I addressed, in my diary, at seventeen, with asterisk and footnote:

"Must refrain from these tendencies or won't attain true maturity."

Monica, let me explain. I've carved a place here, you see, a foothold. I've brought light, jocularity, and living ferns to the mausoleum. I've got the whole motley lot under my gastronomic finger, including the jays and finches. I am chief cook and bottlewasher, master of all I survey, in the kitchen, and I have just, this weekend, found in Richard an axis for my life.

Richard leaves Monica on the phone and comes to me.

"We'll have to hold our news, Emma."

I agree, and cry.

"Tell me," he says. "Tell me."

Oh, it has to do with patterns of termination deeply ingrained. Inability to take root due to erosion of soil. Lousy weather conditions for some years now. Yanked out of St. Anne's, catapulted out of marriage.

We regret to inform you that you can't remain here. Your term has expired. We can no longer justify your presence. Woman was wanted, and now there are two. A surfeit, you see.

I stand here impaled, Richard, on emotional pink slips.
Wendell enters the hall carrying two big rolls of canvas and a gallon of linseed oil. He stops in his tracks and looks at me, in Richard's arms.

"What the fuck is this?"

"Emma's crying," says Richard.

Monica is screaming into the phone.

"Mu-*ther*, it is *not* a mistake!"

She slams the receiver down and enters the living room, crying. Richard extends his other arm to her. He is a bulwark amidst our broken dams. While the three of us huddle there, at the eye of a sudden storm, Wendell throws the canvas on top of Monica's duffel bags, curses, and runs out to the car. The Volvo roars into the night with a whimper and a bang and the three of us are left, cuddling, in the living room. I could not, for all the beads in the Pope's rosary, explain what is happening. But I would say these events, taken as a whole, are not auspicious.
And what a pretty girl she is. Nubile, I think. At the

kitchen table, waiting for her groom to return, she eats Brie on fresh Ritz crackers. It is a croaky voice, like Joan Greenwood in *The Importance of Being Earnest*. Or Debra Winger. She can't even go to bed, because Wendell keeps the key to the bolted bedroom. She says that this was the second proposal. The first, two months ago, was sweet and loving. Yesterday's was manic and she knew it. He had been combustible all day long, ranting and railing against his father, and the circumstances of his mother's death. Repeatedly, he asked, "Hey, what about Wendell? What about *him*?" Monica suggested meditation, a mantra guaranteed to soothe the hypothalmic or pituitary, or whatever was chemically amok. He said his life was camel dung and therefore they ought to get married. He purchased the rings and then they went to a dingy little farmhouse where the wife had spent the day canning mustard pickles.

"It smelled like a vinegar distillery. It couldn't have helped Wendell's bug."

We are all limp, fatigued, and clock-watching, when Wendell falls in the back door. He is convulsive, his limbs jerk and jangle uncontrollably. It is a genuine seizure. Monica rises but he bellows, as if to a hound:

"Sit, Monica, sit!"

He paces back and forth in front of Richard, stuttering, searching for words, like Jimmy Dean in *East of Eden* on the parlor carpet before Raymond Massey's glare. We are dumbfounded as his announcement unfolds.

"I drove all the way to Westport and back. I don't know who got married. Jesus, did *I* get married? Was I there? Can't you see I'm on the fucking *rack?* I actually stopped at Yale New Haven and considered checking into the tenth floor."

He pauses, and Richard mutters, worriedly.

"The Psychiatric Unit."

Monica bolts from her chair.

"Sit, Monica, sit! I didn't. I came home. To do the responsible thing, Emma. Maybe this will pass. Maybe it won't. I have to be alone in my room. Monica can sleep in Mother's room in the meantime. I cannot, you see, under any circumstances, *cohabit.* Sit, Monica, stay! And for God's sake, don't whine!"

We hear his keys clanking as he bounds up the stairs to his room. Richard takes Monica's hands in his.

"Monica, I'm so sorry. I think there's nothing to do but go to bed and see what happens in the morning."

She is withdrawn and lumpen as we support her up the stairs. Richard rolls down the sheets on Marion's bed and pulls the window blinds. I set out fresh towels and unwrap a bar of almond soap. Richard hovers nearby, handling the speechless girl like priceless porcelain. She is weeping quietly as we leave the room and outside, in the hall, we hear that Wendell, also, is weeping.

"We are being sorely tested," says Richard.

We cannot share a bed this night, yet we are loath to leave each other.

"God, Richard, what a double whammy! We'll have to prod them into jobs. Search the Classified, maybe take them down to Yale Placement. Pull some strings. And what about transportation? Lord, there'll be three of us on the Volvo."

He strokes my brow in a gesture of appeasement.

"Oh, my darling girl, you make it all sound so normal. You don't know Wendell."

"Neither, apparently, does Monica. This is no time for leniency. Tomorrow morning he must be ousted from his room. He mustn't be allowed to hibernate."

Falling against a wall, he sticks his hands deeply into his pockets and ruminates.

"Perhaps his instincts were right. Perhaps he should have committed himself for a while. He's done it before. Six weeks once, after his mother let Rae-Ann into the house."

"*Six weeks?* My God, that must have cost a bundle."

"A fortune, yes."

"Richard, I have an opinion on psychiatric wards."

"Yes?"

"I think they're a crutch and an indulgence."

I am looking for an argument, but he stares at me as if there is a sudden barrier between us—as if I am the neighborhood *naif*. I feel our cultures, philosophies, and monetary values clashing. He kisses me lightly and leads me to the landing, where he sighs, resignedly. He is too defeated to differ. He lumbers off into his bedroom, the veteran of too many Wendell wars.

In the third-floor bathroom I take my dial-a-day birth control pill. I think of the two of three times when Michael and I came to blows and I fled to the comfort of home. I flew in the door looking like what Peg called an electrified cat: eyes dilated, claws bared. I proclaimed, stentoriously, that I could no longer *cohabit*. Truly, I don't understand this St. Ronan penchant for having people committed. The underprivileged of south Boston could not afford such luxuries. We counted, instead, on the maxims of our ghetto:

Fish or cut bait.
Piss or get off the pot.
Roll with the punches.
Take it with a grin.

And Peg said:

"When the going gets tough, the tough get going."

And Kevin said:

"Non carborundus illegitimus."

Don't let the bastards grind you down.

There was never any mention of psychiatric help. The mater and pater would bill and coo over me until my pupils and claws had retracted. We would linger in the hall covered with thirty-year-old cabbage roses and hang our hopes on the clean slate of the morning. We would go to our rooms where cocoonlike beds enveloped us and curtained sleep shut out the day's debacles. Then Peg would bang on my door, martially, at seven when the sun rose.

"Rise and shine, Em! Time to do battle with another day."

Listen, Richard, I think, over the years, the Psychiatric Unit has served Wendell *in loco parentis*. I think I will, in my new, promoted status, fix that.

Nineteen

After a harrowing week, Monica looks like the Madwoman of Chaillot, Richard like the Two-Thousand-Year-Old Man, Wendell like Brian Conway after Twenty Months in Alcatraz, and I am beginning to see a distinct resemblance between myself and the photograph of Nanny Culligan.

Wendell refuses to speak. Three separate psychiatrists have visited the house. They say his condition could be either aphasia, aphonia, laloplegia, or a ruse. All recommended treatment. I sat with Richard on these three occasions pleading, begging, cajoling to keep Wendell at home. I don't know what drives me so maniacally in this mission to save him from another trip to the tenth floor at Yale New Haven. I am only aware that extraordinary forces are at work; that this is not a time to surrender to them. And I'm too busy, too pressured Nannying all three of them to spend much time questioning motives. Occasionally, alone in my bed, I pull back and see a collective lunacy that, if given form and put on the boards at the Buskin, would run for a year, standing room only. I sent a postcard home to Kevin and Peg.

"Am up to my——in alligators. Long letter follows."

I won't mention to them my new alliance with Richard because that alliance suddenly seems beside the point. The present emergency has caused the focus to shift, and there are dark, troubling questions circling the premises like

174

vultures. Does Richard *want* to incarcerate Wendell? Does he think it the poet's portent and portion, like Ezra Pound at St. Elizabeth's? Or was it possibly *Wendell's* intention in the first place? The poet's prerogative when caught in a bind. Is this some test of *me*, to see what lengths I'll go to to prevent Wendell from another six-week stint on the ward? Is he showing his father that his bag of tricks is infinite; that he will cause no end of trouble until he exorcises ghosts and settles scores? Or does he just want the adults to step in and bail him out of this whimsical marriage?

He sits in his room with zipped lips. Fully dressed, he sits for hours in a straight-backed chair at his desk and takes his meals there, at the desk. Perhaps it's because he now leaves the door open that I believe he's crying for help. Or maybe he just wants to hear, and wallow in, our constant consternation. Monica has the patience of a saint. Each time that she passes his room she stops and implores:

"*Talk to me*, Wendell! Tell me what you *want*."

He lifts his shoulders, drops them with a thud, answers nothing.

"Please let me *sleep* with you, Wendell! We don't have to *do* anything, just be together."

He moves his now misshapen beard from left to right and stares at his untied shoelaces.

"Oh, Wendell, what do you want me to do?"

He has before him a stack of three-by-five cards. He writes:

Get a bubble. Paint.

"Wendell? It's Emma. Is there anything *I* can do?"

He scribbles:

Ignore me.

Richard, straining for control, tries to reason.

> "We can't ignore you! You have to decide if you
> want the three of us to help you, or if you want
> to go to the hospital and get professional help. If
> you want us to help you, you must begin by saying
> something."

Wendell removes the top from his felt-nib pen.

Get a bubble for Monica.

On the fourth day, after the third psychiatrist, I have at
him again.

> "Wendell, it's my belief that when people are in this
> mute, depressed state, they are sending up a flare.
> They are drowning and crying for help. Give us a
> *sign*, Wendell."

Another card. We are filing them now, for eventual pre-
sentation to the psychiatrists.

Sod off.

> "That's a very coarse, uncalled-for, punk rock expres-
> sion. You're being a *punk*."

I persist.

> "Wendell, you're a very good-looking boy. You have
> excellent health and an attractive body. You have
> above-average intelligence. You're funny. You're well-
> educated, well-fed, and well-housed."

He interrupts my litany with another card.

Some of this is true.

"Are you purposely trying to drive us all crazy? Your
father has aged perceptibly, Monica weeps the night
away, and I am smoking like a chimney. What in hell
do you want?"

This reply takes a moment.

One, I want to know why you didn't take me seriously. Two, I want some of your cream-of-leek
soup.

"Wendell, does it help at all to know that your father
has ended the affair with Nee Marchant? She will
never come here, and she will never again go to the
Vineyard. Does that help?"

His body goes akimbo again. With flailing and jerking
limbs he ushers me out and slams the door. Monica screams
at me.

"*Now* see what you've done? God knows when he'll
open the door again."

He opens the door and hands me another card:

It helps a *little*.

Two men from the Gambardella Construction Company
come and saw a hole in the roof. They put a plastic sheet
over the hole while we await the arrival of a "Skyrama,"
from Meriden.

Richard runs back and forth to the office frantically
now; we both feel an obligation to attend Monica. Unfortunately, her mind is divided into two compartments: Wendell, and the nuclear freeze movement. Her painting has
but one theme—nuclear holocaust.

"I believe I've been summoned, perhaps divinely, to
depict the wasteland."

She invites us to the storage room to see her morbid renderings of an obliterated world: radioactive rubble on the ground and thick green skies that remind me of the French Canadian pea soup Aunt Colleen learned to make. She asks us if we're able to hear, through the paintings, the howling agony of the dead. Richard, the physicist, feels this subject is too complex for simplification and finds these sessions an ordeal. Wendell has drained his energy, demolished his smile, and frequently now, profuse sweat trickles across his upper lip.

"Do you hear the messages from the souls of the dead?"

Courtesy is left to me.

"Yes, Monica, I hear them."

Richard and I have been unable to cohabit because Monica wakes in the night and calls, in a childlike voice, for one or the other of us. We take turns sitting on her bed, holding her hand. She is docile and somewhat flirtatious with Richard, but she is wildly irrational with me. Twice she has delivered a diatribe against physicists. Richard's profession is responsible for the evil technology that threatens the world. Physicists are the whores of the military.

Then, a wildly irrational call from Richard, at work.

"Come to the office," he demands. "Come over here right now."

"I *can't*, Richard! I can't leave them."

"What about *us?* What about the sane ones? Leave them. It's urgent."

When I arrive, he is waiting at the front door of the lab. With no explanation, he pushes me into an elevator and pulls out a set of keys. We ascend about ten feet when he locks the doors and falls on me, kissing me feverishly.

"Please, Emma, please."

"Jesus, Richard, are you out of your mind?"

"Please. Now. *Here*."

"Oh, mercy, you can't be serious!"

"Here. Please. On the floor."

"I will *not*! I will not do it on the filthy floor of a jammed elevator!"

Suddenly, the alarm goes off; a janitor below is calling and banging.

"What am I doing?" wails Richard. "What in hell am I *doing?*"

Hastily, we pull ourselves together and descend to face the janitor. I am beet-red and Richard is erect. He stands behind the bulk of my raincoat and leans sideways to answer the query.

"Something wrong with the Otis, Dr. Goddard?"

"Yes," says Richard. "I think it's on the fritz."

He hobbles along behind my raincoat, to the door.

"I have *got* to commit him. We are *all* of us on the goddamned *brink!*"

I look out sadly; across the grass to the traffic moving down Whitney Avenue. They are all functioning normally, the people in the cars. Accelerating, braking, shifting, heeding traffic lights and speed limits, waiting for pedestrians. There seems to be an impenetrable layer between us and them.

"Tomorrow morning," says Richard. "I'm taking him to the hospital and then I'm taking Monica back to Bennington. And then you and I will try and pick up the pieces."

I bolt up the stairs into Wendell's room, lift him by the armpits, and sling him against a wall.

"Is this a test? A test of my loyalty? I have fought for you as long as I can, but the situation has become dangerous. If you don't talk to me, right here, right now, you're going to be committed tomorrow."

He folds up and crumbles to the floor, moaning.

"Is there *anyone* you will talk to?"

He wriggles his fingers toward the desk. I give him pen and card and he writes:

Lydia

Of course! How could we have been so stupid. I smile and help Wendell back to his chair. He, too, smiles and bobs his head up and down, idiotically. He looks like one of those fuzzy animals that undulate on springs in the rear windows of some people's cars.

There is no answer at Lydia's. Richard, reaching her son, finds that she has gone to Bridgeport for the weekend, to visit her sister. We debate as to whether or not our emergency warrants ruining her weekend and fetching her back. We decide to put it to Wendell. He takes longer than usual to pen his reply.

Lydia's sister's name is Velveeta. Because Lydia's mother liked the cheese. Don't disturb her holiday on my account.

Monica secludes herself in the attic. I detach, I try to trance, I bury myself in newspapers. The New Haven papers carry advertisements for Long Wharf Theatre and Yale Rep. One is doing O'Neill and the other, Feydeau. I wonder, Michael, if what we're playing here is a farce or a tragedy.

The working title on this piece is *Waiting for Lydia*. There's bountiful humor in these events, some of it black, some of it absurd, but no one is laughing. Perhaps because there is, in all the dementia, an undeniable certificate of marriage lying on Wendell's dresser. It's not Wendell's machinations that have caused Richard and me to go through two bottles of Tylenol, it's the gravity of that piece of paper. This morning I found Richard searching the bathroom shelves with quaking hands, hoping to find some of Marion's old Valium. And this morning I found myself sounding a little unhinged.

"Wendell? Sweetie? It's Sunday morning. Let's go watch Jerry Falwell. Please? Come on. It'll give you a rise. Maybe even a chuckle."

He emitted a sound. He said,

"Wha. Wha?"

"*Television*, Wendell. Something to divert us until Lydia arrives. Remember Jerry Falwell? Exhorting our feckless nation steeped in crime and vice? All the little kids watching? From their bowls of Apple Jacks? Please. We'll watch together. Just you and me."

He wouldn't budge. Richard and I watched the entire hour without so much as a grin.

Was there ever, in the recorded history of man, such a honeymoon? I am actually taking Monica's meals to the attic. Preparing two trays in the kitchen, carrying one up the stairs to Wendell, the other up another flight of stairs to his bride. I mutter a lot. I feel like some half-witted scullery maid from "Upstairs, Downstairs." If I stay with Monica and listen to the howling agony of her dead, she eats. If I don't, she doesn't and I tote the tray back, untouched.

A stiff dose of paranoia has settled in. I believe we are all part of a master persecution plan. What was a flight of fancy a month ago appears to me today as truth. When I put Monica to bed I stand in Marion's bedroom and feel her ghost. Her soul will not rest. She is agitating through Wendell, her earthly medium. She is suing for damages from the grave.

Twenty

October and Lydia arrived on the same day. We made sure that Monica wore nothing black, and the three of us lumbered about in the hall while Lydia went into Wendell's room. She herself bolted the door against our interference. We could hear Wendell talking immediately. There were one or two moments of impassioned exchange but mostly it seemed to be Wendell's babbling monologue. After ten minutes Lydia came out and gestured us down to the living room. She held a three-by-five card in her hand. She stood in front of the fireplace, momentously.

"Well, he talk and talk and talk. First he be so sad. He say, Lydia, when de spring come and de crocus bloom he goan say, Go back, crocus, into de groun. Dis world ugly, scurr'lous place. I say, Wendell, what causin' dis? Why you sittin' like a pillar of salt? I say, come on, boy, you tell ol' Lydia what causin' dis. He say it be de Bide-a-Wee Motel. I say, boy, what you talkin'? He say dat motel be scurr'lous place. Daze got cardboard lampshades an' rubber pillows an' wax grapes in de plastic bowl. Daze got paper bath mats advertisin' Naples Pizza. Daze also got de Magic Fingers Massage dat promise tingling relaxation but doan keep de promise an' jis jiggle de bones. Daze got steel bottle openers all over de walls, an' den he talk nasty. He say you pays your money you shoots your wad. He say, Lydia, you know I be *acutely sensitive*. He say dis scurr'lous roadside place

183

no place for a poet. It causin' him brain fever. His head bust in two and he buy rings at de Ben Franklin. I say, Wendell, you buyin' rings cuz you wantin' *married*. No. He ain wantin' married, he wantin' gladness. Dat's what he want. Gladness. Den he say, Give dis to Emma.''

She hands me the card. It inquires, in bold print:

WHERE THE HELL IS THE CREAM-OF-LEEK SOUP?

We just don't know how to react. Is this nonsense or does it bear scrutiny? If scrutinized would we see before us the emperor's new clothes? Lydia is due at Mrs. Hogan's and is an hour late for work. As Richard assists her into her coat she offers her own opinion.

"Dis bad. Dis serious. He need help. I say dat boy need a strong laxative. Flush dem impurities right down de sewer.''

We escort her to the car, where Richard fastens her seat belt while thanking her for her assistance. He then walks around and bangs on the trunk like an angry ape.

"Are we to *believe* there's some connection between the motel's decor and the marriage? It's a hoax! He's playing crazy. It's contrived obfuscation. It takes more cunning than sanity. Enough is enough. He's got us by the gonads. He goes, tomorrow!''

Lydia rolls the window down, shouting at me.

"Git dat man in dis fancy frog car 'fore he bust his coronary!''

Finally, I am defeated. At dinner, over a near-argument with Richard, I relent. It is time to seek professional treatment. But then at midnight Richard chances coming up to Nanny's room. He is torn with doubt; he wants another

conference. He drops his trousers and crawls into bed with
me and once again we go over the pros and cons of
removing Wendell from the house.

There is a knock on the door. We assume it is Monica.
Richard hides behind the blanket chest, and I slip into a
robe. Wendell stands there, fully dressed. His shoelaces
are tied and his beard has been clipped.

"Emma, I have to talk to Dad about an annulment. I
can't find him."

"Oh, blessed Mother. You're *talking*."

"Where is he?"

"He must be snacking, in the kitchen."

He turns, and with inordinate presence of mind I rally a
suggestion.

"Wendell, I know it would take great courage, but
would it be possible for you to tell Monica? Before
you tell your dad? Wouldn't that be fair?"

"Yes," he says, "you're right. I wasn't thinking."

He reaches out and takes my hand.

"I'm thinking now. I have to act while I'm thinking.
I can't believe I got married. I just can't believe the
last three days."

"Three days? Wendell, it's been *nine*."

"Jesus, what a mess. I'm so sorry."

"What happened to you?"

"I just . . . cracked. I knew I'd cracked when we got
to the J.P.'s. All I could think of was getting home,

where I'd be safe. Where I wouldn't hurt anybody. I know I've hurt everybody, but at least I haven't done bodily harm. I mean, I didn't get a gun, or something. Do something really stupid.''

"You've hurt Monica very badly. You must be very careful with her.''

"I will.''

When we heard him knock on Marion's door, Richard dashed down the back stairs to the kitchen. I waited for the reverberations from Monica, and they came quickly. Monica and Wendell were locked in a donnybrook on the second floor.

"Why, why, *why?*'' screamed Monica. "Why did you marry me, and bring me here, and then fold up your fucking tent?''

"I'm sorry! I'm no good for you! I'm too fucked up! You've said so yourself a dozen times. Why did you marry *me?*''

"Because you *proposed*, you bastard!''

"I *am* a bastard! I'm just no good. I have no *confidence!* I'm scared shitless every day of my life. I can't even put a poem in an envelope. I can't even pay my way! I'm getting an *allowance*, for Chrissake! You want to be married to *that?*''

She screams. There's a slap and a scuffle.

"I swore to love and obey, you bastard! I've been billeted in your mother's room! I've been treated like a *leper!*''

"Emma! Come down here! She's clawing me to death. Please, Monica! Get away from my *eyes!*''

I rush to the landing and take the sobbing girl into my arms. Wendell's face is tortured with guilt and for a minute I see his resolve wavering. The scene, the confrontation with the consequences of the rash marriage have, as we say at home, taken the mickey out of him. Slowly, holding the banister, he plods downstairs.

Monica falls onto the bed with little grunting sounds. Before I turn off the light I see what a terrible toll has been taken. Her skin has broken out and she has something resembling eczema on her cheeks. Her eyes are swollen and she is quietly nibbling at her cuticles with her teeth. There's an odor to her hair; she hasn't shampooed since she arrived. She seems unaware of my presence but I sit with her for a few minutes, patting her back. I have an impulse to lie down with her. To let the rest of the night happen and simply get a report in the morning. But the impulse seems disloyal to Richard, who needs my support. There's more mess to come, the mess of lawyers, explanations, and apologies to Bennington and Bloomfield Hills.

I am on my way to the kitchen to discuss the annulment. I hear the crack of an ice cube container against the sink, the assembling of glasses, the pouring of, I would guess, Scotch. And then Richard asks Monica's question.

"Why Wendell? Why did you marry her?"

I pause, in the dining room.

"I married her because I'm in love with Emma."

There is a long hush, the shuffling of feet, the tinkling of ice cubes. I feel shooting twinges in my left shoulder.

"I'm very sorry to hear that."

"I thought it was just a crush at first. Then I saw you treating her in a very womanly way. I got all bent out of shape over that. The jealousy was very real. And the proximity was killing me. Every day I fantasized about joining her in the shower. I tried to tell her and she called me infantile. I'm not infantile. I'm twenty-three. I'm a man.''

I walk into the kitchen, quivering, avoiding Wendell's face. Airborne messages wing through the air like swarming locusts. Jesus Christ, did you hear *that?* I did. It's nonsense, isn't it? asks the great elm, under attack. Absolutely. Arrant, ludicrous nonsense.

''You aren't a man,'' says Richard. ''But you are certifiably married, and you are certifiably out of touch.''

''Please, Richard, tell him.''

Richard pours another Scotch. Wendell takes my arm.

''It's over, Emma. It's been a nightmare, but it's over.''

''No, it isn't. Tell him, Richard.''

''Wendell, I left Nee Marchant's ten days ago, forever. I had been treating Emma in a womanly way because I was falling in love with her. The feeling was mutual. That was confirmed when I arrived back at the house.''

''Confirmed?''

''Consummated.''

''Where?''

''What do you mean, where?''

''Where was it consummated?''

''Here. In the house.''

Wendell whirls on me. His face is menacing.

"Where in this house did you fuck my father?"

"Wendell, we were waiting for you, waiting to tell you when you returned from Bennington. To tell you, and ask for your blessing."

"He was with you tonight, wasn't he, when I came knocking?"

"Yes."

Wendell's right arm shoots back and his elbow breaks the glass front of a china cabinet. He swings, hitting Richard squarely in the left eye. As the glass shatters to the floor the force of the punch sends Richard reeling across the dishwasher. He cries out in pain as the wire prongs in the dish rack dig into his chest. I am like a dragon, fire flashing from my nostrils, beating on Wendell's back.

"Get out! If I were Monica I would run a knife through you and never look back! Here are the keys. Now, go! *We'll* get the annulment, and we will say whether or not we'll have you back, and under what conditions!"

He grabs my shoulder with such fierce force that the car keys gouge into and break the skin on my clavicle. He growls at me as blood runs from the wound and seeps through my blouse.

"You slut! You were hired to keep house. You weren't hired to lick Dick's prick."

Richard is after him, out into the yard. I flick on the floodlight and watch the frantic chase as Wendell climbs into the Volvo, locks the doors, and turns the ignition.

"Come back here, you crazy bastard! Come back!"

Wendell, adding one final fillip, leans on the horn all
the way down the driveway, all the way into the street.
The horn drones distantly into the night as house lights go
on up and down St. Ronan. Richard doesn't come in. He
paces around the asphalt in circles, his torn shirt rippling
in the wind. I remain in the doorway, holding a wad of
Kleenex against the seeping contusion on my clavicle.
Monica is now pacing back and forth on the second-floor
landing, keening.

"Why, why, why?"

I resort to a trance, to diffuse the relentless, lowering
madness. I think of my clavicle. I think of Kevin, years
ago, in his cups:

There was a young virgin from Donegal
Who sat on a wall reading Peter and Paul
I went there to flirt and I lifted her skirt
I showed her my sausage and offered to squirt
She said, Oh, Mother Mary, your suggestion is radical
Then she brought down her Bible and busted my clavicle.

Twenty-One

M onica is in the living room, wafting, like the de-ranged Ophelia.

"That's him out there on the horn, isn't it? He's left me, hasn't he?"

Richard takes her in his arms and wipes her tears with the dishrag I gave him to wipe the blood from his left eye. He says the evidence is in; the annulment is the only sensible thing to do.

"And Monica, you'll be well out of it. Wendell hasn't even begun a process of maturation. My own, private, fatherly belief is that he may never achieve maturity. I don't know—perhaps poets shouldn't. I can say this to you as family, because you *have been*, for a while. I'm reluctant to say it, but there just may be something fundamentally wrong with Wendell. The behavior is just too psychotic.

"Emma and I are in for a long haul with the boy, but you have your whole life ahead of you, years and years, and you deserve better. You're a beautiful girl—Oh, I know, not at this moment. I'll take you back to Bennington and these horrors will recede and one day soon you'll look in the mirror and you'll be beautiful again. And some nice, normal young man from a good, sane family, with a sound degree and a bright future, will take you down the aisle properly. With bridesmaids, and your family there. If you think about it, it's really no more than a bad wrinkle in the overall scheme of your life. So let's call your family and then, in the morning, I'll drive you back to school.''

"I'd like to go tonight, if you don't mind.''

"Well, I think I should stay in the house tonight. If Wendell returns, God knows what state he'll be in. I shouldn't leave Emma alone.''

"Wendell won't return until I'm gone. He'll let you do the dirty work and then he'll call.''

Richard, as only a father could in these dire circumstances, takes umbrage at this.

"I know you don't have a very high opinion of my son, and there's no reason why you should. I'm compelled to say, though, that Wendell did intend to drive you back. Certain things transpired during our talk, things I can't, appropriately, discuss with you now. And that's why he ran away.''

"Is that why he punched you out?''

"Yes.''

"I want to go back tonight. It's the least you can do.''

Richard and I haul the death-rattle paintings, canvas, linseed oil, and duffel bags out to his car. One of Monica's keepsakes, a book, falls out of a stuffed grocery bag. It is L. M. Montgomery's *Anne of Green Gables*.

"To Monica, on your twelfth birthday, with oodles of love from Mama and Papa.''

Fathoming the instincts, I find this inscription deeply affecting. It's vile that little sugar and spice girls in ruffles and curls grow up and get screwed. Or, in Monica's case, don't. Don't even get talked to. And it breaks my heart that the tousled, auburn boy who sat on his bike behind his mother's new Volvo is now wheeling around New Haven in the selfsame car. With no one to welcome him anywhere but the staff in the nuthouse at Yale New Haven. Richard, on my wavelength, consoles me.

> "They're going to be OK, eventually. You must try to sleep. Please, at nine in the morning call the Psychiatric Unit. If he's not there, call the police. They'll want the license number and a photograph. They've got both from past escapades, but they may not keep a file. I have four or five photos, the passport type, in the top drawer of my desk. I'll get back tomorrow afternoon."

Monica gives me a chary hug under the harvest moon.

> "Thank you for liking my pictures. And I'm sorry those men sawed that hole in your roof."

I couldn't sleep. I stripped the bed in Marion's room, removing the tear-stained pillowcases. I had found on the pillows, when preparing the bed for Monica, pillowcases monogrammed with a large "M." It struck me that the initial well served the two Mrs. Goddards, neither of whom had shared the bed with their husbands. Now, in replacing the cases, I sought out another monogrammed set. It seemed proper and fitting—epitaphic—to keep Marion's initials on the bed. I ran my finger over the raised, shiny welt and felt like Mrs. Danvers at Manderley, in *Rebecca*. I thought of Richard's long, difficult journey up I-91, counting the hours and the sodium lights until he could deposit Monica at her dorm. And return, and be conjoined with me. I wondered if, in our conjoining, there was sufficient mucilage to withstand Wendell's infinite bag of tricks. Surprisingly, I found myself praying in my bed.

Even Kevin used to say, paraphrasing, I think, Abraham Lincoln, "Sometimes there's no one to turn to but God."

At nine in the morning, Yale New Haven said they'd heard nothing of Wendell Wharton Goddard for quite some time. The police had no report of a 1971 red Volvo, but said Sergeant Moffo would come by before noon to get a photograph and a description. At nine-fifteen I called a glazier to come and replace the cabinet glass. At nine-thirty, Lydia called.

"I's callin' from de phone in Miz Lippman bedroom. Miz Lippman doan allow no personal calls, so I be hangin' up if she come in. Dat Wendell, he be sleepin' jis now on my Hide-a-Bed."

"Oh, God, Lydia, how did he know where you live?"

"He come down with his paw when daze helpin' me petition to de city about snakes I got in de downstairs hall. Miz Riley? He say you in bed with his paw. Now, Miz Riley, dat de truth?"

"Lydia, it is. Yes."

"Where your head at, Miz Riley, miscegenatin' wid de massa? Nothing' but a heapa trouble ever come from dat. Oops! Here come Miz Lippman. I be home at four. You all come git Wendell offa my Hide-a-Bed. I ain sleepin' on de Barca-Lounger one mo' night."

Richard called from Springfield, Mass., to say his trip back was delayed. Someone had replaced Monica in her room and there was an argument. And he was drinking so much coffee to stay awake, he had to make pit stops every twenty minutes.

"Richard, I have good news. Wendell is at Lydia's. We have to go there and get him at four o'clock."

"Jesus, I haven't got the stamina! I don't know if I can get to St. Ronan safely, let alone drive to Lydia's and deal with Wendell."

"We have to, Richard. He's sleeping on Lydia's bed. And we have to straighten this out. If he won't listen to reason, maybe he'll have to stay at the Y or something. Don't worry, I'll drive."

There was frost this morning and there are always more black people hunched over more stalled cars in the cold weather. These are the people who replenish their own antifreeze, perform their own oil changes and lubes, clean their own carburetors, and always have jumper cables in the trunk. The women in these neighborhoods are a contradiction. They spew out in platoons each morning to clean the city's houses while they themselves live in filth and garbage. I know that Lydia's rooms will be spotless, but outside, on Howard Avenue, she has to contend with rusty, wheelless shopping carts and alleys filled with discarded couches, their upholstered guts spilling in clumps that look like moon matter. Something an astronaut would bring back. The gutters are filled with broken glass from beer and liquor bottles, used condoms, tin cans, Stryofoam coffee cups, old sneakers, and hordes of crumpled, nondegradable plastic bags. A British journalist on TV recently said that Americans have withdrawn into lives of private affluence and public squalor. Yes. I see it.

Richard looks like William Holden in *Stalag 17* after the Krauts kept him awake for three days. Lydia thinks he looks as if he might have been a contender. She examines his eye.

"Looks to me like you lost dat one. You gotta git de beefsteak on dat shiner *toot sweet*."

Wendell does not acknowledge us. He sits in a silent, saturnine fog, watching "Sesame Street" on Channel 13. Lydia gives him a hefty whack on the shoulder.

"Boy? You can't stay here. Your papa here now. He take your wife back to de school, and now he and Miz Riley goan take you home."

Lydia has very nearly crocheted herself out of her apartment. There is a big basket of brightly colored yarns beside her lounger, which faces her television set. There are doilies of bursting stars over the arms of every chair and on the surface of every piece of furniture. There are crocheted afghans over the Hide-a-Bed and a love seat. On a card table she has half-completed a jigsaw puzzle of the heads on Mt. Rushmore. The famous faces are in, but the sky and the cliffs, the least interesting aspects of the picture, lie waiting. A collection of well-tended cactus plants sits under the one window in the room. Richard promptly seats himself beside Wendell.

"Bucko, I'm exhausted, and I don't have much interest in negotiation. I've taken Monica back and I'll get Alex Bloom to work on the annulment.

"We'd like you to come home because I think you're going to need all the support you can get. Your head is off on a tangent and you're stuck in a goddamned, capricious marriage. You have to drop this fantasy about Emma. She and I are a couple now, and that's a fact. If you can't live in the house and accept that fact, respectfully, then I'll have to get you a room at the Y."

"You hear dat, boy? You doan clean up your act, you goin' to Howe Street. You know what happen at de Y.M.C.A.? You goan get it up de ass, cuz all daze got at de Y.M.C.A. is ex-cons and vagrants and queers."

Lydia suddenly remembers my marriage to Michael.

"Oh, Miz Riley, dat's jis an opinion. No offense meant."

Wendell's eyes have not left "Sesame Street." He is presently learning the difference between to, too, and two, and is impervious to our presence. Richard marches to the set and turns it off.

"Wendell, it's honesty time. I've found a wonderful woman and I have a very real expectation of happiness. And I think with Emma on board it could be your expectation, too. But I have to say that I haven't liked your bolted door, I haven't liked your manner, I've found it hard to like *you* much of the time."

"Easy now, suh, easy wid dat boy."

"Lydia, sometimes things must be said."

"I know dat. But you done spared de rod year after year, now you got to go easy."

"Here. Here's eighty dollars. It's all I have with me. Call me when you need more. I don't care where you go, but hopefully you'll have the courtesy not to impose further on Lydia."

As we start for the door, Wendell stands up.

"I'll come home."

Richard is not surprised.

"Well, all right. I don't think you should drive in this state. Emma will take the Volvo, and you can come with me."

"Whatever you say."

Wendell touches my arm and looks directly into my eyes. He is without histrionics; there seems to be an inner layer of truth shining through.

"We will never speak of this again."

He turns to Lydia and swathes her in his arms. It's a long, tenacious hug. At the end of it, he guides her a few feet away from Richard and me. He wants privacy, but there's none to be had in this small, antimacassared room. He speaks quietly and earnestly.

"Lydia, I drank six glasses of water today, right from the tap. I did it to prove that your water's OK down here. If I'm not dead by tomorrow, I think you should stop hauling water from your ladies' houses. It's a hell of a hassle, and quite unnecessary."

Lydia begins to weep. I don't think these tears are about Wendell's plight or toxic water. These tears are about some ancient pain, something deep in her psyche, some crisis of color that confined her life to the impasse of a minimum wage, taken under the table. She is embarrassed. She waves at Richard and me, wanting us to leave, and then she kisses Wendell goodbye.

"You right in goin' home, boy. Daze goan make mincemeat of you at de Y.M.C.A."

At home Wendell goes directly to the phone and calls Monica. He says he hopes she is settling back into the dorm. He says that he can't expect forgiveness and that she is very nice not to hang up. He urges her to finish the year. He says that she is beautiful, that someday a sane man will take her down the aisle properly, with her family there, and bridesmaids. He then calls the lawyer, Alex Bloom, and asks him to come to the house to meet with Richard and discuss the annulment. After showering, he wears a jacket to the dinner table and there he proposes a toast.

"There was a perilous time when I thought I might have Miss Marchant at this table. I'm delighted it hasn't worked out that way. So, I raise my glass to the future happiness of Dad and Emma. And, just for the record, you may rely on my respect.''

There is contentment on Richard's face, and he savors his food with gusto. Over coffee he suggests that he and I make our social debut in two weeks. He has been invited to a party at Henry Salisbury's, on Livingston Street. Henry has just embarked on a second marriage with a new, young wife, and she, too, will be acquainting herself with the community. I will accompany him and he will say to the gathered throng:

"I would like you to meet my lady.''

I search Wendell's eyes with trepidation. He allows nothing but polite complacency. Finally, smiling, he recommends that I wear my black cashmere sweater and gray challis skirt. Richard says I should put my hair back in that French sort of knot, and Wendell agrees, yes, that would show off her fine Celtic bones. They natter on about jewelry, rather like Higgins and Pickering preparing Eliza for the ball. When the phone rings, I go to answer it. It is Mr. Gambardella, announcing that the Skyrama has arrived from Meridan. He and his brother will install it on our roof at eight in the morning.

This discussion of the wardrobe for my debut strikes me as slightly crass and untimely. Monica has been dispatched summarily, and there seems to be no lingering trace of remorse in either man. Richard prophesied that Wendell would take what he needed from people and then leave them by the wayside. Perhaps Monica is the first of our poet's casualties. But Nee Marchant, the expedient fixation, is now alone among her singular, suspended mobiles, a second Goddard casualty.

Sharp, flash feeling of fear. Who will be the next? Kevin would say:

"It's in the lap o' the cards.''

I'm inclined to think it's in the knot o' the blood.

Twenty-Two

Wonder of Wonders, Miracle of Miracles, as Austin Pendleton sang in the original production of *Fiddler on the Roof*. Wendell is flirting dangerously with adulthood and Richard's ensuing smile envelops the three of us in sovereign gold.

A momentous event, this shifting of clothing to Richard's closet. He has cleared three drawers in the huge Empire dresser for my "intimate apparel," as he says. I am embarrassed that the bulk of my intimate apparel requires only one drawer. Richard's contents are folded and packed into cardboard boxes, which Wendell kindly volunteers to carry to the third-floor storage room. And Wendell thoughtfully removed from my room an old cotton shoe bag that Nanny made. It has twelve calico pouches for six pairs of shoes, and it is interesting that Nanny and I had the same quota of shoes. Wendell hammered three nails on the back of a door and transferred the bag to Richard's room. My *Reader's Digest* rests under the lamp on my own night table, along with a volume of Anaïs Nin. My slippers squat nearby, and in the bathroom my green toothbrush stands, unashamed, alongside Richard's white one in the fat ceramic holder. My velour robe hangs from a hook beside the tub, my birth control pills have their own shelf in the medicine cabinet. The plastic dial-a-day disk shares space with my array of color-coordinated Cover Girl makeup, purchased at prices guaranteed not to rip you off. Richard, upon seeing this collection, showed me an ad from a magazine. Princess Marcella Borghese was announcing "nine exquisitely sensate beauty treatments that are now available for the first time in the history of the world." He chuckled at the ad.

"I love your thrift," he said. "I love your dollar-ninety-nine mascara. I love *you* more than anyone has ever loved anybody *in the history of the world.*"

And because we are frail, we harbor secrets. Richard selects a private place for Metamucil, Gelusil, Stress Tabs, corn plasters, suppositories, and Fleet enema. I have a private place for an old retainer I should but don't wear, a douche bag, hair depilatory, mud mask, wrinkle repellant, a bottle of wart remover, and then of course, a spectrum of sanitary pads and tampons. Minis, maxis, ultra-thins, slenders, and supers to absorb the light, the medium, and the heavy flow. Flushable and nonflushable. With tabs to hinge into belts, with adhesive strips to fasten to underpants. Michael mused that the poor, deprived woman behind the Iron Curtain had only one choice of napkin, whereas, in the West:

"You bleeders have spawned a dozen industries competing for your capitalist blood."

"So? *So?* You shavers have spawned a dozen industries competing for your capitalist whiskers!"

And then I surreptitiously drop my St. Christopher medal into a drawer. Peg says you should always carry one of these when traveling, not to protect against the exigencies of locomotion, but against the aforementioned syph lying in wait on public toilet seats. Finally, I hide a pair of thick wool bed socks for frigid feet caused by poor circulation due to cigarettes. Slip 'em on in the middle of the night when he has gone to snooze.

Wendell announces that he will no longer require an allowance. He scans the want ads and takes the Volvo to an interview. The manager of the Touch Base Answering Service is looking for someone to work from four to

midnight, hand-recording messages. The manager is looking for someone who doesn't say wou-unt and cou-unt and
shou-unt, all of which Wendell doesn't. At dinner he
announces that he has been hired on at four dollars an
hour. He will need the Volvo every day until he can
stockpile enough for a down payment on a second-hand
car. It goes without saying, says he, emphatically, that he
will pay his own insurance premiums. He will leave the
house at three-thirty with a sandwich and a thermos of
cream-of-leek soup, please, Emma, and won't return until
twelve-thirty. He describes the virtues of this schedule
gleefully before Richard and me. This job at Touch Base
will allow him to sleep eight hours, rise at 10 A.M., and
write until three. It will, of course, require a little flexibil-
ity on Emma's part. She will have to run errands prior to
three o'clock. Oh, says Richard, she's very good at organ-
izing her day. Yes, says Wendell, she does have her
priorities in order. But when Richard leaves the room to
search for his brown Shermans, Wendell's glee disappears.
He wanders to a dining room window and stands for a
moment, with his back to me. He turns and faces me.

"White man speak with forked tongue."

"What do you mean?"

"I mean that I have arranged to be conveniently
absent when you two have dinner. I've arranged to be
absent when you go to bed. I would appreciate it very
much if you could contrive to enjoy your moments of
conjugal bliss during those periods when I'm absent."

The words are flippant, but there is sorrow in his eyes. I
thought we were not going to speak of this again, and I'm
on the verge of reminding him, but then there is pleading
in his eyes and a catch in his throat.

"I would really appreciate it if you'd contrive that, in
my behalf."

I find myself on the verge of tears. I find myself whispering:

"Yes, I understand. I'll do my best."

He smiles, Richard returns, and both men sit at the table engaging in gleeful chat about second-hand cars and Blue Book values. I sit quietly and consider the exchange. How innocently it happened, the way the words fell randomly across the carpet. To outsiders, or flies on the wall, it would be no more than a second's communication. But it was, in fact, a pact. I am party to something again, still straddling the breach between the two men, but differently. Wendell has sought to relieve Richard and me of his presence in the evenings. And I have agreed to schedule our sex life around Wendell's employment at the answering service. I've agreed to try to protect Wendell from Richard and me. Richard sits there, puffing on his Sherman, savoring his wine, and Wendell sips his coffee. Wendell no longer leaves his spoon in the cup while he drinks, no longer licks his knife or has what Peg calls "the boardinghouse reach." These improvements in etiquette happened gradually and naturally, for my benefit but without my intervention.

Wendell seems assured by my brief pledge. He looks relaxed: he really is inordinately handsome. A *tender juvenal*. I am struck that there is pleasure in merely looking at him—physical pleasure in his youthful, present, physical presence. Traces and whiffs of dialogue run through my head, vestiges of some near-forgotten play—what is it? *Love's Labor's Lost*. There's a moment when Costard, the clown, takes Moth, the page, the "tender Juvenal," aside and confesses his fondness for the boy. He says, "Had I but one penny in the world, thou shouldst have it to buy gingerbread." I look at the two men and feel again that sense of inheritance that I felt initially: Goddards begetting Goddards. Continuity. Sudden, impetuous urge to be genetically included. To participate in and perpetuate their line. Fleeting flash of an engagement ring. Our Lady of the Barren Womb hankering after a ring from Richard. Not looking for the Holy Grail, Michael, rather a sire to father

a child. A child for whom I would feel the primal commitment known only through parentage. A child to whom I
would give my last penny.

They natter on about used cars. Richard says he wouldn't
buy Japanese. He remembers Pearl Harbor too well and
that, he says, shouldn't ever be forgotten or forgiven. And
Wendell shoots me a furtive, startled glance at the choice
of words. They talk ''Detroit'' and begin with quadruped
mammals. Colts, Pintos, Mustangs, and Broncos. Skyhawks,
Skylarks, Firebirds, and Sunbirds. Gremlins and Hornets.

Listen in, girl. Concentrate, and perish these thoughts of
rings, progeny, and perpetuity.

Gracie, upon hearing of my miscegenation with the
massa, suggests something perhaps only Cat'lics understand.

''Jesus, Mary and Joseph,'' she says. ''Do you want
to go to church?''

Yes, in the circumstances, that sounds like a good idea.
Lydia has eavesdropped on my phone conversation.

''Miz Riley, you goan light a candle at dat church?''

''Probably, yes.''

She goes to her canvas bag and digs for her change purse.
She hands me a quarter.

''My sister, Velveeta, she feelin' poorly. You lights
one for her.''

''Thank you, Lydia. I'd be happy to.''

Then, a moment of uncertainty.

''Can't do no *harm*, right?''

''Right.''

Although my father and mother would beg to differ.

I climb into the Volvo and go to meet Grace at the "Cathedral of New Haven," St. Mary's on Hillhouse Avenue.

A hundred years before the patricians lived on St. Ronan, they congregated on Hillhouse Avenue. It is only two blocks long, from Grove Street to Sachem, where it runs smack into the enclave of physics buildings. The mansions must have been spectacular at one time; now they have been taken over by Yale and one sees file cabinets in the windows rather than damask and Chippendale. There are imposing Italianate structures, porches with doric columns, porticos calling out for horse-drawn broughams, round rooms in turrets, and mansard roofs with pearly gray slates. A few stables remain behind some of the houses. If I'm here in the spring I'll come back and watch the cherry trees, dogwood, and forsythia do their thing. And all the wondrous florification that occurs when florets burst forth out of Holland bulbs.

Grace points with pride to the tall red brick residence of A. Bartlett Giamatti, the president of Yale, a fellow Eyetalian. We pass a modern building that houses Yale's Department of Health Services and an ancient, brooding sandstone heap that houses Yale's Collection of Musical Instruments. Michael, this old seat of learning is, like Dolly Parton whom you love, well endowed.

We are attending the twelve-noon Mass, and Grace has spent the morning at the library. She carries a fishnet satchel containing six heavy best-sellers, and when the weight is too great, she hands the satchel to me. I lug it up the stairs of this Dominican church, through the wooden Gothic doors and then, since we're early, I wrestle with it while Gracie, as she says, indoctrinates me to St. Mary's.

The interior of the church has been painted a rather dreary olive green and there is, for a Catholic church, a sparsity of graven images. Joseph, the carpenter, stands with plane and square to the left of the altar and Mary is suspended rather oddly, in red and gold, on a pillar to the right. There's a nice bronze Christ on a bronze cross hanging from the ceiling and he is, thankfully, without the ubiquitous gaping wounds. But we are here today to celebrate the Infant of Prague. According to Grace, the more we honor this small doll, the more He will bless us. Legend and holy writ have it that a Spanish Princess donated the statue to the Carmelite Fathers of Prague upon her marriage in that city. According to the pamphlet fetched at the door, War, Strife, Sacking, and Looting followed and the city of Prague was sorely Plundered. As devotion to the Infant declined, so did Prosperity. The Babe was cast aside and lay behind an altar for seven long years. A priest, finding the damaged doll in 1637, heard a strange, heavenly voice as he lifted it from the rubble:

"Have pity on me and I will have pity on you. Give me back my hands, and I will give you peace."

The statue was restored and many blessings, both Spiritual and Material, were showered on the clients of the Divine Infant. While Gracie lights a candle, I examine the Babe. He is two feet high and wears a tiara on his blond curls. He is dressed in a white satin robe embossed with a red rose. His right hand is raised and he is blessing me. Listen, Kevin, I know this is all bilgewater but I have never quite escaped the clutches of these teachings. You must have had that in mind, you old fart, when you sent me to St. Anne's in the first place.

I leave the quarter and light a candle for Velveeta who is feeling poorly in Bridgeport. I light another and leave a dollar, and pray that Wendell and Richard will someday find a path to each other. So great is my munificence that I drop another dollar and light a third candle. I pray that Daniel will always be kind and loving and faithful to Michael. I know that God, in His wisdom, forgives flaming faggots, Jerry Falwell and Anita Bryant notwithstanding.

Grace doesn't take the sacrament because she hasn't confessed the sin of her illegitimate child, and I choose not to partake of the wafer because I am divorced. We two sinners sit at the back of the church and watch the people file by the altar. We chat quietly in the stillness. What, asks Gracie, did Wendell say when he learned that I had gone to bed with his father?

"You don't want to know."

"I do! Desperately. Come on, spill the beans."

"Oh, Grace, not *here*."

"Why not?"

"He said I was hired to keep house. I wasn't hired to lick Dick's prick."

Her eyes widen with mischief. She delves down into her satchel, pulls up a book, and flips it open to a red plastic paper clip. She hands me the book. It is Helen Gurley Brown's *Having It All*. And there, while the devoted citizens take the blood and the body of Christ in the dim hush of St. Mary's, I read:

A delicately rosy, silky-satin, somehow innocent, always-vulnerable erect penis is probably *the most fascinating object in the world. There is nothing like a big (anything over 4″ erect) longing-to-be-appreciated, grateful for anything you do to it, show-offy, lovely, male penis to bring tears to the eyes and joy to the psyche.*

I slam the book closed and thrust upon Grace a gaze of righteous indignation. She responds heatedly.

"Don't tell me this is Mouseburger hogwash because I happen to agree with Mrs. Brown."

"Swallowed it whole, did you, Gracie?"

And we erupt in raucous laughter, giggling our way out of the church like randy schoolgirls, passing under the stained glass images of St. Catharine of Siena, St. Agnes of Montepulcano, St. Rose of Lima, and St. Catharine of Ricci. The four saintly ladies frown down on us as our knees buckle at the madness in the world. Grace gives her satchel an affectionate pat and I fold the Infant of Prague Novena safely into my shoulder bag. It can't do any harm.

At home, Alex Bloom has arrived to discuss Wendell's annulment. Richard introduces me to him and Wendell insists that I sit down, join them, and keep the record straight. He says he can't remember much about his short-lived marriage and Emma's input might help. Bloom seems to know about Richard and me. He says he looks forward to talking to me socially sometime. Then, pulling a long pad—"legal size," I suppose—out of his briefcase, Bloom says that the annulment will rest on Wendell's proof that he "misrepresented" himself to Monica.

"May I hear, in your own words, Wendell, how you misrepresented yourself to this young lady?"

"Well, she thought my proposal was synonymous with love. The proposal, in that context, was a misrepresentation. I didn't love her."

Wendell is sweating. His complexion is motley and piebald. He is trying valiantly not to sound juvenile, and although Bloom is kind, he is a lawyer and sixty and automatically infers malfeasance. Bloom looks askance at Richard, and Richard does the same at me. The two suddenly look like Daumier judges, and I refuse to become one with this adult dismay. In keeping my eyes fastened on Wendell, I'm trying to tell Bloom that anyone can make mistakes. I'm telling Wendell he'll get no conde-scension from me.

"If you didn't love her, why did you propose?"

"I think it was a seizure. I was not, at the time, responsible for myself."

"How long did this seizure last?"

"Exactly as long as it took to make the proposal."

"But you went ahead and bought rings and got a certificate. You were not in a seizure then."

"Then I was in a daze. It wasn't until we got home that I fully realized I couldn't make love to her. Frankly, I had trouble looking at her."

"So you never actually consummated the marriage?"

"Well, we'd consummated off and on over the last three months, but we never did after we took the vows."

Alex Bloom will draw up a "Summons and Complaint," asking that the marriage be dissolved. He will file it with the court and a sheriff will mail it to Monica. Monica should, on Wendell's amiable and cautiously worded request, agree to the annulment in writing. Bloom will then request a court date, for a hearing. After a mandatory three-month lapse, Wendell and Bloom will go to the Superior Court House on the New Haven Green and show evidence as to why the marriage is invalid. Bloom prepares to take notes and looks grim.

"Richard, do you think she'll want compensation?"

"You mean financial compensation?"

"Bucks, yes."

"God, I don't know. I hope not. What do you think, Wendell?"

"Jesus. Her father earns a half million a year at General Motors. And I didn't cost her anything. Anything *material*."

Bloom addresses the three of us.

"Just in case, now. Just in case she wants to recuperate psychologically for a year in the best hotel in Tahiti, would you say that there was aggravation on your part? Did she cost *you* anything?"

Richard and Wendell wag their heads in a unanimous "no." For some inexplicable reason I hear myself clearing my throat. Bloom looks up, quizzically.

"Yes?"

"Well, just, you know, for the record. Certain aggravation, yes, and certain cost. There's a five-hundred-dollar Skyrama on our roof, installed in her behalf. I don't mean to speak out of turn but I imagine these legal fees, at, say, a hundred an hour, will also add up. So I would say, just for the record, technically, Monica did cost us something."

Gaffed, again. Didn't think before I spoke. Peg says if the populace thought before it spoke the world would be mute. Bloom clears his own throat and mutters,

"Two hundred an hour."

Oh, dear. If I had two hundred an hour I'd work all the time, never sleep, and retire at forty. Richard is embarrassed. There are certain occasions when he does suffer from too much good breeding. He offers Bloom brandy and goes to fetch it from the butler's pantry. Wendell excuses himself and goes to his room to draft an amiable letter to Monica. Bloom leans against the mantel and looks very judicial.

"There's something about all this that speaks to me of a rebound. An unrequited love. I'd wager that Wendell married Monica on that account."

"I really couldn't say."

"Richard says he carries a torch for the old black cleaning lady. Now, I know he's a genuine crazy person, but you don't think that's *serious*, do you?"

Oh, Mr. Bloom, I think it is. But even a crazy person would realize the unlikelihood of such a union. As Tevye warned, also in *Fiddler on the Roof:*

> "A fish can marry a bird,
> but where can they live?"

Twenty-Three

I must pass inspection before going to the Salisbury party. Richard has given me a bottle of perfume, Ma Griffe, which I apply sparingly. And since all of my jewelry veers toward the cheap, I dig for my one good piece, a cameo set on onyx in sterling silver. I wear my hair in the prescribed French knot, the black sweater and the gray skirt. I look like a mortician's wife, but the point is, I think, to look like somebody's, anybody's, wife. So I don't wear the black stockings that would make this ensemble really nifty. Michael loved the black stockings. He said they made him think I was about to lift my skirt and russle my petticoats, like a Lautrec woman on the verge of either a Can-Can or an electric sexual encounter. Richard thought I looked picture-perfect. Fleetingly I'm sad that Wendell is at work. He never sees me dressed, and I think he would approve. All one ever wants in this life, really, is unqualified praise.

And how handsome is this senior Goddard, smelling of the green juniper soap he orders from England. Gray slacks, navy jacket, and fine woolen turtleneck that some skilled Florentine has made to feel like silk. His white hair glistens in the light. He is like those distinguished gentlemen who appear on certain commercials, going to the mansion next door to borrow a cup of Johnny Walker, leaning out of their Alfa Romeos to borrow a jar of Grey Poupon, presiding over a Tuscan feast, touting wine from grapes grown in their own vineyards. Brief, flash feeling that I couldn't live without him. That the earth would lose its green, turn gray and morbid like one of Monica's paintings, without him. Frogs would lose their chirp, roses their scent without him.

> "Except I be by Sylvia in the night,
> There is no music in the nightingale."

It is quite thrilling to sit beside his dapper self in the car, both of us so sleekly groomed and me a bit of a dish myself. And how raffish he is when he slides his hand under my skirt between my folded legs and leaves it just above the knee. Exactly where raffish qualifies, rather than predatory. Six inches further and the hand would be an invasion. It's nice that we know all this about each other, without words.

Contrary to prematurely formed prejudices, the gang at Henry Salisbury's turns out to be lively. Richard, as promised, introduces me all around as his lady. But then there is the matter of Henry's new wife, Blodwen. She is a Welsh Valkyrie with a rambunctious manner, a pronounced openness, and a modified punk haircut. She is thirty years old while Henry is a paunchy sixty. She is tall, with wide, swaggering hips and pendulous breasts as large as casaba melons. I thought Richard would find her voluptuous but no, I can hear his teeth grind.

> "Blodwen doesn't talk," he says. "Blodwen brays."

And indeed, while I had dressed so conscientiously, was so afraid of a wrong impression casting aspersions on Richard's good judgment, Blodwen now makes me feel distinctly aristocratic. It's not that her clothing is cheap; it's a case of what the Italian art restorers call pentimento: the original layer asserts itself no matter how many layers are superimposed. It's a case of what Michael would call, less flatteringly, the slatternly. It enables me to sally forth with the confidence and aplomb of The Honorable Millicent Fenwick. Stick by me, Blodwen, it makes me feel classy.

Blodwen had worked at Victuals and Grog, a wine and cheese shop on Temple, and Henry's first wife used to send him in every Friday after work to pick up a pound of

St. André Triple Crème for the weekend. One thing led to another, said Blodwen, unabashedly. One weekend Henry picked up the cheese and never went home again. He left his wife in a 1790 Colonial house on six acres in Cheshire, filed for divorce, and moved into Livingston Street with Blodwen. Henry was a professor of physics and was also Deputy Provost for the Sciences.

"You'll be fine," brays Blodwen. "Very few of the middle-aged professors have remained with their wives. The first lot were all Radcliffe, Vassar, and Bryn Mawr. The second round are somewhat more eclectic."

Henry fills my hand with a glass of Plantation Punch and looks eager to make amenities, but Blodwen takes Henry by the shoulders and plants him alongside Richard.

"Richard," she commands, "talk to Henry."

She steers me past a bookcase that contains rows of green soft-back physics journals identical to Richard's collection.

"Just be sure, if you ever have a party, to run the gamut. Physicists tend to be clannish. Never invite more than two at a time. That woman over there is a track coach. That old fellow writes books about the Old Testament. Those two men are, well, a couple. Poets. One teaches Milton and the other's stuck in Wallace Stevens. I'm told they are very well-connected in the literary world. That fellow over there is rather rank and file. He's an accelerator operator. I invite him because he is guaranteed to sit down at the piano at midnight and do his imitation of Louis Armstrong singing 'Hello Dolly.' "

I am trying mightily for confidence and aplomb but I find myself clinging to Richard, nervously eating altogether too many chicken livers wrapped in soggy bacon. Richard, on his second helping of Plantation Punch, is a little giddy. He holds the toothpick in the air and examines the liver.

"Can you imagine the cholesterol content in these things? Maybe she's trying to kill poor Henry off. Take his booty and go back to Cardiff and live in the house on the hill."

This libation is mostly rum mixed with an insignificant portion of some tropical fruit juice. My head spins while Richard engages in home-computer talk with the very old, Old Testament man, Ethan Shepard. I pretend to listen but I am fastened on Blodwen's description of the poets.

"I'm told they are very well-connected in the literary world."

Round and round the sentence goes in my head, spurring me to action. I want to sit with the homosexual couple, and they sense it. They smile at me compassionately. They know that I know. That I know volumes about the intricacies of their lives. That I've had intimate experience with one of their number. I have announced, chemically, in airborne messages, that I am privy to the naked truth. But I can't, comfortably, leave this chair at this moment. This bits and bytes talk is a far cry from the social banter I'm used to. I don't think this crowd will ever play "Did," nor will they discuss the films Laurence Olivier made at Pinewood. I say, would anyone here care to know the sad details of the sordid life and untimely death of William Inge? The two across the room already know, but I don't think they speak of it socially.

Henry? Don't be such a nebbish. She's barking at you, isn't she? All about sticking the livers under the broiler. Take the sog out of the bacon. Replenish the ice cubes. Fetch more Triscuits. Hold your stomach in. Jesus, Henry, who needs it? You apparently do. What you've got there, Hank, is a first-class harridan and one can only hope there's commensurate compensation in the sack. If you'd come sit by me, Henry, you'd see that I'm able to discuss, albeit superficially, the thirty-nine plays in the First Folio, with a cursory nod at the Sonnets. And you wouldn't expect that from a girl from Dorchester. But I'm full of surprises; surprising myself just now with a compelling need to get with the poets and go to work for Wendell.

One of them, the small Milton man, flames so intensely he needs a fire extinguisher. What no one understands is that if I said that to him, he'd laugh. He'd have himself a great, gurgling chortle. Because that's all they've got, you see, in their survival kits when they show themselves publicly, amidst the righteous straights who were born on the right side of the sheet, who run accelerators and jerk off in the john with *Penthouse* magazine. Richard is speaking loudly because the Old Testament man is deaf.

"What you want, Ethan, is a general purpose micro, rather than a word processor. You have more options that way. I'd say the minimum you'd require is sixty-four K of memory, display screen, two floppy disk drives, and a printer. I suspect you'd like daisywheel copy better than dot-matrix."

Ethan Shepard is well over seventy, with a keen sense of the ridiculous.

"I wouldn't like either, Richard. I don't want any of it. I don't want memory and I'd abhor floppy disks. I don't even want options. I learned to write in the first grade with a *quill!* Yes! In 1912 in a North Dakota schoolhouse I set my thoughts down on paper with a turkey's tail-feather."

And that's the way Shakespeare wrote the thirty-nine plays and the sonnets. So the question is: with a five-and-one-quarter-inch diskette holding two hundred K of memory, or approximately two hundred thousand characters, or even with an eight-inch diskette holding six hundred K, or approximately three hundred and sixty pages . . . will we ever see his like again? And I'm off now to ingratiate myself with the pansy poets.

They are a good-looking couple in their forties, both
wearing Liberty silk ascots. A soigné couple, Michael
would say. The small, pyrotechnical one is called Ben
Lindsay and the tall one is named Martin Martin. He was
born in New York City and went to Antioch as an under-
graduate, spending four years there introducing himself as
Martin Martin from New York, New York. They look at
Blodwen, raise their eyebrows, and expect a comment
from me.

"Yes," I say. "But perhaps she's a diamond in the
rough."

"I don't think so," replies Ben Lindsay. "In the
rough I fear she's more a chunk of her native
anthracite."

They have been discussing the decor in the room, and
Ben observes that there are distinct Commie origins in the
provenance of these pieces. Martin agrees.

"It's these peripatetic physicists. They're forever jour-
neying to Russia on funds supplied by the taxpayer
via the Department of Defense. During breaks from
their various symposia they set out on chartered excursions to markets in Kiev, Leningrad, and Tbilisi.
They bring back these icons and samovars and
matrushkas. And those little scatter rugs are, of course,
Armenian."

"Crude and provincial crafting," says Ben. "But
falling, I suppose, under the general rubric, Oriental."

Listen, fellas, I am sorely in need of advice and guidance. I have a young friend, Richard's son, actually, who
writes poetry. His poems are, in my opinion, quite fine,
but my opinion is hardly informed. What he needs, because he tends to isolate himself, is a connection with the
profession. He's very disciplined; he writes every day for
at least five hours. But he's scared diarrhetically shitless of

showing the poems to anyone. And I believe, if he could just break this vise and *trust* another opinion, he might begin submitting. And until he does that—gets the stuff out and receives reactions—he has no knowledge of the marketplace. He's just another closet writer. And I know, in my heart, that he's got the mark. The makings of something really mad and spectacular. I'm sorry if I'm imposing, you must be sick to death of sampling poems and advising, you must be drowning, I would suspect, in the scribblings of vapid, vernal Yalies, but this boy is really special. Quirky, shy, bombastic, insecure, obscene, schizophrenic, and very handsome. And an old Blue himself. Boola-boola. So as not to break ranks.

I'm not entirely sure that I can coax something out of him, but if I *can*, would you consider giving them a quick peruse?

"Gladly," says Martin Martin. "See if you can lift a few. Bring them around to our apartment on Orange Street."

"I can't tell you how much I—"

"No bother at all," says Martin. "Always glad to help the youth."

Ben has one of those narrow mouths. I think he whines and is afflicted with hardening of the emotional arteries. He is not pleased at the prospect of Martin taking time to read Wendell's poems. I suspect, when they get home, it'll go something like this:

MARTIN:
How about a little nightcap?
                    BEN:
No, thank you.
                    MARTIN:
What's the matter?
                    BEN:
Nothing.

MARTIN:

The Riley woman, right? You didn't like her.

BEN:

I thought she was all got up to look like Millicent
Fenwick.

MARTIN:

I thought she looked fine. The beige stockings were
a mistake, but the cameo was nice.

BEN:

You liked her description of the mad young boy.

MARTIN:

Oh, Benjamin, *this* again?

BEN:

You're turned on by this handsome St. Ronan scriv-
ener. As if you haven't enough to do. As if you're not
fucking buried already in mountains of versification.

MARTIN:

Well, let's go to bed.

BEN:

You go. I'll be along later.

It's nice to go parties, to look at authentic matrushkas,
learn about daisywheels, be fed at the hands of a hostess,
and feel the buzz of the booze. It's nice to feel a protective
wing across the room, and loving eyes that will rescue you
if they receive a baleful signal. To know that, at the end of
it, one will not have to brave the night alone, sitting
fearfully in a cold, idling car at a red light, wondering
what evil lurks in the minds of the single men in the other,
waiting cars. Peg always said when Mick-faced blue-bum-
scum approach your car the smart thing to do is lock all
the doors and lean on the horn. Until a Mick-faced cop
arrives. And that hanger under the seat from the last time
you locked yourself out is good for mutilation, if you need
it. She said they've got these great throbbing hammers,
you know, and a dire need to sink them in female flesh,
even on the gritty asphalt under the red light at the witching hour. I said yes, I read of one Portnoy who sunk *his* in
a jar of liver from his mother's refrigerator. And Peg
replied, and I'll never forget it:

"Was this Portnoy Catholic?"

"No. Jewish."

"Oh, well, they're all circumcised."

When we got home we dove together under the fat, down quilt and it went like this:

"Emma, tell me, honestly, what did you think of Blodwen?"

"I thought she was a rather odd mix of the primitive and the pretentious."

"Ummm. She's been here ten years and she still says 'alu*min*ium' for foil, and 'meegraine' for headache. And when she sends an invitation, she writes her 's's' in the Old English way."

"What do you mean?"

He grabs a pen and pad from his nightstand and illustrates the manner in which Blodwen writes "Mister."

Miʃter

"It's got to be," he says, "the last word in affectation. You'd think Henry would say something."

Well, it's not so easy to say something. I did once and it backfired. My friend Madeline, back in the days of Finnegan, long before Bitsy appeared in the kennel, frequently complained that she was "pressurized" by work. It began to rankle to such an extent that I would actually anticipate her use of the word long before she misused it. Finally, her persistence in using it caused a sensation in me not unlike flagellation, so I said,

"Madz, I think you mean you are pressured by work."

"No," she said, "I'm pressurized."

"I don't think so, Madz. Pressurized is what happens to food in a cooker."

Our friendship was never quite the same because she never quite forgave me. And one day she and I and Bitsy and Michael were looking at geese and swans on a pond. Madeline said, "Oh, look at the baby geese and the baby swans." And Michael said, "Uh huh. Goslings and cygnets." And it ruined the afternoon. But never mind.

"Henry will take a lot of flagellation," says Richard. "He's impaled himself on his libido."

We, in our somewhat similar May/December alliance, are somewhat different. In our goodnight kiss we indulge in no more than a peck. Wendell is home, across the hall, and Richard understands, tacitly, that Wendell's presence on the premises is a wedge between our two bodies.

There is something inherently false between us and I can't as yet label it an outright lie. I can't, because I'm unable to fathom the truth.

Twenty-Four

Saturday morning in Wendell's bedroom.

"Oh, Jesus, Emma. Oh, Christ. I can't! You have to make some kind of excuse. You have to get me out of it."

"I won't. If you can't do it, *you* call and make your own excuse."

"Why did you do it?"

"I'll tell you why. You're in a no-win situation. I almost think that you don't *want* to succeed. As long as you hibernate here, you're holding your father in thrall. I've done a lot of speculation and it may be all wrong but it seems to me you're trying to pay your father back in some way. Because your childhood happened not to be some idyllic version of Norman Rockwell. You're so damn unreasonable about your work, so obstinate, I actually thought of *stealing* some poems. Taking them to Martin Martin secretly. But that's another cop-out and this household is glutted with cop-outs."

"Martin Martin sounds like a redundant man."

He is trying very hard to revert to the old, familiar, easily facile, but he can't quite pull it off. He can't be-

cause this is a matter of import. His work is too vital and
I've got him, I think, where he lives.

"Martin Martin is a honey-bunch. His boyfriend is
something else, but Martin's the one we'll deal with.
I want you to select three or four poems and I'll take
them over, personally."

"I can't! You just don't understand what's at *stake!*"

"I understand too well! You have to jump this hurdle
now! Good God, man, what do you need? A stick of
dynamite?"

I'm reaching him. He doesn't respond but I feel that he
wants me to persist.

"If you go on like this, sooner or later you won't be
able to write *anything*. Because you have no *life*. You
stand impaired. You're thoroughly disconnected from
all of the forces that feed the mind and the soul.
And this malnutrition, so to speak, is bound to
show in your work. I would even go so far as to
say that somewhere in you there's a secret desire
to follow your mother. To be committed, by someone else's decision, to be removed from the job of
life."

"Lady, you are really unbalanced this morning."

"Then you could abdicate responsibility completely
and it would all be your father's fault. I love him,
Wendell, and I won't let that happen. And the irony
is he feels that, in marrying your mother, he disquali-
fied himself from some important race. That's his
great regret. And you seem to want to emulate that,
too. I'm saying that if you don't get off your ass and
show these things to somebody, take the *chance*,
you're risking permanent disqualification."

He shifts his long body in his straight-backed chair. We hear in the background the scraping of Richard's rake as he tackles a yardful of fallen autumn leaves. Wendell is so frightened, so pensive, so in need of assurance I have an immediate urge to run and hug him, console him, and then I think we both would cry.

"You might not believe this, Wendell, but I love you, too. And the thought of your never getting on with this job of life just breaks my heart."

"If you do love me, you'll be the first adult that ever has."

The statement is not self-pitying. It's his honest, open, quiet, sad appraisal. His view from where he sits. I feel such empathy it's hard to keep my eye objective, my tongue in the groove of truth.

"Your father loves you enormously. All that stuff about settling scores is shit. All that shit about forgetting nothing, forgiving nothing is *dreck*. Don't you see that the both of you are hurting? He extended a great big olive branch. He opened the door and took you back in the house and that took *courage* because you were hardly repentant. And what did you do? You came to this room and bolted the door."

He whirls up out of his chair, angrily.

"All right, all right! I'm a no-good son-of-a-bitch. I'm an ingrate, a cad, and a bounder. What do want from me?"

"I want you to give some poems to Martin. And I want you to understand that you're doing it for Richard, not for me. You're doing it to open the door."

"And if Martin hates the poems?"

"The door will still be open. There'll be options. Fresh air. *Leverage*, as my mother would say. He won't just hate them. He'll offer suggestions and guidance. So then we'll reconnoiter. Move on from there. The point is to move on. To run the bloody race."

There are papers strewn everywhere but he hones in on a specific pile. He knows, without reflection, which of the poems he wants seen. He hands me "Interloping Woman," "Forgiving Fog," and two others, "Hazardous Waste" and "Annulment." While I read them he stands at the window and watches Richard rake. The former poem suggests that he has keen knowledge of his own morass. The latter suggests that he couldn't love Monica, could not love anyone, until he lays down his sword and accepts the love of his father.

I drive, hell bent for leather, pushing the Volvo to its limited limits before he changes his mind. Martin Martin receives the packet at the door and takes our phone number. He would invite me in but grumpy Ben, the wife, walks past and scowls.

"Don't forget, Marty, you have to pick up the dry cleaning."

If Ben lived with Blodwen they'd flay each other to death in a week.

And on this cold November day I have the pleasure of bagging leaves with Richard, wearing his big floppy work gloves, breaking twigs, twirling plastic bags, and winding ties. Telling him, with a tremendous sense of accomplishment, that Wendell, just this morning, discarded his crawl and decided to walk. He stands upright, holding the rake and I, in flat shoes, feel very small.

"Thank you," he murmurs down to me. "God in Heaven, thank you."

We sit on the back stoop and share a cigarette break. He pats my head. It's an oddly parental pat, a sort of neuter approval.

"I think it's finally happening," he says. "God, it's a miracle. I just may be on the verge of having order in my life. Bless you."

He talks again of Wendell succeeding. He had always imagined that the stifled, burned-out part of him would be passed on to Wendell. He had desired it all the more fervently recently.

"For most men," he says, "science goes out of physics by forty. The real advances, the really significant contributions happen early, if at all. For most men *administration* sets in with a vengeance. Few will admit it, but it's drudgery."

He had dreamed that, in his old age, he would find meaning and sustenance in the passing of the torch. He looks out on the dormant back yard and there is longing in his eyes, yearning in his voice. If only it could happen. He speaks of Wendell the way one speaks of a lost lover one meets up with again after a war, a scourge, a pestilence. He speaks of second chances, a just compensation at the end, a glorious reunion, a sunset to walk into. How slowly I am understanding Marion's impact: I think, for a moment, that she was a plague or a pox on the house and all of the resulting blisters and lesions that she caused in her husband and son went like cankers and tumors into their viscera. And I, with my housekeeping husbandry, my creative cuisine, my Mary Poppins cheer and bustle, am swabbing salves, bromides, and common home remedies where surgery is needed. He repeats,

"Bless you. You're the catalyst."

My brain cells are at sixes and sevens; I feel a frightening wave of doubt that I am not germane to the picture he is painting. I'm somehow leftover, a subtraction, a mathematical remainder. Where, Richard, in this network of interacting elements, do you perceive *me?* A cloud passes over his face.

"This is probably very unreasonable, but there's something about your being in the house all day that disturbs me. At first I thought it was just because Marion was holed up here all the time and that was so depressing. But I think it's healthier than that. I think it has to do with your potential. I think I'd like you to be more ambitious about yourself."

Reeling now, feeling the irksome chip on the shoulder, feeling *criticized*. Potential is for Wendell, at twenty-three. Potential gets my dander up, at thirty-five. I'm *actually sensitive* on this point. Potential implies that I'm in an inconclusive stage of limbo. Presently inadequate, deficient, but rife with possibilities of measuring up. Measuring up to what? For what reason?

"You're so quick of mind. Intelligent and curious and adventuresome. What would you like to do?"

Interact, Richard, in your network of elements. Include me in. Perhaps even genetically.

"Isn't there something in your past that you aspired to? Some secret accomplishment you covet?"

"Well, I wouldn't mind taking piano lessons."

"You'd like to be a pianist?"

"No, I'd just like some lessons. I've always wanted to sit down at parties and play show tunes."

"Anything else?"

When I was in high school I wanted to be a nurse. I don't think this was purely south Boston cultural conditioning; I thought nursing a satisfying, noble calling. Salves and bromides and splints and tourniquets applied educatedly. A sort of Nanny with certification. But there wasn't any money and I learned to type instead.

"I don't think you'd want to nurse nowadays. It's hard labor at low pay. What about a doctor? You could do it, if you put your mind to it."

Not this mind, sir. This one was set more on plumping-pillows, hands-on care. A daily defraying of psychological as well as physical pain. And the entire staff would take note and proclaim, with a flourish of cornets:

E.R.R. brings cheer to the ward.

"I'd be the oldest living M.D. at graduation. I'd pass directly from residency to retirement."

Then again there is this business of fine art. Michael hauled me around to look at rather a lot of it over fourteen years. I wouldn't mind a few lessons with the brush. Not to ever call myself an artist, but to understand what I look at. Michael used to say that every critic should be required to write a play and see it through the perils of production. Kevin said every carpenter should be required to design a house and see it through the vagaries of construction. So it seems to me that if I learned about the ingredients and actually had to wrestle the pigments and tinctures from the palette to the canvas I'd better appreciate what I see. But even there I'm not ambitious. Nothing cosmic in the vision. I wouldn't attempt Monica's ghoulish graveyards, or any kind of statement. I'd capture a cosmos, but I mean that representationally. I mean, I'm afraid, the fragile flower.

"Come into the study," he says.

He shows me literature from Yale's Office of Summer and Special Programs. He explains. In 1977, two hundred and fifty years after its founding, Yale finally gave a democratic nod to the community at large. The Program

for Special Students is available to people who were unable to attend college upon graduation from high school.
There is a non-degree option, and a degree option that
leads to a B.L.S.—Bachelor of Liberal Studies. I read one
of the phamplets while Richard looks on, happily. The
B.L.S. candidate must complete thirty-six term courses, at
roughly eight hundred dollars per course. The program has
been drawn especially for those who are otherwise engaged in earning a living, but who wish to augment and
achieve.

I must pull in my reins now and understand how important this is to Richard. We sit down in the study. The first
snow has begun to fall outside.

"We were at the eleventh hour, weren't we, with the
leaves?"

He frowns, seeing that my enthusiasm for a degree does
not match his. He is bewildered. He wonders how I have
escaped the rhetoric, if not the influence, of the Women's
Movement.

"I haven't, Richard. But I've worked and I've been
married, and I think the most sustaining thing in any
life is to love someone absolutely. Without that, pay,
even when it's equal pay for equal work, is just
something you cash at the bank."

I am trying very hard to show interest in this B.L.S.
thing. But I'm still reverberating from his vision of the
future—I still feel like a free-floating remainder. I wonder
if Richard isn't hoping to achieve order by having both
Wendell and me at separate desks, fulfilling our potential.
Does he see himself as an overseer, I wonder, a resident
don? I am not entirely untouched by feminism. Don is
from the Latin *dominus*. And the man is talking about *four
years*.

He comes and sits beside me on the couch and holds me
tightly to him. He enumerates the courses offered: ancient
and modern literature, architecture, classical civilization,

history of art, philosophy. How exciting it would be for me to go off, three or four times a week, expanding my spheres and widening my horizons. He would convert Marion's bedroom into a study for me. Buy a globe and a typewriter and a filing cabinet. Bring me coffee there in the evenings while I toil over papers he thinks I would write clearly and concisely. It would give him great pleasure to initiate me into the wonders of the Sterling Library, to guide my research, to share the joy of an "A." He'd try to get Lydia in more frequently so that I could be a full-time student.

The snow is falling heavily; I can see its accumulation on the cars. They look like two igloos standing in the driveway.

"I'll give this some serious thought, Richard."

"Good! Terrific. Look all this stuff over while I finish up the leaves."

Sitting in the study, cogitating, my gaze falls on the dictionary. It seems years since I went there in search of Wendell, to look up "puerile." Now I look up "remainder." In search of something exact.

"An interest in property that follows and is dependent upon the termination of a prior intervening possessory estate created at the same time by the same instrument."

What a mouthful. As I digest it I think the property I'm interested in is Richard, that my interest is dependent upon the termination of a prior intervening possessory estate. And that is Wendell. And suddenly, after ten weeks of thinking that Wendell and Richard were engaged in some sort of struggle at the heart of a blood knot, I wonder if the struggle isn't actually listing toward Wendell and me. I have claim to Richard sexually, but Wendell has prior, possessory claim. And this will not be solved until something is terminated. My blood runs cold: I think I can't blame it on poor circulation due to smokes. I shiver, pull my jacket over my shoulders, and the dictionary falls to the floor, opening and advancing from the *R*'s to the *S*'s. now my eye falls on another word.

Superfluous.

Wendell comes in, with the mail.

"Did you deliver the poems?"

"Yes."

"You look awful. What's the matter?"

"Just thinking."

"About what?"

"Actually, superfluity."

Years ago, on television, a brilliant performance by a young Dustin Hoffman. In a superb play called "Diary of a Superfluous Man." By a playwright named Ronald Ribman. And after it we heard less and less from Ribman. The critics dumped on him several times and Michael mused at the paradox. You'll like this part, Wendell. The paradox that you can't be an artist without on open, bleeding, exposed heart. And therefore the people in this world least equipped to face the critics are the artists. And without the art the critics would have no employment. Because they themselves don't create, generate, invent, initiate, originate. Oh, this is close to home. It's getting him all riled up.

"They don't give *birth*. That's what they don't do."

Right. Michael said they mostly classify. According to what they've learned in their lives. And their lives are arrested because they left their open, bleeding, exposed hearts behind in their childhoods.

"Read Corinthians and put away childish things."

"Right."

"So what happened to Ribman?"

"I don't know. Michael said he couldn't take the heat, so he got out of the kitchen. But the play's probably in a metal can somewhere. It was adapted from Turgenev's story, 'The Journey of the Fifth Horse.' It was all about four horses being needed to pull a carriage. And a fifth, superfluous horse. A remainder. Hoffman was it. God, Wendell, as if he was born to it. I'll never forget Michael watching it. He cried. He said, 'This is the most exciting thing in life. A good actor in a good role.' "

Wendell sits down and reflects on all this for a moment. He didn't really listen to the latter part—he fastened on the stuff about the critics and that's where I lost him. He did that because he takes what he needs and nothing else is relevant, really. And that just may, someday, get him to Stockholm. I'll watch him on my telly, through bifocals, while soaking my bunioned feet in Epsom salts. Someone named Gustav will hand over the glittering prize. And I'll see Richard, the octogenarian, in the front row in black tie, in the luminous nimbus he couldn't achieve in his own life. Because he was bent on order. And still is.

The telephone rings at my elbow.

"Emma, I've read them."

It's Martin Martin. I cup the receiver and whisper.

"He's read them."

Wendell blanches, holds his stomach with one hand and covers his eyes with the other. Martin tells me that this young man has a "voice," a fledgling, sometimes unruly voice, but nevertheless a distinctive voice. Martin would like to help him. Whispering again.

"Wendell, he's impressed. He wants to help you."

Wendell now grabs his throat, gagging, fighting back nausea. I've seen it a thousand times when they vomit their guts out from nerves in the Buskin crapper.

"But, Emma, does he know what he's in for? Does he know he's in for a lot of rejection?"

"Yes, he knows. He anticipates it."

"But has he got the wherewithal? For the life? It's such a hazardous life. Has he got the stuff?"

"Martin, how can anyone know?"

He is, at the moment, Prometheus Bound. But he's breaking out gradually and there is, on the horizon, the love, enthusiasm, and encouragement of his father. And when that happens, when they get the tumors out of their viscera, I think Wendell will have the wherewithal.

"Well, I really do feel that I've found something here. Really, the voice is distinctive."

"Martin, could you hang on a minute?"

"Of course."

"Wendell? He says you have a distinctive voice. Will you accept his help?"

"Gladly."

"Martin? How can you help him?"

"I know a few people. I'd like to submit all four poems around with a letter of introduction. His Yale connections will help, but of course there's no guarantee. I'll try Shawn, at *The New Yorker*, but that's a long shot. There's more of a chance at—"

"Martin? Hang on a sec. I want to write this down."

Wendell thrusts me pad and pencil. Martin says there's more of a chance at *The American Poetry Review* at Temple University, the *Prairie Schooner* at the University of Nebraska, and *Poetry Magazine* in Chicago. He will send them off on Monday.

"How can we thank you?"

"My pleasure, Emma. Always glad to help the youth."

"Would you like to come over and meet Wendell? Or would you like Wendell to come there?"

A pause. I think the wife looms small and poisonous in the background. Martin says:

"Uhhh—"

"Well. We don't want to impose any further."

The wife exits. Perhaps to the kitchen. To grab a box of Betty Crocker. Get a little lovin' from the oven. Historical She.

"I'd love to meet Wendell, but I don't think he should come here. Things are a little dicey here over this matter."

"I understand. Maybe you and Ben can come see us, sometime."

"Great. Anytime. Give a jingle. And please, tell
Wendell he must be patient. I'll ask my friends to
respond directly to him. But replies take time. At
least a month."

"Thank you so much."

I rise from the couch and hand Wendell the list of
publications. I kiss him on the cheek. The call has ren-
dered him insensible. He looks drugged, anesthetized.

"Congratulations."

He doesn't answer. He has dropped the mail on the
Chinese table and I see that there's a letter for me. A bulky
packet from Kevin.

"Oh. This is for me."

He staggers up and wafts out of the room, headed for
the back door. He stumbles down the hall looking at the
list, totally immersed in himself.

"Wendell? It's snowing."

He doesn't hear me.

"Wendell, take a coat."

Outside, he walks into the driveway and halts. Fifty
yards away, Richard halts and leans on his rake. He
doesn't issue a greeting, he just watches Wendell standing
there under the falling snow, bending over the list, protecting it from precipitation. I can tell from Richard's stance,
the heightened awareness in his posture, that he knows
Wendell is at the starting line. I feel acutely superfluous
and it is comforting that I have this packet in my hand, this
little cushion that is postmarked Boston.

Kevin writes:

Your mother isn't at all well, but won't go to a doctor
because they're all charlatans and lolligags. Country-
club men more at home with the golf cart than the
stethoscope and she'll die before she further lines the
pockets on the men who began their careers odiously
in the first place, with an oath of Hypocrisy. If the
Old Sow dies don't worry, I won't come and live
with you. I've wanted independence all my life and it
appears there might be a little space between your
mother's parting and my own when I can luxuriate,
finally, in my private self. We'll visit each other, of
course, sing a few songs and tell a few tales, but we
won't mix up the generations under one roof as has
proved so unworkable all through the neighborhood.
Of course, she sends her love and hopes that you're
keeping your nose clean.

What I really want to ask point-blank is what's
going on with you. Your letters are cloudy and vague.
Your mother suspects mystery here because your custom has always been the brutally candid. She says
that brutality has very nearly killed us over the years,
and are you trying to protect us from something now,
out of deference to our age? She inquires if you've
committed *murther*, or robbed Brinks, and she says
there'd better be a man in the picture because she
never meant to raise a bloody nun, or a quitter.

We've gone on direct deposit now for the Social
Security. There were just too many scofflaws hanging
about the banks on check delivery day, waiting to rob
the elderly. It's a sin and a shame when you're faced
with daily physical decay that you have to be on
guard against these young dope fiends. I heard yesterday that old Mr. Fitzgibbons (84) was seen buying
canned cat food and he has no pet whatever. Your
mother says he's eating the putrid stuff so she sent me
up with two coffee cans of kidney stew. There were
tears when I presented the cans, great drops running
out of his dim old eyes and I nearly screamed at the
injustice of it all. I don't mean to depress you but it
does make you count yourself fortunate. I came home

and told Herself that when she does kick the bucket
I'll refrain from informing the Social Security. She
said, 'Oh, you black Irish turd, that's illegal.' I said
so is the Mafia, and there's been no social conscience
in this country since Franklin Delano and his Missus.
I meant it, too, Em. It isn't as if I'll go buy Gucci
slippers and Godiva chocolates. I mean to collect the
paltry sum and pass it on to Fitzgibbon. And if the
Lord our Father fails to recognize the generosity of
this act, then he isn't the Lord or my Father and to
hell with it all.

I had a dream last night that I came to visit you at
the New Hampshire place. I brought along all my
carpenter's gear because the place was falling down—a
real Irish shanty. We bolstered it but then we got on
each other's nerves and I left.

No, we've not seen hide nor hair of Michael and
we wish you'd stop inquiring after him. Your mother
says that chapter is finished, for God's sake get on
with the rest of your book.

There's a cabochon ruby down at F and P that I
really wish you could see. I've tried their patience
down there for forty years and never spent a dime,
but the salesman tolerated me sufficiently the other
day to tell me they got this ruby from the son of a
Maharajah. It came originally from Burma, it's the
size of a Concord grape, and the man called it a
bright carmine gem. By that he means what you and I
have always called pigeon-blood. Their opals lately
have been a feeble lot, wan and pale affairs with little
internal play of color. Not worth the trip on the ''T.''

Too much rain lately, four solid days of it. Gray
and gloomy and I've had to go to the cellar and hitch
up the sump pump to the big hose. Which then dumps
all our water directly into the Faheys' yard, and you'll
remember what a commotion they make when that
happens. They've got a big powerful sump twice the
power of our dinky one, and Fahey's got the Veteran's benefits along with the Social Security, but they

are and will always remain the sort that just can't shut up.

The days darken early now. We've got the drapes pulled shut by five o'clock. Your mother wants to order some rubber liners from Monty Ward, to put behind the drapes and keep out the draft. She says it'll cut the fuel by half, which is patent nonsense. She doesn't get easier but I'll say no more in that regard and let you read between the lines.

Heavens, this great ream is going to take two twenties in the post or they'll send it back undeliverable. For God's sake send us some real, hard news, lass.

Love,
Da

P.S. Don't call us again on the long distance. You know how it scares us. We always think you're calling to tell us you've died.

Twenty-Five

I'm cranky, ill-tempered and premenstrual. The days pass by eventfully, but there is a certain propulsion missing from them. The pursuit of a B.L.S. engages my mind because Richard can talk of nothing else. I don't understand why, given my history, I don't just submit and go along with this idea. God knows, I've gone along with a multitude of unsavory things in the past, just to keep the peace. I went along with explicit descriptions of Daniel Graham's sexuality to the point of revulsion. I went along with reprehensible treatment at the hands of a certain supervisory witch at Kelly Girl for three whole years. Still, I'm on the rack with this B.L.S. thing, feeling talk of it a daily harassment. And yesterday the intensity of the feeling surprised even me. I felt like an underprivileged ghetto child being offered a trip out of a slum for a sojourn in a suburb. A sort of charity case more disgruntled than grateful at the prospect of an advantage. I had a terrible, childish impulse to throw the literature across the room and sing Popeye's sweet-potato song:

"Richard, I yam what I yam."

(Must refrain from these tendencies or won't attain true maturity.)

Normally, I have one of those truly absorbent minds. I attempt to wake in the morning and unfurl it like a vast expanse of canvas. Like a desert or a seascape susceptible to and happy to accommodate whatever dromedaries or schooners happen by. But lately each daybreak finds my mind a tangled thicket. I'm not lambent or trenchant, I'm far from mordant, and I can't latch onto my entity.

It appears to me now that Richard is transferring to *me* aspirations that belong more suitably to Wendell. It's Wendell who ought to be completing applications and applying to graduate school. It's Wendell who requires that added degree, the ability to teach and earn a living. It's almost as if I've become a conduit, a courier sent out daily to span Richard's gap. No longer mere conciliator, more of an intermediary now, with messages for Wendell winging along my wires. It seems to me, Wendell, that what's addressed to *me* is intended for *you*. What is this damned breach that prevents Richard from direct contact?

Why do I feel so fundamentally *endangered* when everything around me is, at least superficially, safe and ordered? The house, the refrigerator, the stomachs have their daily demands, and Martin has given us much to anticipate. Additionally, something's out of whack with Wendell's advancing maturity. I should delight at every sign of it but instead it has let the steam out of some part of me, it has left that part oddly disengaged. While he was the squeaky wheel I dredged up a dollop of oil to quiet him. While he was Peck's bad boy there was a tension between us that defined the boundaries of our modus operandi. There is now, in both of us, a *denial* of that tension and we are both floundering somewhere between fate and foreboding, not knowing what it portends for us. When I am not laboring under Richard's B.L.S. presumptions, I'm in a quandary as to how to behave with Wendell. I am like every blond bombshell, ditz, bimbo, space cadet, airhead I've ever seen on TV. I want to open my mouth and say,

"Oh, I am so *confused*!"

As Wendell's behavior becomes less and less suggestive, I feel more and more threatened. I awaken in the night and think of him, across the hall. The less he makes

demands on me, the more I feel in touch with his exasper-
ated soul. He has put the list of magazines under his
pillow: he sleeps on it. He's received a letter from Monica
in which she agrees that he misrepresented himself. The
fact that there will be no complications, no legal demand
for bucks in the annulment has enabled him to step back
and look at the experience with a more composed and
philosophical eye. I see less and less of the cool and the
cocky and hear less and less of the self-indulgent and the
obscene. And Richard is no longer the master Dick.

Wendell "brings home" a hundred and thirty dollars a
week. He gives me twenty-five toward room and board,
banks seventy-five, and keeps thirty for spending money.
He now puts gas in the Volvo regularly, as soon as the
gauge hits the half-mark. He does his own laundry, makes
his own breakfast, takes out the garbage, and twice weekly
bundles and cords the mostly unread newspapers that arrive at this house: the *Journal Courier,* the *New Haven
Register,* the daily New York *Times* and the Sunday Behemoth. He no longer steps out of his loafers, leaving them
in doorways. He has finally learned to restore the toilet
seat after he urinates in the downstairs bathroom, so that I
don't rush in and plunk down on the cold enamel bowl. He
leaves his bedroom door open while he writes, and he goes
for Lydia's rose every Tuesday. He watches her leave with
a sense of satisfaction and achievement. Through his good
offices she no longer hauls her jugs of water. He watches
the mail attentively, as if waiting for Godot. And most of
the time he is very quiet. He isn't morose in his silence:
his face assumes the same inscrutable, felicitous expression whenever he is in my presence. Exactly the same.
Every day. A carbon copy. This felicity grates on me more
than Richard because I at least see Wendell each morning,
whereas Richard now sees him literally on the weekends.
He spends most of Sunday at the Silvermans', hieing up to
their third floor to help Raymond Serio with his homework.

I'd like to think that there is peace of mind underlying
this rather dogged accepting of responsibility, but last
week I found a sheaf of papers by the telephone in the
study. There were sixteen versions of a long poem called

"Silver Hill Sanatorium." Hearing him on the stairs, scurrying from the room, I eavesdropped while he proceeded to call the hospital. He was trying to track down the psychiatrist who had attended his mother; he told the receptionist he was bent on research. The doctor had moved to Texas, to Baylor University. Wendell took down the address. As I entered the room his face, which had been contorted, returned once again to the inscrutable.

"Wendell, does this poem *have* to be written?"

"Yes."

"Why?"

"You have a short memory. I have a score to settle."

"Your memory is even shorter. I thought we agreed that this score-settling stuff was dreck. You can't exonerate your father on *paper*. The forgiveness is in your heart."

"That's the trouble. That's not what's in my heart."

I dream of Wendell often, sometimes locating him in the Costume Shop at the Buskin. In my dreams he selects a masque from a dusty shelf. He keeps it in a box, near his bed, the way Peg always kept her teeth nearby in a glass. When his alarm goes off he reaches for the masque and fastens it behind his ears before he rises. Every morning I search his visage for some residual hint of the old, unadorned crazy person, but he is all papier-mâché and varnish now. Yesterday, when the Volvo wouldn't start and we had to call Triple A, there was no reaction at all. No temper, no fucks, no anxiety at being late for work. I could stand it no longer and confronted him.

"What's happened, Wendell?"

"Must be the battery. Needs a charge."

"I mean with you."

"Me? Nothing's happening. I'm just watching the mail. That's all that's happening with me these days."

"I don't like it."

"Hey, it's like that old paperback. *I'm OK, You're OK*. OK?"

"You're so damned complacent. You should at least find a girlfriend."

"Let's not talk of *should*. It's the most uninhabitable word in the language. I shouldn't have left Berkeley, I shouldn't have married. I should have my own car. I should forgive and forget. But I can't. And I'm here. And this is what is. And the car's on the fritz. You shouldn't ever harp on should."

"I just want to say that I don't like it. You've become a sort of crustacean. You're all shell these days with the tender parts withdrawn."

The Triple A tow truck arrived and he walked to the back door.

"Emma, I will not be roused."

"Damn it, man, why won't you *communicate* with me?"

"Because," he growled, "I said we wouldn't speak of it again."

"We can communicate without speaking of *that!*"

"That's just what we're doing."

And daily the both of them are obsessed with the mail. Wendell haunts the mailbox and it's Richard's first inquiry when he returns for dinner. They know that we probably won't hear anything until after Christmas but they share a curious exhilaration in the waiting. It's there between them Monday through Saturday; it's like a drawn bow or a coiled spring. And Sunday, when there's no delivery, the starch goes out of them and they languish about the house in a state of laxity, uncoiled and unsprung.

I've learned to make Gracie's Panforte di Siena. And now, in the wintry chill, I'm into the preparation of hearty soups and stews laced with burgundy. I've tacked weather-stripping around the front and back doors and have personally hauled the lawnmower and lawn furniture to the basement. I have, with faint heart, registered for the Scholastic Aptitude Tests and written to Hillford High for a transcript of my grades. I'm trying to romanticize this thing that Richard wants me to do. Trying to imagine:

E.R.R. at Yale.

Full-time student in darkly paneled Gothic chambers carrying five-subject notebooks with shiny wires down the back. A Bic clipped to the cover of the subject at hand. A Danish school bag over the shoulder. Wearing Shetland, Orkney, Paisley, Melton, and Harris tweed from the Co-op. Having this conversation:

"What are you doing over Christmas break, Muffy?"

"Oh, I'm doing some schussing with my family at Gstaad. What are you doing, Emma?"

"Oh, I thought I'd run up to Boston for a few days. See my ailing mother. Share the floss."

Walk across the Common at twilight and watch the myriad miniature lights flick on in the trees. Trot down Newbury, that enchanted street where the elite meet to eat. Get custom-fitted and photographed by Bachrach. Bachrach

whose secret, Michael said, was that his camera made
women's jewels appear larger and their waistlines smaller.
And then I'll come back to St. Ronan and lay claim again
on Richard until Wendell, who has prior possessory claim,
does whatever it is that's in the cards in order to settle his
score. May I confide in you, Muffy? I can, I think,
because you come from Santa Barbara, where excessive
mammon has permitted rampant venery for three or four   .
generations now.

Once, in a dream, Wendell removed his masque and
we went together through Joyce's Dublin. I took him
by the hand and guided him through every nook and
cranny along O'Connell Street. And crossing the bridge
I pointed out each vessel of interest on the Liffey, and
in the afternoon we went to a horse show at Ballsbridge,
and at the end of the day whole segments of Joyce's
voluminous, virtuoso work came into my head.

And when the sky put on its nightcap Wendell laid
me down on a bed of straw in Parnell Square and
under the sanction of the moon he asked would I say
yes my mountain flower and first I put my arms
around him, *no*, Wendell, and drew him down to me
so he could feel my breasts all perfume and I said,
no, Wendell, this is Richard's perfume I said *Ma
Griffe*, and his heart was going like mad and *no*, I
said *no* I won't *no*.

But I did. And he possessed me. And then he said:

"Emma, this act is not synonymous with love. I'm
afraid I've misrepresented myself again. What I really
want to possess, you see, is my father."

Muffy, white as a sheet, would reply:

"Wow. There is nothing in my experience even in the
debauchery which wreaks havoc along the Santa Barbara shore, to match this carnal chronicle."

Clearly, I sorely need a real human being to confide in.
I go to the Silvermans' kitchen to share a few selected

thoughts with Grace. Carefully, judiciously, selected thoughts.

"For some reason, Grace, I feel endangered by Richard and threatened by Wendell. I feel there's something unsavory going on."

"Let's start at the beginning. Why do you think Richard was attracted to you?"

"I think he wanted, unconsciously, to form some semblance of a family."

"What's wrong with that?"

"Everything. Because he wants this family *after the fact*. He wants it for Wendell. He wants a second chance at the kind of unit he didn't have in his marriage."

"Don't put yourself down. He could have had *that* with the seashell lady."

"No, he couldn't. Wendell hated her. And she has a life in New York. I showed up without a life. I was sort of like a blank slate waiting to be written on. Aching to be written on, after the divorce. And I came as his housekeeper. I carried with me all the tools of the trade. So I fell into some prescribed slot. What I'm saying, Gracie, is that Richard saw me as his conduit to Wendell."

"Has he gotten any closer to Wendell?"

"A bit. They inch along like worms. But something's about to happen. Wendell has finally submitted some poems. Whatever the response, it's going to throw them together. I feel it in my bones."

"So you're asking, where does that leave you?"

"I know where. At school. Getting a degree over four long years."

"So? There's lots to gain and nothing to lose."

"Plenty to lose."

"Like what?"

"Like me."

Don't ask me to describe what me is: I'm too confused. I only know that something crucial, something deeply ethical is at stake. Because when I talk to Richard of this degree it becomes a siren song. The prospect of my having credentials in the world is an aphrodisiac for him. Maybe it has something to do with his age, something to do with falling testosterone levels, some textbook thing having to do with fighting off death in bed. Jung's theory, maybe, that when a middle-aged man scales the hill he gets a glimpse of the other side. The down side. His own ambitions are behind him and the glimpse scares him to death. Even Kevin, turning fifty-five, said,

"This birthday is making me shit bricks."

And there's a need, somewhere in the permutations of Richard's personality, to fill the down side with people who give off sufficient glow for him to bask in. He *needs* me to be someone else. Something more. These misplaced B.L.S. plans are unquestionably a turn-on for him. His ardor becomes damn near unquenchable. And mine dwindles because I feel strangely in arrears. So that after love-making, when his weight is removed from me, it's replaced by another, spiritual weight that spreads over me like a lead tarpaulin. I can't breathe, I gasp, I think I'm drowning. I have a deep, frantic fear that Richard does not, in his heart, accept me as I am.

"Jesus, Gracie, there's a lot to lose."

"*What*, for Heaven's sake?"

Well, risking the grandiloquent, this:

"My honor as a woman."

"Oh, Emma, you just *think* too much."

Yes. Thinking of what I want. Trying desperately in all the confusion to define what I really want. It isn't four years of surveys, analyses, and comparisons of the ancient and modern in art, philosophy, history, and lit. It's a child. An infant to love and nourish and rear. I want to bask in the glow of my own progeny as I glimpse my own down side. A Paul or Pauline to bounce on my leg while I sing:

> Ride a cock horse to Banbury Cross
> To see a fine lady upon a white horse
> With rings on her fingers and bells on her toes
> She shall have music wherever she goes.

I want to design a unit of my own. I don't want to accommodate to an ersatz one where I am surrogate mother to Wendell, full-time student to Richard, chief cook and bottle washer in Another Person's Kitchen. I should like to be master of all I survey in my own domain. If I'm to have monogrammed pillowcases in my linen closet, I should like them to say E.E.R. I want my raison d'être, my meaning and my justice rooted not in Stockholm or Heaven but in now, in me, in my womb. To banish the old, hypocritical emissary to oblivion once and for all.

I leave the Silverman house more intact than I've been in weeks. Twice now Richard has hinted that there will be something very special for me at Christmas. Surely, if he is able to imagine me at Yale for four years, he has permanency on his mind. Surely the special present is an engagement ring.

My mind wanders back to the town of Malden, Mass., where Michael had a cousin in the wholesale jewelry business. I was twenty the day we drove out to the small gray building. We passed the iron bars on the windows and the sign that said "To The Trade Only." We bought a simple fourteen-karat gold band for thirty dollars. Fourteen years later I stood on the Longfellow Bridge in Boston and tossed the ring into the Charles.

This ring of Richard's will contain a diamond. And it will be, as the DeBeers people say, forever. The minute I receive it I must bare my soul and tell him what I really want. I must find a way to make my deepest desires coincide with his. Otherwise, I'll consign myself to an ethical shambles and forever lose, well, there's just no other way to put it—my honor as a woman.

Twenty-Six

December twenty-third is my birthday and it's always been a gyp. Kevin called it the "December double-whammy" and decided early on to combine it with Christmas, divvy up the days, and give me presents for both occasions on the twenty-fourth. Michael and his theatre pals called it a "twofer" and did the same. I never did reap double spoils and still feel my nose edging slightly out of joint at the fate of an April conception. I end up with tags of snowmen, poinsettias, and silver bells, which inevitably read:

"Merry Birthday"

Now, while I'm baking Peg's fruitcake, Peg's mother's plum pudding, pumpkin bread, cranberry bread, and Irish shortbread, Richard lunges from the breakfast table with a sudden inspiration.

"I've got a really cunning idea. Let's split the difference and give you a little party on the twenty-fourth!"

We send out invitations to Blodwen and Henry Salisbury, Martin and Ben, Ethan Shepard, the old Old Testament man. We invite Richard's lawyer, Alex Bloom, and his wife, Ruth. We also invite Leonard Ascher, the accelerator operator, in hopes that he will sit down at the piano at midnight and imitate Louis Armstrong singing "Hello Dolly." I hand-carry two invitations across the yard to the

Silvermans, and to Grace, insisting that Raymond, too, is welcome.

Richard and Wendell began by driving an hour to a tree farm in Killingworth. They'd done this once when Wendell was a boy; in the interests of sentiment and nostalgia they hoped to repeat the trip and capture a speck of the past. They wore plaid wool jackets over clashing plaid flannel shirts for this outing, and each carried a length of rope to tie the tree on top of the Peugeot. When I handed Richard the saw he said that Wendell also must have a saw.

"Won't one saw do to cut down one little tree?"

"Two men," he said, "need two saws."

They clobbered about in what they called their Trail Boots, ransacking cupboards and drawers in search of another saw. They were overcome with sudden, earthy machismo. They looked precisely like all those movie men who shout "Thar she blows" and "Timber" and are, more recently, led through everglades and other nasty natural places by Burt Reynolds. They swaggered and imagined themselves lumberjacks and they made asinine jokes about tools. Heavy hand tools, the horror of being caught in the forest without the appropriate tool, ha, ha, ha. When they left, Richard carried the saw and Wendell carried both pruning shears and a Swiss Army knife. When they arrived at the tree farm they found a stand of condominiums in its place. So they drove to North Madison where they cut down a seven-foot burly blue spruce, roadside, illegally.

We engaged Wendell to help us drag from the attic yards of ancient red and green velour ropes and a dozen boxes of glass bells and balls. OPDs. Other people's decorations. We strung the ropes across the living room ceiling and bought a big, fold-out red paper bell to hang in the middle. At the confluence, Richard said. He and Wendell hadn't decorated the house in nine years and I was so overwhelmed with a century's accretion of ornaments that we left no corner or surface untrimmed. We didn't step back and appraise, we just kept hanging things, some of them very beautiful Victorian antiques, some of them home-made monstrosities. I found a large star that Nanny Culligan had contributed, forty years ago. She had cut it out of cardboard, glued raw macaroni all over it, and sprayed the whole enterprise with gold. I thumb-tacked it over the arch. Wendell put his great Aunt Rosemary's gingerbread house, whose chimneys were held together with cracked brown masking tape, on the mantel. I set, alongside it, Richard's Yule log made in eighth-grade carpentry shop. Richard said,

"It looks like something large dogs leave in the yard."

I found a length of green velour and draped it around the portrait of the great, great, great grandfather. Wendell said,

"We've got festoons up the gazoo."

They were happy together. I wondered, not for the first time, what would happen if some mystical spirit waved a wand and excluded me from the room. Would they revert to their old, pinched selves, or had they really inched along into some permanent truce?

I made mulled wine with honey, cinnamon, whole cloves, and allspice. The three of us sat in the room that now felt subterranean: an overdecorated, congested cave. We lit a fire and had only the lights from the contraband spruce for illumination. Richard suggested that we sing along with "Mitch" and put on an old Mitch Miller recording. We listened to "Winter Wonderland" and "Rudolph the Red-Nosed Reindeer." Afterwards Wendell, heavily into the warm wine, and in a fit of silliness, gave us his rendition of "Good King Wenceslas."

> "Hither page and stand by me
> If thou knowst what's good for thee."

Richard offered:

>"While shepherds wash their socks by night"

and a jumble of babble from his college days:

>"Deck us all with Boston Charlie."

I, departing the season, took center stage, clicked my heels like Jose Greco, snapped my fingers, and recalled my flamenco from my St. Anne days.

>"Toreador-eh, don't spit on the floor-eh
>Use the cuspidor-eh
>That's what it's for-eh."

And from Hillford High days:

>"Don't know why
>There's no buttons on his fly
>Got a zipper
>Me and my guy think it's quicker
>We do it all the ti-eye-me."

Wendell recalled, from the bottom of the barrel:

>"Oh, they don't wear pants
>When they do the hula dance
>And they don't wear brassieres
>In the southern hemisphere
>And the natives go around
>With their organs hanging down . . ."

Richard interrupted, feeling the returns were diminishing, and made a request of Wendell.

"Wendell, do your cow."

"What cow?"

"The one you learned at camp, in Maine."

"Oh, yeah."

Whereupon Wendell mooed. It began as more of a tentative lowing and then it quickly escalated into a full-blown bovine rumble, reverberating through the house. It was astonishingly true to the barnyard and Wendell, cheered on by our reaction, did it five or six times until we were, as we used to say at St. Anne's, in stitches.

As we ladled down to the dregs of the wine and agreed it was bedtime, Wendell didn't know how to make a graceful exit. I felt his discomfort keenly. The night was so warm, the ambiance so mellow, the enjoyment so mutual, I thought for a moment that if Wendell were a little boy Richard and I might bundle him off to bed with us. That image brought a flush of blood to my face and I was thankful for the darkened room. Finally, Wendell put on his inscrutable masque and excused himself. His exit was awkward and pathetic. Richard felt and noticed none of this. He sat within singeing distance of the fire and we talked about the food and liquor requirements of the upcoming party. I rattled on about baked ham and baked beans but the blood didn't leave my face because the urge didn't leave my body. The Parnell Square urge to take Wendell's hand and accompany him to bed. Mary, these thoughts, once etched on the neuropanel, do not perish easily.

The day after I turned thirty-six the doorbell rang incessantly. They all came and sat in our cluttered cave and ate, drank, dropped, and spilled, took their social stances and played their societal games. Raymond appeared only to sing, courageously, "Away in a Manger" in a sweet, pubescent tenor, and then ran home having satisfied an obligation to his mother. Wendell hosted felicitously and eventually got into a corner with Martin and Ben. They discussed Rainer Maria Rilke, Günter Grass, and Ted Hughes, excitedly, and moved on to disparage Sidney Sheldon, Judith Krantz, and Rod McKuen, maliciously. The Blooms and the Silvermans talked about a winter vacation in Jamaica and Ethan Shepard explained Chanukah to Gracie. At midnight Leonard Ascher imitated

Satchmo, and Martin and Ben together imitated Carol
Channing. And once again, as in olden days, I observed
that, even though Planter's Deluxe Mixed Nuts promise
not to contain more than fifty percent peanuts, the ca-
shews, almonds, hazels, and Brazils go first. And the sad
little orphan peanuts, last.

Through it all Richard felt compelled to announce,
repeatedly,

"Did you know that Emma's going back to school?"

"Has Emma told you? She's entering the Bachelor of
Liberal Studies program."

"Yes, the Program for Special Students."

"That's right, the B.L.S. And after that, who knows?"

Through it all there was, for me, an excitement and
titillation I could hardly conceal. I had found, lying openly
on Richard's dresser, a yellow receipt from Sykes-Libby.
It did not say what had been purchased but the total was
six hundred and forty-five dollars. Surely this was the
ring. I would know soon: I watched the clock tick away
the night. Richard would bestow upon me legitimacy in
only a matter of hours; he would declare his intentions of
permanency. In a matter of hours I would declare my
intentions of full-time motherhood rather than full-time
scholarship. Throughout the day I rehearsed my speech.
And now, as I mixed and mingled and hosted, I listened to
the school talk and automatically refuted it. My mind leapt
forward to the end of the evening when Richard would
proclaim his true intentions. And in my mind the ring took
on almost supernatural powers. It would clarify my position, allay my confusion, banish all of my unsavory questions and urges: I would arise in the morning with a new,
sure sense of principle, probity, honor.

It was at twelve-fifteen that I noticed Blodwen staggering
and I felt disaster looming over my party. She was up to
her gills in Richard's potent eggnog when she proceeded to

advise Ben Lindsay never to go to Jamaica. She said, within earshot of the Silvermans and the Blooms, that it was overrun with Jews. All conversation screeched to a halt as she went on to say that Montego Bay, in particular, was teeming with them. Grace reddened and coughed and went to stand by the Silvermans, as if somehow to protect them. No one knew what to say and it was Grace who, for some inexplicable reason, found herself uttering one word. She said,

"Nevertheless."

The word dangled in air thick with embarrassment. Richard looked to Henry to rescue the party and Henry looked ashamed. Wendell's hand went to his stomach and Martin and Ben appeared to be petitioning Heaven, rolling four eyes at the fold-out bell. I stood silent as a sphinx and Gracie repeated,

"Nevertheless."

Blodwen, with glazed eyes and thick tongue, examined the stunned faces around her.

"Oh, dear," she said. "I think I've caught my tit in the wringer."

"What is that?" asked Martin. "An old Welsh expression?"

Blodwen laughed. If her speech was a bray, her laugh was a cackle.

"No. But here's an old Welsh joke. To take the curse off my blunder."

Henry winced and she began. And I felt forebodings of doom.

"This one's about the annual meeting of the Cardiff Garden Society. All of the ladies gathered, all the doyennes and dowagers, to hear Miss Agatha Llewelyn discuss the African Violet. But one of the members came in inebriated. She seated herself noisily and adjusted her hat, and the chairwoman chose to ignore her. The chairwoman began her introduction:

"*Today we are honored to have at our lectern a woman of international horticultural renown.*

"Everybody applauded.

"*Miss Agatha Llewelyn is the winner of a dozen blue ribbons for her prize* Saintpaulia ionantha.

"Again, everyone clapped.

"*She is a generous patron of our Society and she's been a tireless traveler spreading our gospel.*

"At that point, the inebriated woman stood up and shouted:

"*Agatha Llewelyn sucks cocks.*

"Madame Chairwoman, undaunted, replied,

"*Nevertheless—*

"and continued."

It was a complicated story and while my own inebriated guest held us all in horrified thrall there was a small measure of awe as we listened to her negotiate her tongue around the characters, and the *Saintpaulia ionantha*. The story did little to remove the curse from the blunder and the Silvermans and the Blooms quickly rose to depart. Henry Salisbury came running with Blodwen's new fur coat. Blodwen blithely asked Ruth Bloom what she thought of the magnificent lynx coat.

"I think," replied Ruth, "it makes you look like a Jewish princess."

Richard kept murmuring "Now, now," and ran to the front porch, where he grabbed Naomi Silverman's elbow and repeated, "Now, now." Wendell and I scurried about frantically apologizing to everyone.

Gracie stayed on to help with the clean-up and the four of us expressed, in our different ways, amazement at Henry's choice of mate. Richard called Blodwen Henry's barracuda, Wendell called her Henry's pariah, and Grace called her Henry's hot fuck. The men fulminated while carrying trays of dirty dishes to the kitchen. Grace and I brushed a bourbon-soaked chair with detergent and vinegar, covered everything with foil and Saran, and then reloaded the dishwasher properly after the men had put the big bowls on the bottom, the coffee cups sideways, and the fork tines down. When Richard walked Grace across the yard, I felt Wendell's eyes watching me as I stacked leftovers in the refrigerator.

"You don't want to go back to school, do you?"

"No."

He took me in his arms and kissed my hair.

"Merry Birthday, Em."

I stayed, enveloped, with one hand resting on his hard, taut stomach, the other on the back of his thigh. This was so incongruous, to be in this position while waiting for Richard to return and give me a ring. The embrace was not platonic, nor was it fevered. I stayed, I think, because of a momentary sense of well-being. Wendell, like Michael before him, accepted me as I was.

"Emma, what will make you happy?"

The ring. I wanted to say the ring. But I said,

"A child. I want a baby."

He cupped my face in his hands.

"I thought so."

He was like a sweet old relative offering a palliative.

"Dear lady, I'm so sorry. He doesn't."

"Does he think himself too old?"

"He thinks himself unrealized. He's had his child. That's where he wants realization. As a poet and as a father. You should have had Michael's child."

"You should take your own advice. You shouldn't harp on should. It's not a habitable word, remember?"

"What's a habitable word?"

"Marriage."

"I see. Oh, Emma, you shouldn't have shipped with Ahab. Ahab's appointment is with me. I'm the white whale."

He said this quietly but with authority and the kind of prescience he talked of possessing months ago. It was like a death knell and I knew, when Richard returned from the Silvermans', that the receipt was not for a ring. Richard related the details of his trip; he had taken Grace into the house. They had found Professor Silverman in the kitchen, determined to write Henry Salisbury a letter. I was trancing again, I tuned in and out of Richard's voice. I heard something about buying a muzzle for Blodwen and putting it on her in the New Year. We went into the living room, sat under the tree, and began to open our presents. I felt estranged from the men, the house, the world, as I went through the gift-giving motions.

I gave Richard the lavish *Nova, Adventures in Science*, earmuffs, and a challis tie. I gave Wendell a new *Roget's Thesaurus* to replace his old battered one, and a subscription to *Writer's Digest*. Wendell gave me *Everyday Cooking with Jacques Pépin*, and Richard a new life of Einstein. Through all of the ripping and tearing, the pronouncements of approval, Wendell looked at me with searching eyes. I hadn't felt this look since my last visit to the neighborhood. In Wendell's eyes I was suddenly "Our Lady of the Barren Womb."

Richard gave Wendell a bulky Irish sweater of uncarded wool and a pair of fleece-lined slippers. And then Richard reached into his pocket and handed me an oblong blue velvet box. Its proportions told me that I was hasty in refuting the B.L.S. talk. That was what he intended for me. Four years of augmenting and achieving, slithering among the Sterling stacks. The box contained a string of graduated Mikimoto pearls. There was an odd, brief, but indelible flash of contrition on Richard's face. I willed away the disappointment on mine.

I ran and kissed him and made the appropriate, obligatory noises and all the while I remembered going down to F and P with Kevin, as a child. Kevin always said that, someday, he would buy me a string of fine pearls. As an adult I stood on the very same spot with Michael and he said I'd have pearls for my fifth anniversary. But consumer consumption was close at hand in our twenties. We needed furniture, a vacuum cleaner, two air conditioners, and the fifth anniversary brought me a washer and dryer. And the tenth, the black onyx cameo. And now I held the round, lustrous, individually knotted, faintly pink rope in my hand. The necklace looked like a noose and I clumsily dropped it to the floor.

Richard, exhausted from the day's preparations, mumbling angrily about a muzzle for Blodwen, fell into bed without taking time for the usual ablutions. Alone in the bathroom on the eve of the birth of Christ, I move in jerks and spasms like a metal-clad mechanical character in some rendition of *Star Wars*. My moves are not premeditated. I've not for a moment calculated that I would reach for my birth control pills, swathe the disk in toilet paper, and throw it in the wastebasket. Yet this I do. The gestures seem utterly instinctual. There's no malice aforethought, there's no future strategy. There is only the lingering feeling of estrangement. In the thicket of my head it isn't clear if I want to give Richard an ultimatum, if I want to fulfill my biological destiny, or if I want a weapon against my mounting frailty with Wendell.

I have closed the bathroom door adjoining Richard's bedroom, but left open the door to Marion's room. Suddenly I hear a voice. It's not within me but outside of me. I don't think it's Marion's voice; it doesn't sound female or male or otherworldly. It has resonance and depth. It cries out into the wilderness of my life. It says.

"Take away a child."

Mary, am I hallucinating? Do I think I'm Joan of Arc? Does the voice emanate from God, or Freud? Why must I take the child away? The answer lay hidden somewhere in Richard's indelible look of contrition. I crawl into bed with the sleeping sire. As the curtain of sleep begins to fall I see myself as a guest at a great banquet. Heaping platters are being passed all around me but my presence is unseen; I am ignored. I ask politely, gently, to be served, not wanting to be thought a pushy Boston broad. No one hears. Finally I shout, demand, lunge for the food, but it is all a dream. Only my appetite and my decision are real. I replay it quickly. The reach for the disk, the reach for the length of tissue, the toss. And all through the night the knowledge is real. That the chemicals will wear off and the body will restore itself. And I will, in a week or two, ovulate.

Twenty-Seven

My New Year's resolution is to take away Richard's child, and I am in what Sean O'Casey called a state of chassis. Michael explained that did not mean the frame of a car. It meant something akin to chaos. Flux, fluctuation, disorder, tumult. Without my pill I walk around in a state of chassis. On New Year's Day Richard sat for an hour at his desk, paying bills and whistling "What's It All About, Alfie?" Wendell came into the kitchen, tore off a length of foil to catch his jam dribbles in the toaster, and inquired,

"Well?"

"Well, what?"

"What's it all about, Emma?"

I'd be the last to venture an opinion but once upon a time, after listening to balding Australians singing in eunuch tones, Michael said it was all about stayin' alive.

I walk around feeling penetrable. I'm like the hemophiliac in Lydia's television program. So exaggerated is my vulnerability, I actually give sharp corners a wide berth and am strangely wary of various household hazards. I heed the American Cancer Society and resolve to quit smoking. It seems to me I should be announcing, through airborne chemical messages,

Fragile, Handle with Care.

but neither of the men sense my new capacity. Or perhaps I mean my ancient capacity, dating from either Eve or some female fish that crawled out of the ocean. I am without barriers and chemical resistance. I am now and have ever historically been, She.

It may happen in January, it may happen in February or March. I still have no strategy, but I think vaguely of the New Hampshire saltbox. My Property. The place of last resort. In the meantime I take a page from Wendell's book and busy myself with what *is*. I'm ironing shirts for Richard's upcoming trip to D.O.D. And I've given myself the chore of partitioning the front hall with draperies. Our fuel bills here in the mausoleum are exorbitant: oil is delivered every two weeks and Richard says our heat costs upwards of twenty dollars a day. And the basement ducts don't quite deliver the heat to the drafty first floor. The front hall is the culprit, it's like a wind tunnel at the core of the house. The draft even causes the fronds on the Boston ferns to sway in the breeze. Richard observed that, thirty years ago, there were sliding double doors on the dining and living rooms, but nobody knows where they are. So it's my intention to sew draperies and hang them over the arches.

Wendell accompanied me to Horowitz, on Chapel Street, where we rummaged through aisles of bolts.

"Are you pleased with the pearls?"

"Very. They're lovely."

"I wanted to get you a blue zircon. Your birthstone. I priced them but I couldn't afford it. Maybe next year. Have you decided on your courses?"

"Richard thinks I should audit a couple of things this spring. See what appeals."

"Good idea."

But I don't intend to be here when the ferns unfurl.

We purchased twenty yards of heavy upholstery fabric. I was happy to have Wendell's help with the bulky packages. Crossing the dreary, cold parking lot I thought fleetingly of Michael's garden in summer. Alyssum, impatiens, salvia, viola. I blocked out thoughts of winter in New Hampshire. I would cross that arduous season when I came to it.

Richard had to travel to Washington for three days to grub for research money. And for an interview with a journalist from *Scientific American*. Something about work being done at Yale on lasers. We took the Peugeot and I delivered him to Connecticut Limousine.

"Lasers, you know, were almost called 'losers.' "

"Really?"

"It's an acronym. Accurately, it's light oscillation by stimulated emission of radiation. Loser. So they changed it to light amplification by stimulated emission of radiation. Laser."

"That's funny."

I shall file that story, record it sequentially, and commit it to the memory bank for all eternity. He mused.

"Do you think it would be a bad idea to call Martin Martin? See if he's heard anything? He *is* friends with some of those editors. He might have gotten a Christmas card or something."

"Well, he might take it as pressure. And he did say we'd hear directly. I think it's a bad idea."

We lingered for a while in the waiting room.

"It was such a wonderful Christmas, Emma. Except for terrible Blodwen. But all the decorations, the feel of the house, all the food. I think it was the best Christmas we've ever had. When they ask me in Washington, how was my Christmas, I'll say great. And for the first time it will be true."

We gave each other tentative, public kisses.

"Hurry back."

I returned home to find Lydia and Wendell in the kitchen. Lydia ceremoniously presented her Christmas presents from her Channel 13 bag, explaining that these were belated because she had to spend the holidays in Bridgeport with Velveeta. The first, large package was a down couch pillow with a crocheted cover. There was a huge "G" in the middle with a "W" on one side and an "R" on the other.

"Dat's for bofe of you."

She gave me a pretty potholder. It had a green background and she had crocheted "E.R.R." diagonally across it. She thanked me, again, for the little cactus plant I had given her and expressed her disappointment that Richard wasn't home. He had sent her a Grand Union grocery certificate for a hundred dollars. She proceeded to write a thank-you note on the back of a brown paper bag.

"Lydia? My mom and dad sent me a box of fine vellum stationery. Would you like a piece?"

"No, ma'am. I prefers dis bag."

Wendell offered her a pen but she refused that, too, saying she couldn't write too good in the first place and she couldn't write at all without a pencil. And she couldn't write with a pencil, either, unless she spat on the pointed lead every three words.

"Spittin'," she said, "gives you time to conjure up de words."

The three of us worked for two hours, taking the decorations down in the living room. Wendell brought in the ladder and dismantled the ceiling ropes, I packed the glass balls away, and Lydia unclipped and stored the tree lights. Wendell and I hauled the dry, dead spruce out the back door with Lydia vacuuming up the needles we left in our wake. At three-thirty, Wendell had to leave for work. I followed him into the back hall to say goodbye. Snow was falling heavily.

"How will you spend your evening?"

"Hemming the draperies."

"I'll think of you, doing that. Will you be in bed when I get home?"

"Yes."

"See you in the morning, then."

Lydia watches him go and smiles like a Cheshire cat.

"Dat boy grown' up. Ain a minute too soon."

"He's submitted some poems, Lydia, I think he's ready to take his licks."

"Praise de Lawd!"

I cut the panels on the dining room table, measured the hems and pinned them. My hands shook, I stuck myself, I bled. I thought of the reality of being unarmed. A Paul or Pauline. Or Mirabile. Leaving Richard without telling him. By nine o'clock my eyesight gave out and I went and wrote a thank-you to Kevin and Peg for my Merry Birthday vellum. I went to Richard's desk to find a stamp and there, sitting boldly in the top drawer, was a Christmas card from Ariadne Marchant. It had been sent to Sloane Physics Lab. I had no business opening it.

"How is your little experiment going? Surely that's what it is."

I felt pangs of jealousy followed by flashes of female conquest. I had, after all, the Mikimoto pearls. But what a Pyrrhic victory. I hadn't fought for Richard as she would have, I had merely succumbed. Fallen into the prescribed slot. Like a rookie, Kevin, getting the pennant after leaving the farm team. I went to bed considering Ariadne and her New York friends. Perhaps I should think about going to New York. Anonymity in those numbers. Two years ago, when Michael first met Daniel Graham, I tried to persuade him to move to New York. "You'll take Manhattan, the Bronx and Staten Island by storm, Michael."

And we'll live in a very expensive rabbit warren, go to opening nights, auctions at Christie's. And I'll stick my nose into Tiffany, Cartier, Bulgari, Van Cleef and Arpels. I'll purchase beauty in a parlor, get masked with mud, tweezed, waxed, streaked, and blow-dried. Get roundly Klingered by Georgette. Wear sneakers with my furs and travel incognito behind my stretch limo's tinted glass. Carry my own whistle, for cabs, my own can of Mace for muggers. Visit Bloomingdale's, buy ice from Greenland a buck-a-chunk. Zoo-Poo for my plants, a buck-a-turd. Berbers and Bokharas for my floors. Meet Halston, Vreeland, and Astor. Mike, Harry, Morley, and sweet old Andy Rooney. Ronald Ribman, and Dustin Hoffman.

"Oh, for Chrissake, stop it," Michael said. "That city's a fucking sewer."

But as I fell asleep I spoke to Wendell's apparition. I said, Wendell, if you can make it there, you'll make it anywhere. And we went to Manhattan together and he took the town by storm. And we lived in a garret and kept the old Volvo because, Wendell said, no thief would be dumb enough to want it. And we took Lydia with us. But even in Manhattan she wouldn't bend, and I still had to swab my garret floor myself. I didn't hear Wendell return from work at midnight.

At noon the following day I was on my way to the third-floor Singer when the doorbell rang. It was Blodwen Salisbury. She stumbled in reeking of gin, her face swollen from crying. When Wendell heard her, he came to assist, and the two of us guided her into the kitchen. Henry had driven her home from our party but did not speak to her for two days. The day after Christmas he packed his bags and told her he couldn't live with a racist. He got in his car and drove away and Blodwen had just today tracked him down. He was registered at the Park Plaza Hotel. He refused to see her. I gave her coffee and cranberry bread, and Wendell and I had difficulty with the conversation because she was beyond reason.

BLODWEN:
Jews aren't a *race*. There's white, black, and yellow. He's such a smart-ass physicist, he doesn't even know that.

WENDELL:
Well, I guess he was surprised, Blodwen. That you held these opinions and that you voiced them.

BLODWEN:
What opinions?

ME:
The ones you expressed at our party.

BLODWEN:
What's so bad about saying Montego Bay is teeming with Jews? Harlem is teeming with fuzzy-wuzzies. London is teeming with A-rabs. Is coal black? Is urine yellow? Does the Pope shit in the woods?

WENDELL:

It's just that the Silvermans and the Blooms were here. And I'm not sure, but I think Leonard Ascher is Jewish, too.

BLODWEN:

He is. But he's a Jew for Jesus. He told me so himself. Listen. This is about guilt. Henry's exchanged his old wife for young pussy, and that's what it's about.

ME:

Blodwen, please.

WENDELL:

Have another cup of coffee.

I've been waiting for Wendell to excuse himself and leave this awkward visit to me. To register extreme discomfort, feign a seizure, and bolt for his room. I'm surprised at the strength and solidity he brings to the table.

BLODWEN:

I have to say, Emma, this coffee tastes like the Ganges on a holy day.

ME:

I'm sorry.

BLODWEN:

Wendell, you're cute. Why did you get married and cause all that trouble?

WENDELL:

I made a mistake. It was stupid. But Alex Bloom is helping me out of it.

BLODWEN:

Good. Smartest Jewish lawyer in town. How much is he charging? Is he gouging you?

WENDELL:
Please, Blodwen. There are limits.

BLODWEN:
I only asked because, with Henry at the Park Plaza, I
may need a smart lawyer. Listen, Emma. The word
on the circuit is that you were married to a gay.

ME:
The word is true.

BLODWEN:
Oh, well. Nevertheless—.

She breaks into her cackle and slaps me on the shoulder.

BLODWEN:
Amanda Llewelyn gives head! At the *garden* party.
Isn't that rich?

WENDELL:
Agatha.

BLODWEN:
Pardon?

WENDELL:
Wasn't she Agatha? Agatha Llewelyn?

BLODWEN:
Right. Agatha Llewelyn gives head.

WENDELL:
Sucks cocks.

BLODWEN:
Same difference.

WENDELL:
Right. Have another cup of coffee.

BLODWEN:

So how was it?

ME:

How was what?

BLODWEN:

Being married to a gay. Did you catch anything?

WENDELL:

Jesus!

BLODWEN:

Well, they're all contagious, aren't they?

ME:

No, they're not. Blodwen, I loved him.

BLODWEN:

Ah, love. Makes the world go round. Henry's guilt finally surfaced. He's old and I'm young. You'll have the same thing with Richard.

ME:

I'm hardly young.

BLODWEN:

Yes, you are.

ME:

I'm thirty-six. That's not young.

BLODWEN:

Of course it is! If thirty-six isn't young, what the hell is young?

ME:

Wendell is young.

BLODWEN:
Christ, yes, look how young he is. But so are you.
Isn't she, Wendell? Isn't she young?

WENDELL:
I think she's young.

ME:
Well, I don't think I'm young at all.

Wendell drove her home on his way to work. I watched
him tuck her into the Volvo, watched him harness her seat
belt, and I felt like a proud parent. He had come such a
long way from the self-absorbed, indolent boy with the
toaster-gash and the red flannel crotch. He'd been patience
personified, he'd behaved stoically. He was not the boy
next door, but he was no longer the family mutant.
    Because of Blodwen's visit, I hadn't collected the mail.
As I carried it to Richard's desk I riffled through it, hoping
there would be some news from Boston. Peg was seventy-
five now and not well, and in fathoming the instincts
around Kevin's letter I'd experienced a sudden intimation
of the world without Peg. And then I spotted the corner of
an envelope.

Poetry Review

It was addressed to Wendell Wharton Goddard. I hadn't
felt so intimidated by a piece of mail since my divorce
decree arrived. I ran and held it to the dining room window, trying to decipher the message. If it was a rejection,
would I tear it up? Dare I steam it open? Why? What sort
of interference was I running here? I wasn't courier or
intermediary, I wasn't acting in Richard's behalf. Why did
I want so fervently to protect him when *I* persuaded him to
take the chance and run the race? I went to the phone and
called Touch Base.

"Wendell, it's Emma."

"Hi. You got news of Blodwen?"

"Wendell, there's a letter here from *Poetry Review*."

Silence.

"I have it here in my hand."

"Well. Well, well, well. Judgment Day. Well, well, well. I guess it's either an acceptance or a rejection."

"Do you want me to open it?"

"God, no."

"Shall I bring it down?"

"No. I want to be at home when I open it. Would you just leave it on the stairs?"

"Yes. The suspense is killing me."

"Emma?"

"Yes?"

"Will you wait up for me? I mean I'd like to *open* it alone. But I'd like you to be awake. I mean dressed and up. Will you?"

"Of course."

At ten o'clock I went up to the sitting room and watched a news. I imagined Wendell crashing into the house, finding the letter on the stairs, tearing it open. I would contain myself and stay put. I wouldn't confront him; he could stay down there as long as he liked. He would tell me in due time. He'd either bounce up or drag up and I had obeyed his instructions. He'd find me upright in the sitting room, dressed. I turned my attention to a wonderful Preston Sturges movie, *Sullivan's Travels*, and watched the lean and large Joel McCrea and the tiny, waifish Veronica Lake tramp their way through the Great Depression.

I must have dozed off. He was standing in the doorway, beaming, letter in hand.

"Two of 'em! They've accepted *two* of 'em! A dollar a line."

"Mother Mary, which ones?"

" 'Interloping Woman' and 'Hazardous Waste.' "

"When will they publish?"

"April."

I rose from the couch and rushed to him. He kissed me and dropped the letter and kissed me again. He took out my hair combs, dropping them to the left and right of me. Joel McCrea was in some southern church. It was a congregation of convicts, chained, laughing at a cartoon being shown on a movie screen in a church. The camera moved in on a close-up of Joel. He seemed to be experiencing some sort of revelation, some deep insight into comedy, tragedy, humanity. Wendell turned off the set and we went, as if it had been agreed upon months ago, upstairs to the third floor, to Nanny's room. And there we ended that particular Judgment Day entwined and enfolded as one.

Twenty-Eight

I awake at six and lie there, looking at him. The pleasure of what we have done and the pain of what lies ahead have reduced me to a kind of existential stasis. I am, for the first time in my life, grounded in my own existence. I am at once sorceress, enchantress, crone, and hag. I'm at the bottom, and base, and the words redefine themselves moment by moment. I'm at the top, the exalted zenith, discovering crooks and crannies in my nature.

I feel mystically attuned to contrary states, opposing forces, good and bad, Heaven and Hell, Father and Son. St. Anne's, the Virgin, the Crucifixion, the snake, the apple, original sin, Michael and Daniel, Kevin and Peg, Richard and Wendell—all of their impacts and influences have washed over me, eroded me, and finally drained away through some great sieve into some great cistern. There's nothing left but the silt and the sediment of me. I remember the matrushka at the Salisbury party, the brightly painted wooden doll that came apart to reveal another doll inside. With another inside of that.

Am I not like a matrushka? The adult shell is the emissary I presented to St. Ronan. The adult has been assembled around all the earlier personas. But since I arrived I've undergone a process of dismantling. I've given a layer to Richard, I've given a layer to Wendell. And what will happen now? Will they fight over the little, final doll? Will they struggle, grasp and grapple until they learn that the little, final doll will not divide?

Wendell was moaning and flailing one arm. A bad
dream. The sky was clear and the moon bright and the
light, reflected off a new heavy fall of snow, radiant blue.
There was a metallic glint off the crystal tray, as there had
been the first time here with Richard.

Who was it that said our bodies are our earthly prisons?
Vinnie Basilicato. No. Michelangelo.

It has only been seven days since I threw away my pills.
I wonder if my mucous membranes continue hostile to
sperm. A gynecologist once told my friend Madeline that it
would take a miracle to conceive before ten days off the
pill.

It is so frightening to think of the future, my mind
withdraws to the past. There are, of course, many prece-
dents, sublime and ridiculous. While Wendell fights a
demon in his sleep I reflect upon older women and young
men. The ancient tales had the bloodiest resolutions. Oedipus. Doomed not by passion, but by declarations from a
pernicious oracle. The oracle announcing, privately, that
Oedipus was destined to kill his father and marry Jocasta,
his mother. Oedipus, fulfilling the prophecy, then tearing
out his eyes. Jocasta committing suicide. Michael Riley
said,

Sophocles was a mean man with an oracle.

Phaedra, wife of Theseus, in love with her stepson,
Hippolytus. Catherine the Great had lofty intellectual pre-
tensions, corresponded with Voltaire, but never could resist the young stuff. Nor could Colette or Bernhardt or
Piaf. On film, randy Vivien Leigh scoured Rome looking
for them, Ingrid Bergman succumbed to Anthony Perkins,
Deborah Kerr opened her blouse and gave more succoring
than sympathy. And we had in my old neighborhood a
certain Fiona Harrigan who, at forty, took in a twenty-
seven-year-old plumber. I had always liked Fiona. Every
time she made almond macaroons she called me in and
gave me three or four. But after the plumber Peg said I
mustn't accept any more macaroons because Fiona Harrigan
was

a two-bit hoor and a chippie.

Could it be this heightened, this extreme, only when forbidden? Was Michael, imprisoned in traditional marriage vows, able to achieve this only with a man? Was it this stinging, this biting, because laws were being broken, tenets violated? How else to explain nine hundred years of prurient interest in Heloise and Abelard? Or the root of the humor when the wild and wicked Brendan Behan, on his deathbed, turned to the attending nun and said:

"Ah, bless you, Sister, and may all your sons be bishops."

And more recently, more up my Dorchester alley, millions watched "The Thorn Birds" nightly and waited with bated breath until Richard Chamberlain finally removed his collar and lost it, there on an Aussie beach. I was at home with it happened. Peg said,

"Oh, for God's sake, will you look at that? He's gone and consummated himself."

Kevin said,

"Indeed he has, and he'll immolate in hell for it, too."

I see developing before me the specter of a most irregular rivalry. A free association of bodies and bloodlines. A fast decline into territorial imperative. A struggling, grasping, and grappling. I will not allow it because I know that the little, final doll will not divide. And again I hear a voice. Not within me but outside of me. I don't think it's Nanny's ghost; it doesn't sound female or male or otherworldly. It says,

"Take away a child."

I creep downstairs to Richard's room and find my shoulder bag. The little Infant of Prague novena card lies folded at the bottom. The gynecologist said it would take a miracle. Well. I'll rely on the long history of success with the miracle rather than the brief history of suppression with the chemical. I must leave quickly now. I'll go to the Infant before I do.

On my return to Nanny's bed Wendell whimpers. A tear runs down his cheek and then he sobs. It is a huge inhalation. He wakens and looks at me with haunted eyes. He slithers down and cuddles up, resting his head on my shoulder.

"You were moaning."

"A nightmare," he says. "Terrifying."

"Tell me."

"Do you love me, Emma?"

"Yes, I do."

"How much?"

"As much as I love Richard."

"That can't be. I don't believe it can be *equal*."

"Yes, it can. I love him because he's struggling with the results of his life. And I love you because you're struggling to live. He's all epilogue, Wendell, and you're all prologue."

"What time does his limo get in?"

"Six o'clock."

"You'll pick him up?"

"Yes."

"And tell him?"

"Yes. I can't stay here now, Wendell."

"Neither can I."

"Yes, you can. You must."

"You can't go until we understand all of this."

"I think I do understand."

"Nobody's life will ever be the same."

"I think that's all there is to understand."

"I'll find you. I'll track you down."

"You don't have to say that, Wendell. You're not obliged to say that."

"I am! Because I love you."

"Tell me about the dream."

Morning light filters through the dormers and the room is very cold. Wendell reaches for his T-shirt and pulls it on. He reaches for his cardigan and wraps it around my shoulders.

"I was in some huge, urban center, a strange combination of Manhattan and Tokyo and Cairo. I was looking for Dad. I scoured the city, running in and out of tall glass buildings, up and down escalators and elevators. I kept rushing through lobbies that were filled with trees in tubs. I prowled on roof tops and pried open steam grates. And then I began to find Dad. This is awful."

"Go on. Tell me."

"I found parts of him. He's been distributed around this megalopolis in pieces. I found a hand at a post office, an arm in a bank vault, a leg in a locker in a Grand Central sort of station. And finally I understood that this monstrous crime had been committed by my mother, and she had done the grisly distribution. And just before I woke up I spread a blanket on the marble floor of this Grand Central place and I put him back together. And the thing is, the amazing thing is, he went back together very easily. I felt like an expert working on a Rubik's Cube. He fell into place, took form, very quickly."

A moment passes.

"Emma? Say something."

I'm horrified by the gruesome details, gladdened by the result. I don't know what to say. I want to cry or laugh and Wendell's quizzical eyes seem to warrant the latter.

"Will you say *some fucking thing?*"

"All right. Some fucking thing."

He smiles and rolls back with sudden merriment. And then he is shy and sheepish.

"Was I all right?"

"You were wonderful. Because you have a sensate soul."

"Does Dad?"

It begins.

"Yes. But he's been into more battles. His soul has more scars."

"Is he—"

"Wendell, I won't do this."

He's embarrassed and ashamed.

"I'm sorry."

"I'll pick him up at six and tell him in the car. I think you should get the night off. You should be here."

"Oh, Jesus, I can't."

"What will you do? Take shelter in some Salvation Army bin? Run to the ward at Yale New Haven?"

"All right, I'll be here. I'll face him. What do you think he'll do?"

"I don't know. He may not want me to stay here tonight. If that's the case I'll go to the Park Plaza."

"Jesus. You and Henry Salisbury at the Park Plaza. Where are you going?"

"To shower."

The water streams down on me and I use the small chip of strong, Yardley sandalwood soap that was here when I arrived. When Wendell opens the shower door I jolt backwards, dropping the soap, slipping on it. He is all attack. I fall against the wall of the stall and receive him. Sunshine pours into the bathroom and I think of Richard, wanting him again. Not out of some diabolical desire for equality or reciprocity or balance, not out of some need for fearful symmetry, but out of simple, ordinary affection and familiarity. Wendell's orgasm is like a detonation and when it's over he whirls against the stall and begins to bang his head on the yellow tile.

"I love you! You're not *hearing* me. I love you."

He grabs me roughly.

"Can't you, anywhere in your mind, see a future for us?"

"No, Wendell, I can't."

"It's the age difference, isn't it? But, Christ, he's twenty years older than you. Are you so hung up on *years?*"

"No. Years are external. Years are disapproving looks in the eyes of other people. I'm hung up on the internal. I've broken faith with Richard."

"That sounds so fucking *Catholic.*"

"Maybe it is. Do you know about Madame de Stael? She was another Catholic lady, eighteenth century. She was a writer, a very independent woman, a feminist. She married and bore three children and then left her husband. She traveled widely and lived fully and had many affairs. And at the end of her life she said, 'This is all I know. No two people can be truly happy when their union makes a third person miserable.' Perhaps, in French, it doesn't sound quite so Catholic."

With towels folded around us we walk down to the second floor, to our rooms. He stops and bangs his head again on Richard's door.

"Oh, God, I'm sad. I've never been so sad."

At noon, while I make breakfast, I sense an insurrection. He goes to the phone, angrily, and asks a man named Brian Palmer to take the four-to-midnight shift at Touch Base. He sits down to breakfast with quivering lips and he has no appetite. He gulps air, swallowing hard, and sits in smouldering silence. He rises and prowls around the vast table and I feel certain that he has never actually given voice to these thoughts, never before expelled them.

"This has all happened, Dad and you, you and me, your being here, it's all happened because he committed mother. And she died."

Fighting tears, losing the battle, he stops the prowling and stands on one spot, swaying.

"I tried, Emma! Jesus Christ, I tried. When I left for college I knew she'd go off the deep end. I must have known because when I review my actions I see how desperate I was to prevent it. I went down to the Lawn Club and found a couple of women she'd known and I asked them to call her once in a while. They looked horrified, as if I was asking them to socialize with a leper. I said, 'Look, it would help her so much if you'd just go have a cup of tea.' I went next door to Mrs. Silverman, and I asked her to visit occasionally. I asked Lydia to impose herself, talk to her, force her out of her shell. No one called, no one visited. Lydia just got all superstitious and talked about voodoo. She thought mother was possessed. And I went blithely off to college. That's what caused her total isolation. That's why she let Rae-Ann into the house. That's what finally sent her around the bend. Are you *hearing* me? It wasn't Nee Marchant. It was me. I just fucking *took off* and let her fall by the wayside."

He runs to the hall, giving me the canine order he once gave to Monica.

"Stay, Emma, stay."

I'm afraid he's going to run away again but he puts on his boots, a jacket, and hat, and shouts that he's going out to shovel the driveway. I watch him, from the study window. He digs the shovel into a ten-inch accumulation of snow and leaves it there. He falls on a mound banked from previous shovelings and cries uncontrollably. When he finally straggles in he is spent and docile, having delivered himself of an awful burden. He takes my hand and we go once again to Nanny's room. I mutter my bromides as we walk up the stairs, but he doesn't listen.

"You'd have become her caretaker. Her custodian. It would have destroyed you. That's why your father went to Ariadne. Because there was a profound illness in the house and he didn't know how to save himself. There's a difference between self-centered and self-interest. Saving yourself is paramount, elemental, a basically religious idea having to do with the essence of life."

"Stop it, Emma. It's dogma. It's just words."

And once again we are in the throes of passion, an estrus state divinely designed by our Maker for one reason only, according to Sister Helene. To ensure the propagation of the species. It's a sunny, wintry afternoon with rhinestones scattered across the snow. The furnace chugs, burning the costly Persian Gulf petroleum, our daily fleecing. Our bodies are connected but our thoughts are private. I am struck anew at the relative ease of physical penetration and the extraordinary difficulty of verbal communication.

Twenty-Nine

At five-forty-five I take the Peugeot and go to meet Richard, leaving a wistful Wendell at the back door. He wore his corduroy jacket, a shirt, and a tie. I saw Richard distinctly in the nape of the neck, the line of the jaw, the arch of the eyebrow.

As I drive past the Connecticut Limo building, Richard is waiting inside. He's standing near a huge poinsettia plant. When I enter the building he runs to me, swings me off the floor, and kisses me lengthily on the lips. It's a *Rashomon* moment. The people in the waiting room assume we're a married couple and they smile their approval at the heat of our greeting. Richard's tenacious embrace commands their attention; they feel warmed by what they see, happy to have his confirmation of connubial solidarity. Perhaps they'll go home affected by it, striving to be a little nicer to each other. If an hour from now, I am found brutally murdered on St. Ronan, these people will be called as witnesses. They'll recount what they saw in this waiting room. And a detective will sigh and say,

"Ladies and gentlemen, I'm afraid what you saw was not what was."

Richard hands me an armful of newspapers and magazines while he balances himself with briefcase and suitcase.

"How was Washington?"

Fuses blowing on the neuropanel as we leave the building. The onlookers blur and the bold, Czechoslovakian circus posters on the walls meld into each other. Washington was abuzz, he says, humming with rumors of failing nuclear power plants. One after another closing down, mid-construction, around the country. The projected costs were one-fifth the actual expenditures. Utility stockholders were losing their shirts and of course the electrical consumer would pay in the end. But he had garnered five grants for the Department.

"How's Wendell?"

"Richard, I have to leave."

"Leave where?"

"New Haven."

"Is your mother ill?"

"I've broken faith with you, Richard. I went to bed with Wendell."

He had been prepared to drive home. He reels back, his head jerks, and he drops his keys into the thick gray slush at the curb. The slush is wrist-deep and as he digs for the keys he whispers.

"He raped you."

"No."

Rising, towering above me, his face contorted with rage, he pins me against the fender of the car.

"He must have!"

"No, Richard, he didn't."

"I . . . can't drive. I mean I think I . . . shouldn't."

I take his cold, wet keys and we get into the car.

"Where? Where in the house did you go to bed with Wendell?"

"In Nanny's room."

"And he's gone now? He ran away in the Volvo?"

"He's waiting at home. He got the night off. We'll try and talk about it. If you'd like, I'll stay at the Park Plaza."

"This is lunacy! This is so outrageous I don't think I can handle it. This son of mine, this *malignant tumor* of mine—this really is criminal!"

They haven't taken the Christmas lights down around the New Haven Green. Each street lamp has an arc of red bulbs around it. Our faces redden and turn garish, lamp to lamp.

"Richard, I felt, when I arrived, that I'd walked into the center of a blood knot. There was a schism in the house, caused by Marion. The two of you were in your own spheres. You never shared the dilemma that she caused."

"This is hardly the time for criticism!"

"I'm not criticizing, and I'm not blaming. I'm talking about the breach. Almost immediately you called me a catalyst. I think all the two of you ever wanted was a direct line to each other, and you looked to me to provide it. Within a week of my arrival I had the two of you serenading at my window. It's culminated in this."

"It is utterly *amazing* to me that you're saying these things! How could you *do* it? He's wet behind the

ears, he's unstable, he's twelve years your junior!
And he has absolutely nothing to offer you. Are you
considering going off with him?''

''No. But he has a great deal to offer. He'll eventually offer it to you. I did it because I love him. I love
you both. Equally. Differently.''

''Oh, for Chrissake, do you expect me to believe
that?''

''I told you there were signs of intimacy in Wendell's
behavior on my very first day. You didn't take it
seriously! *He* told you he'd married Monica in an
attempt to extricate himself, somehow, from these
dangerous feelings. You didn't take him seriously. He
was always the wet-eared prodigal. What in the world
must happen before you take the man seriously?''

''The *man?* Well, now I suppose I must take *the man*
seriously.''

''And you must realize, Richard, that all of his erratic
behavior, all of his deranged escapades are grounded
in his guilt over Marion.''

''My God, you've made love to my son! Why are we
talking about Marion?''

''He thinks he betrayed her, abandoned her by leaving the house for college. He thinks if he'd stayed,
and tended her, you wouldn't have committed her. He
blames himself for her death.''

I am crying, weaving up Whitney Avenue.

''Stop the car, for God's sake. You can't see. I'll
drive.''

I pull over to the curb and he walks around to the driver's seat.

"You talk of him as if he's remote. As if he hasn't, just this day, fucked you. You talk of him with such . . . tenderness. Oh, Christ."

He takes my hand, holds it and murmurs.

"I have never felt quite so reduced."

"Nor have I."

We pull into the driveway and park. Neither of us moves to retreat from the car. He drops my hand and leans forward, resting his arms on the steering wheel.

"I don't want you to go to the Park Plaza. I'd like you to stay here tonight. I almost gave you an engagement ring for Christmas. I'd like to explain why I gave you the pearls, instead."

"Please, Richard, when we go into the house, let's not hurl insults. Let's try and talk the truth."

He bridles.

"I intend to."

"I mean about all of us. About these feelings of reduction in all of us."

With quick, kinetic energy he vaults from the car.

"I don't know where you're coming from! I don't understand your *context*. He's cuckolded his father. He's got me wearing horns, for Chrissake. *That's* the truth."

Slamming his cases down in the back hall, marching into the living room, he finds Wendell standing at the mantel. It looks like a stance of authority and strength, but the mantel is the prop that holds Wendell up. Wendell's face is a wracked commingling of alarm, fear, and dread. Richard growls.

"I should think you'd be down on your knees, begging for mercy! How do you account for this? What's your explanation? She attacked you? Great brawny Emma overpowered you? Or did you have one of your convenient seizures?"

"Richard, please—"

"Stay out of this! I want to know, Wendell, how it happened, *why* it happened?"

Wendell's manner turns transparent. He is childlike, without guile, barely audible.

"I was very lonely."

"Lonely? *Lonely?* I will not have a dialogue about loneliness! Try it for a quarter of a century, buddy, as I did! Try it for two solid decades and then we'll talk about loneliness."

"Why didn't you come to *me?* Why didn't we talk about it when it was happening?"

"You were a little boy! You were her *son!*"

"I was your son, too."

"So it said on the birth certificate. For the *record.* I never felt it. You seemed to sense, right from the beginning that I was in the wrong marriage, in the wrong profession, in the—"

"*Weren't you?*"

"*Yes*, I was! But you didn't *approve* of me; there was always disappointment in your eyes, you never had a good word to say about me or my work. You gave everything to your mother, your total attention. So don't ask me why I didn't come and talk to you."

Richard whirls around, addressing me.

"Why in Christ's name are we talking about Marion again? I left here three days ago, intact. I come home to the vilest news of my life and everybody's got Marion on the brain. What the hell has Marion got to do with my *son* taking my *woman* to bed? Loneliness is a feeble, lame excuse and I won't accept it!"

"You got on the train and went to Nee Marchant and left me alone at the cemetery! You did that when mother wasn't even fucking *cold!* You gave me no explanation and I sat alone in this house all night. And the hours went by and her fucking Bibles were up there with all of her clothes and her nail polish and her Vitabath sitting on the tub and I *despised* you, man! Why? Why did you *do* that?"

"Because I despised you, too! Because you thought me some weak, adulterated, compromised man. Because all the while you and she were ensconced up there in that room I was out there *functioning!* And you were fucking *wrong! I* was putting on the tie and going to work and hiring and firing and earning a living, paying the bills, keeping this roof over your head. I went to Nee because you had never, ever *been* there for me, Wendell. You *made* yourself enemy territory. It was terrible, horrible, leaving you alone. But I was a basket case and I was desperately—"

"Desperately *what?*"

"Lonely."

They stop for a moment and shift positions. Richard falls in the wingback chair.

"All right, Wendell, all right."

"All right? Shit, nothing's *all right*. It's not all right that you call *my* loneliness a lame excuse. What's good for the *goose*, man!"

"That's why this happened, isn't it? That's why you took Emma to bed. An eye for an eye. You had a score to settle. If you weren't so big I'd give you the flogging of your life. If I had a gun I swear I'd shoot you. What are you doing? Oh, for Chrissake, don't *cry!*"

"Why wouldn't anybody come and visit her?"

"Because she was *dangerous!* Please, Wendell, don't cry."

"She wasn't dangerous! Why did you have her fucking *committed?*"

"Because she was fucking *crazy!* Christ, will you get a handkerchief or something? Emma?"

I shuffle in my bag for Kleenex and hand it to Wendell. Richard is up again, pacing, rocking back and forth with his arms folded.

"Look. I know you made efforts. Naomi Silverman came over one day and Marion was upstairs, mending something. She had a sewing basket on her lap. In the middle of the conversation she walked over to Naomi with a pair of scissors and cut the hem of her skirt. Then she went back and finished mending."

"Why didn't you *tell* me that?"

"I'm telling you *now!* I was trying to protect you! Does it *help* to know? Does it make any difference? But while we're talking truth here, Wendell, let's talk truth. You didn't need *me* to tell you. You knew. You had to, you were with her every day. You saw the signs. And you know what stayed my hand? Your loyalty to her. Your devotion. You guarded her as if she was incompetent—"

"She *was!*"

"Yes, Wendell, she was. I should have committed her long before I did, but every time I saw your dependency I had qualms. I thought I'd wait until you grew up a bit, until you got into your teens. I thought maybe when you learned to drive and you got away from the house and got a little objectivity, the word might even come from *you.* But no. You couldn't deal with it, and neither could I. I was damned if I did, damned if I didn't, and you set about smashing cars and running to psychiatrists. Then Rae-Ann came on the scene and you let yourself in for six weeks. That's when I realized that there'd never be a word from you—you'd never tell me you were ready to let go. You'd just go on telling me with these gestures of hopelessness.

"You came out of the hospital and came home for spring break and went to the gym that day. And she traipsed over to the office. I thought, Jesus, this is it. This will send him right back to the ward. It's either him or her. So I called Silver Hill and told them to come and get her. And you, you sniveling bastard, you've had it in for me since! She *wanted* to die, Wendell! She had for years. I think she only got up every morning because of you. And most of the time you were the only reason *I* had to get up. And then

Emma came and I thought, Jesus Christ, there's still a *chance*. And now there isn't''

I take a wad of Kleenex to Richard but he refuses it and wipes his eyes with his cuff.

"I'm finished, Wendell. I want you out of here tonight. You're a goddamned malignant tumor, and I want you to take the Volvo and get out of my house and don't ever come back.''

Wendell strides past him and grabs me by the shoulders.

"Come with me.''

"No.''

"Are you staying here tonight?''

"Yes.''

We hear the engine rumble and feel the house vibrate. Richard, sullen and sluggish, fatigued, leans against the living room arch.

"Did you make the draperies?''

"Yes. But I don't have the rods to hang them.''

"Are you determined to leave?''

"Yes.''

"You were disappointed by the pearls, weren't you?''

"I thought that you might consider marriage, if you cared enough for me. You were evidently able to imagine four years with me.''

"Come, let's sit down. I can't explain it now. I haven't the energy. I'll try in the morning."

"Richard, you never really seriously considered divorce, did you?"

"No."

He lifted his eyes to the portrait of the founder, and smiled ruefully.

"Goddards don't divorce. They lead lives of discomfiture, they keep their contracts, they long for doses of prussic acid. And now they seem to have committed a sort of incest."

"Are you sure you don't want me to go to the hotel?"

"God, yes! I don't want to be alone tonight."

There's a hushed stillness in the house as he loosens his tie, removes his shoes, and puts an arm around me. In an exhausted, relaxed state, he asks,

"What was he like?"

"Young."

Something masculine and peculiar afoot here. He wants my assurance that his son, his malignant tumor, is a manly performer in bed.

"Did he put me to shame?"

There is such innocence to the question, such charm. It seems so improper to find him irresistible now. The lines around his eyes are deep; there's silver in his five-o'clock shadow. I make the advance. I kiss his lovely, generous mouth. Shame, Richard, is such a Catholic word.

"My God," he says. "My God. You have such *promise* in your eyes. Are you a witch? I don't want you to go."

I used to think that, as I aged, I'd have very wise eyes. I thought I'd understand the complexity of life, the intricacies of fidelity, the sanctity of love and friendship. The complexities have fallen away, replaced by simplicities.

"All I know, Richard, is that two people can't be happy if they've made a third miserable."

"Christ, this is odd. Let's go upstairs."

It isn't odd at all. It's explained by the forbidden, the irregular, the free association of bodies and bloodlines. All that was incorporated, back at St. Anne's, in the word "taboo."

But in the lovemaking I am ineffably sad. I don't find the affectionate familiarity I thought of so fleetingly while in the shower with Wendell. This is too extreme. I'm not included in. This is all about rivalry, performance, fearful symmetry, measuring up, settling scores. I'm painfully detached.

Something residual just now about measuring up. An old story about a man in a veterans' hospital. He's got a tattoo on his cock. When the old, sagging, sixty-year-old nurse bathes him, it says TONY. When the young, buxom, thirty-year-old nurse bathes him, it says,

TICONDEROGA, N.Y.

Gratitude that God, in His wisdom, granted females a reprieve from measuring up in the crotch. Pardoned us from sexual hyperbole, liberated our bodies from the phallic appendages of swords, billy clubs, rifles, fixed bayonets, missiles. They're right when they say we're all the same in the dark. If we're the gentle sex it's because we walk about the world in a kind of clitoral amnesty. Our minds have been freed for the higher pursuit of maring the brood. Mother Hood. Mother Church. Mother Country. Mother Tongue. Mother Earth. Mother nature gives life and Father time takes it away. There is no such thing as mistressful. Mistresses sublimate, masterful Masters dominate. And even Peg observed that the belligerent, war-hungry Krauts sought to develop a master race to live in a Father land.

Afterward, he sleeps fitfully. I will go tomorrow to St. Mary's Church. I'll make a novena for nine hours, on the hour, to the Infant of Prague. I'll take away a child and I won't know which man is the father. Sudden image of the church falling down around me. God, seeing me there in my contrary state, will strike the church with lightning and reduce it to rubble. But I don't think so. The day I was there with Gracie I felt an affinity with Mary, suspended stage left on a pillar. The saints over the doors were all women. From Siena, Montepulcano, Lima, Ricci. Forgive my sacrilege, but they were all the same in the dark. There's sisterhood in that. I will pray that there's power enough in that to prevail against the words of Madeline's gynecologist. I'll pray to be allowed a state of grace.

Thirty

We awaken with grumbling stomachs and I realize that dinner was missed in the melee of yesterday. We stretch and listen to our dueling growls and there is, for each of us, a moment of harrowing recall. Yes, it's true.

"Emma?"

"Yes?"

"In a couple of months, when we have some hindsight on this, could I meet you somewhere?"

"Why?"

"I don't know. To . . . confer. Provide a coda. Try and understand."

"I think I do understand, Richard. This, now, is the coda."

Both of us cry. A veritable waterworks. Desperate kisses and his two hands grasping my hips, the thumbs gouging my empty stomach, bruising me. Teeth on the neck, tongues everywhere, drops of sweat falling from his brow into my eyes: madness. Hunger in the gut, hunger in the loins, the pathetic urgency to turn the clock back, erase. A half hour later in the sweat and damp sheets, the reality affirms itself. Yes, it's true. Both of you.

"Where will you go?"

"Montreal. I have relatives there."

"Oh, yes. Aunt Colleen. Would you let me give you some money?"

"No, thank you. I've saved two thousand. I'll be fine."

"When do you want to go?"

Immediately. Because Wendell will return today, in your absence. Because I cannot endure a gang-bang at the heart of a blood knot. Because I have to protect myself from shame.

"What would be best for you?"

"Well, I should drop into the office briefly. I've got five post-docs waiting for my news. Could I go in this morning for a couple of hours? I'll come home at noon."

"Fine."

"Would you like to have lunch out? We could go to Mory's."

"Why don't we? Pick me up at noon and I'll take an afternoon train."

"All right."

"We're starving. I'll go make an omelet."

I've become quite familiar with this omelet pan. It has a turquoise enameled botton that conducts the heat fitfully. I know its quirks, and the quirks of the burner it sits on. The burner, too, heats unevenly. I've learned how to outwit them both, how and when to turn the pan to balance an omelet. The various knobs on the range gleam. They were grimy with grease when I arrived and I've scoured them regularly with Ajax and an old toothbrush. Houses are more resilient than people. Perhaps because they don't mourn the folk who pass through them. A little Ajax, a little paint. Houses accumulate dirt instead of memories. Richard and Wendell and I may mourn each other forever, but this house lives in the moment. The stove has forgotten the pablum it cooked for Wendell, and Richard before him. Open the oven door and fill the gaping mouth with a repast for whoever is present and hungry today. Their shapes, sizes, ages, bloodlines, and names don't matter. The walls have forgotten Nanny's songs, Marion's misery, Rae-Ann's sermons, Blodwen's insults, Wendell's moo. So I think this house will not mourn for me. It only recognizes the Hoover, the broom, the dust mop, the scouring pad. A little Ajax, a little paint.

He's got his terry robe on over his shirt and there is something penultimate in his eyes. It's as if there's a deficiency between us, an omission that holds us in limbo and won't let us get to the end.

"I'd like to explain about the pearls. I'd decided to surprise you with an engagement ring. But I knew when I went to the store that it was a mistake. And I bought the pearls instead. I didn't know *why* I'd changed my mind so compulsively, when it was such an important matter. I went back to the office, refused all calls, closed the door, and just sat there. I didn't want to confront it, so I tried to avoid it. I read several articles, I rearranged some journals, tidied the desk. All I knew was that I'd have done you a great disservice if I'd given you a ring."

He looks haggard, and he is chary with these truths.

"I do love you, Emma, but I really don't know what I wanted from you. I do know what I didn't want. I didn't want anything resembling marriage. Marriage, as I knew it, was a slow, suffocating death. A daily curse on every sunrise. Now I'm going to tell you terrible things about me. Deliver my own verdict. They're awful and, God, they're a bitter brew to swallow.''

He's like an addict going cold turkey and the monkeys riding on his back are ghosts. I once listened to Ibsen's Mrs. Alving say that ghosts were as countless as the grains of sand, that we were miserably afraid of the light. I listened but didn't hear. Yes. I see.

''I felt blind panic at the thought of ever coming home and finding you idle. I thought if you ever did anything, said anything, behaved in any way remotely resembling Marion, I'd hate you. When you first came you borrowed her sewing basket, remember? To mend Nanny's chair. I saw you carrying it upstairs and I felt pure dread. God. Another woman. Another millstone. Such unfair thoughts. So cruel to encumber you that way.

''Every now and then I'd see your face in repose. You were sad about Michael. I thought, Christ, will she end up on lithium? And that day that you went to church with Grace it was such an ordinary thing. But I'd had the Seventh Day Adventists up to my eaves and I wondered if I had another fanatic on my hands. I wondered if you'd run to the Bible every time I raised my voice.

''I must have sensed all this when I brought you the B.L.S. material. I wanted you to leave this house every day, mix with people, never, ever be static. You see how disordered I am? How pathological all this is? Something in me has been bent and mangled. I hate these admissions, I hate every compromise I've ever made, I hate my lost youth and every birthday's a trauma. But mostly I hate what's happened to Wendell.

"So I sat there, stuffy me in my stuffy office. I said, listen, you unfeeling bastard, do you feel *anything* for *anybody?* And I remembered being very confused, back in my Shelley days, as to what I really believed in. Young men are in such a quandary to nail themselves down, carry the right set of credos. My father said, 'Well, what would you be prepared to *die* for?' I thought it was such a pivotal question and that day, last month, I asked it again. The answer was Wendell. That was it. That's the truth. Please forgive me. I'm so sorry."

I sit in his lap, stroke his hair and whisper.

"The letter came from *Poetry Review*. They accepted two of his poems."

"No!"

"Yes, two days ago."

"I don't believe it! They'll publish them?"

"Yes. And pay him, too."

"I don't *believe* it! When?"

"In April. He was ecstatic. If only you'd been here—"

I stop mid-sentence because "if only you'd been here" broke out of my throat in a threnody. He rises, we separate, we begin to clear the table, methodically gathering cutlery onto plates.

"That's when it happened?"

"Yes."

The phone rings as I enter the kitchen.

"Hello?"

"Hello."

It's Wendell. It's eight-thirty and Richard generally leaves the house at eight.

"Is he still there?"

"Yes."

"I want to see you."

"Not today. Where are you?"

"At Lydia's."

"Just a minute."

Richard walks past me, carrying glasses and cups.

"It's Wendell. He's at Lydia's."

There is no reaction. He rinses the plates and stacks them in the dishwasher. I go back to the phone.

"I hope you slept on her Barca and let her have the bed."

"I did. Are you all right?"

"Yes."

"I gather he's staying home today. Do you think he'll leave at eight tomorrow?"

"Yes."

"I'll park on the street, and when he goes I want to see you."

There's a crash in the background. Shattered glass falls into the sink, careens across the counters. I hear the frenetic squawking of birds. Richard has put his fist through the window; glass has hit the bird feeder outside. Terrified sparrows take wing, blood gushes from Richard's knuckle. He wraps his hand in a towel and says, calmly,

"Give me the phone."

He takes the receiver.

"Wendell? Congratulations."

Wendell doesn't respond. Richard's face takes on a grim determination.

"Wendell? Emma's told me about the acceptance. Congratulations."

Relief registers, and he replaces the receiver.

"What did he say?"

"He said, 'Thank you.' "

"But *how* did he say it? Bitterly? Cynically?"

"No. Nicely."

He embraces me awkwardly, trying to hold his bloody paw at bay.

"He doesn't know you're leaving today."

"No."

"Will you send him a note?"

"No."

"How will he know?"

"You'll have to tell him, Richard."

When he's ready to leave, he can't get his glove over my bandage. It's ten degrees below zero and I struggle with it, making the gash bleed all the more. Finally he stands on the back step with the bare hand dangling.

"It's just *killing* that you're leaving. I don't know if I can stay here alone tonight. But I'll try. Do you remember that dinner when you told us all about Michael?"

"Vaguely."

"You said you stepped back graciously on little cat feet. Because you saw misery in his face, and pride and ego and rivalry had become meaningless. Yesterday, when you told me, I saw misery in your face. Absolute wretchedness. So we'll have lunch and then I'll take you to the train."

"Thank you, Richard, I'll see you at noon."

I tape a sheet of plastic over the kitchen window and call the glazier, the same man who repaired the broken glass when Wendell punched out Richard. Then I rush to the third-floor storage room. I haul my suitcases down the stairs. I open bureau drawers, empty them, empty the pouches of the shoe bag. I stack sweaters and blouses and bluejeans in the case. Shed quiet tears. Trance a little.

When I was eleven I went to Louisburg Square with Peg, when she was delivering laundry. We were sent upstairs to a maid named Holly. It was August and the mistress of the house, Mrs. Eaton, was going to Saratoga. Holly packed her dresses with two layers of white tissue paper between each dress. Peg and Holly talked while I marveled at the stacks of tissue lying on the canopied bed, watched Holly smooth the layers so deftly between the beaded and sequinned garments. Holly noticed my interest.

"This, lass, is the way fine ladies travel."

Then we went up the street to deliver to the Dickson house, where they retained a man who did nothing all day but polish brass fixtures. Mrs. Dickson was going to Saratoga and her maid, too, was packing beaded and sequinned dresses. But tissue paper was not in evidence. When we left Peg stuck her nose in the air and said,

"What did you learn from those two houses?"

"The Dicksons are the richest."

"But Mrs. Dickson wasn't packed in tissue. She's not as fine as Mrs. Eaton, the brass man notwithstanding. Remember that."

Oh, my Pegeen, I have. But it's had little influence on my life. I try to pack my shoes so that the heels don't perforate the sweaters. I wrap bottles in plastic produce bags in case they leak.

I leave my Volvo and house keys, the Mikimoto pearls, and the envelope of B.L.S. material on Richard's Empire bureau. In the kitchen I step over broken glass and fetch Lydia's potholder, Wendell's cookbook, and Richard's egg cup. In the study, I go through the albums and lift a snapshot. It is Wendell's first day at the freshman dorm. He stands outside, a yard away from his father in front of a statue of Nathan Hale. I will know, when I look at this, that Marion stood behind the camera. I'll know the ordeal it must have been for her, getting out of the yellow robe, putting on one of the ruffled Confirmation dresses, willing herself through the orientation exercises.

I take two souvenirs from Nanny's room: the 1938 *Reader's Digest* and the little crystal tray. From Nanny's room I look down through the dormer and see Gracie sweeping snow from the Silvermans' stairs. I resist the urge to run and say goodbye. It would take too much time and I must begin my novena at eleven. And she'd want too much information, which she'd pass on to Wendell, if pressed.

When the cab arrives the driver loads my cases in the trunk and I ask him to wait while I make a last check. A slow saunter then, into the back hall, past the L. L. Bean exhibit, through the kitchen, past the omelet pan which I triumphed over so mistressfully, through the study, the green physics journals, the bulldogs, a glance at the volumes of Shelley on the shelf of oblivion. It is rather mawkish to make these last checks, but it is what one does. Passing through the living room to reach the front hall, the wind tunnel. Thriving Boston ferns to my left, in the dining room, and to my right, the founder up on the wall. The last thing I see is Lydia's pillow, on the couch. The Christmas gift for bofe of them.

R G W

When the cab pulls into the street I look back at the house. The trees are bare and the house is naked and I see Monica's bubble shining on the roof. We head down Whitney, turn off Grove into Hillhouse, and pull up in front of St. Mary's. Sal the cabbie helps me up the stairs and into the church with the luggage. We cross ourselves upon entering and then stack the cases alongside a confessional.

"Would you still be available to come back and get me at seven o'clock?"

He hems and haws. He generally quits at six.

"You making a novena to the Infant?"

"Yes."

He checks his digital watch.

"And the ninth is at seven?"

"Yes."

"Where you going then?"

"To the Trailways depot."

"I'll be here at ten past seven."

"Thank you very much."

There are only five or six people in the church. I sit at the back until it's exactly eleven and then I make my way past Mary, on the pillar, and kneel before the Infant. The last time I was here he wore white brocade; now he wears red velvet. I wonder if, somewhere in this vast building, there is a little costume shop; I wonder who is the doll's dresser. I dig the novena card out of the lint and dross at the bottom of my bag.

O Jesus, Who hast said, "Ask and it shall be given you; seek, and you shall find; knock, and it shall be opened to you," through the Immaculate Heart of Thy most holy Mother, I knock, I seek, I ask that my prayer be granted:

Please let me take away a child.

O Jesus, Who hast said, "if you ask the Father anything in My Name, He will give it to you," through the Immaculate Heart of Thy most holy Mother, I humbly and urgently ask Thy Father in Thy Name that my prayer be granted:

Please let me take away a child.

O Jesus, Who hast said, "Heaven and earth will pass away, but My words will not pass away," through

the Immaculate Heart of Thy most holy Mother, I feel
confident that my prayer will be granted:

Please let me take away a child.

I must foray out on various errands and farewells, but
I'm content to sit quietly in a pew for the first hour. I feel
totally exposed. Reduced. Without my emissary's veneer
of sophistication. My thoughts are taking unusual umbrage
at the egalitarian, the liberal secular, the worldly cosmopolitan. I sit in this church in a state of blind faith.
Michael used the term derisively. He said the words im-
plied a refusal to see, to think, to admit to reality. The
Unitarian Church, he said, was the least of the evils. The
thinking man's religion. Well, to hell with it. Thinking is
located in the brain, faith is located in the soul, and the
soul has yet to reveal itself on any X-ray or CAT scan. It's
as ethereal as faith and both are blind and a thinking man's
religion is a contradiciton. I have blind faith today that the
Infant hears me, that the Sisterhood over the door looks
kindly on me. It's quite amazing, Michael. I'm not a
babbling idiot, my I.Q. remains the same. And I intend to
offer my Paul or Pauline to this church. Kevin will take
offense.

"Oh, sweet Jazus, Em! You *know* it's all bilgewater."

"I'm so sorry, old chap. It happens to be the bilgewater
of my preference."

Now it is noon, and Richard has parked the Peugeot out
back. He's standing in the downstairs hall with his bandaged hand, hollering for me. I approach the altar and make
the second novena.

I have tried mightily to consider a future in Boston. I
begin with Commonwealth, that street of stately grandeur,
move on to Newbury, where the elite meet to eat and the
talk is refined. Across the Common when the gardens are
in bloom and stay there until moonlight glistens off the
panes of the Hancock. But other, urban images overwhelm

me very quickly and persuade me that the city is not the place for an unwed woman great with child. In that condition, I think I couldn't brook the madding crowds, the strident feminists, the bleating gays, the ponderous academics. The legions of pikers and dolts with Walkmans and strangulated hair. The porno houses in the Combat Zone. The inevitable *awareness*. Of the bomb, the deficit, unbalanced trade, hunger in America, subsidies and PACs. Illegal aliens, inebriated Irish, born-again Christians, sorrowing Jews, black people trying to have a dream. Weary beyond description of city faces that carry the world too much with them. Bearing the imprimatur of warring ambitions. Racing against the clock and queuing up like sheep somewhere between sin and salvation.

> I will arise and go now, and go to Innisfree,
> And a small cabin build there, of clay
> and wattles made;
> Nine bean rows will I have there, a hive
> for the honey bee,
> And live alone in the bee-loud glade.

Do you hear me, Lord? I sing of four green acres eight miles east of Keene, a stone's throw from Marlborough, an easy jaunt to Mount Monadnock. I have twenty-one hundred dollars at Colonial Bank of New Haven. I have five thousand dollars stashed away at Boston Five Cents Savings. I'll work as long as I'm able and then stay home for at least six months. I'll practice thrift, write for agricultural and farming pamphlets from the University of New Hampshire. Keep accounts as thorough as Thoreau's. I *will* be fine. This is, after all, in all its mess and glory, America.

Sam Wilkenson, the quarry owner, likes me. He talked to me at length once of feldspar, mica, and beryl. He said he always needed office help because secretaries in Keene wouldn't travel to the quarry. "Who is the father?" he'll ask. I'll say a man I met from Prague. I'll ask my neighbor, Henry Polk, to bring his Rototiller and double the size of my vegetable patch. I'll ask Kevin to prop up the chicken coop and build new roosts. I'll raise poultry. Wyandottes for meat, Leghorns for eggs. I'll watch the classified and buy a second-hand freezer, preserve the summer bounty from the garden and the berry bushes. A second-hand bike to transport me, a second-hand saw for the wood lot. A home, a hearth, and a bantling. Baptized in mine and Michael's name. And they'll come and visit, Uncle Michael and Uncle Dan, and bring gifts. Dolls or trains. *Babar* and Dr. Seuss. If they ask me do I need anything, can they help, I'll say yes. I'd like a camera to photograph the first tooth and a recorder to tape the first words. And please feel free to visit anytime. You know you're always welcome.

Between novenas I leave the church. I venture out into the freezing cold and make the withdrawal at the bank. I go to the Park Plaza and inquire if Henry Salisbury is registered. I don't wish to see him, I just want to quell curiosity. Dr. Salisbury checked out yesterday. Did he leave a forwarding address? No, he went home with his wife. Ah, well. Richard said that Henry would take a lot of flagellation. Then up Chapel to the British Museum to visit their gift shop. I want to buy a postcard of Diana Kirke, the bare-breasted woman who looked down on Richard and me and left us so accelerated.

The New Haven Green is ugly now. Mounds of dirty snow on dark, sodden grass. I pass the three Protestant churches and in my untemporal mood the buildings seem as minimal as the religions they house. What you get in there, Kev, is a fast-food lunch instead of an eight-course banquet.

After the next novena I light candles and say a prayer for Gracie and Raymond. Then I hike up to the Beineke courtyard. I sit for ten minutes looking at Earth, Sun, and Chance. And then, numb with cold, I make my way to Grove Street Cemetery. I pass the Jacobs, Algernons, Ebenezers, and Aarons, arriving at the Goddard plot. Rest in peace, Marion. Your son's poems will be published in spring, and in the summer I hope that he will travel to the Vineyard with his father. I hope they'll stand together and look at the lilies that were, unlike you, indestructible.

I move out, under the massive Egyptian portal, blindly believing that I carry a Goddard away. I might return with it someday, to show it its ancestors. It'll have eyes to die for and a generous mouth; it will be genetically linked but there'll be too much Mick in its face and it won't inherit.

It's late afternoon when I return to St. Mary's and the day has grown dark. I enter the church and am astounded to see a large, dark figure hovering over my luggage. It is Lydia. The heels of her snowboots make her six feet tall and she is bundled in scarves. She sees me and swerves, looking immense and fantastical.

"How did you know I was here?"

"I doan *know*. I suspect."

"Did you tell Wendell your suspicion?"

"No. Cuz I got me a *heap* of suspicion. Mizz Riley, I foun de wad in de trash. An' in de wad I foun de pills. Now, Miss Riley, you tell ol' Lydia. You pregnant?"

"Lydia, will you take an oath of secrecy?"

"Cross my heart."

"I hope that I am. But I can't stay in New Haven."

"I knows, Mizz Riley. I *knows*, and I *cares*. Come."

She takes me by the hand and leads me to the nearest pew.

"I'm goan say dis, den I *gits*, cuz dis place gimme de spooks. Now. We bofe women, right?"

"Right."

"An' we bofe be in service, right?"

"Right."

"An' never was two cents to rub together outta bein'
in service. So, listen. My sister, Velveeta? She done
it twice all by herself, no one but me assistin'. Now,
when de time come and dem doctors daze all wantin'
cash on de line, and you ain got it, here's what you
do. You listenin', girl?"

"Yes, Lydia."

"A month befo', on de calendar, you start drinkin'
saffron tea. You brews dat with cumin seed and
drinks it every day. Den, in two weeks, you switch.
You got to find juniper twigs and brew dem and drink
dat for two weeks. When de pains come you switches
again. Dis time you find trillium root and brews dat.
Dem ol' Injuns dat be here in de firss place, dey call
dat trillium 'birthroot.' Den, de pains get bad you
holds your nose to de pepper can. Dat makin' you
sneeze and push, an' down it come. Doan lay on no
bed, cuz dat *bad*. You be *kneelin'*, hear, jis like dat
man up at de candles. It goan slide out jis fine an'
you be cuttin' de cord an' all you be needin' is clean
scissors. An' after, you brew up tea of sage. Dat be
de blood tonic. An' Mizz Riley, dem ol' Injuns, dey
say if you makin' a fire and burnin' de afterbirth, den
yo' chile never see no evil all his days. Now, you tell
ol' Lydia where you be goin'."

"Lydia, you must swear secrecy."

"I's crossed my heart already, girl!"

"North. Into the country."

"Good! Dat be fine place to find all dem roots. You
stan' up now."

I stand, as instructed. Her big arms go around me, locking me to her. She kisses my cheek. She doesn't say goodbye. She smiles, pats my stomach, looks into the high, vaulted ceiling, and says,

"Hallelujah!"

Thirty-One

Emma Rowena Riley presently leaves the rather rustic offices of Roberts and Rubin, gynecologists. She bounces down the steps of the tall brick house on Emerson Street, wraps her plaid lambswool scarf over her forehead, laps it around her head and across her mouth, tucks it into her collar, and hops onto her bicycle.

The colors of the morning, and the town, are strong and vibrant on this sunny February day. An azure blue sky above the white Federal houses, a fringe of dark green forest ringing the hills, puffs of gray smoke curling up from the chimney of the scarlet-red firehouse. She wheels along the black asphalt ribbon of road that divides two snowbanks, passing Spencer's Bookshop. She waves at Mrs. Chittenden, the octogenarian owner. In April she'll request that Mrs. Chittenden call the larger store, in Marlborough, and special-order a copy of *Poetry Review*.

Pedaling up to the main street, she stops at the corner drugstore and calls Sam Wilkenson at the quarry.

"Sam? It's definite. I am."

"Definitely fragrant?"

"Definitely fragrant. Do you still want me?"

"Damn rights I do. Eight o'clock, Monday morning."

"Sam, are you *sure?* There'll be a lot of questions."

315

"Tell yuh what I'm gonna do, Missy. I got an old folding screen round here somewheres. When you gets to be potbellied I'll jis set up that old screen round your desk. That way you'll have a little cubby, an' screw the questions."

"Bless you, Sam."

Bless him for his kindness, his generosity, his willingness to take her on. Bless him, too, for his folding screen. In the event that she finds herself in occasional disgrace with fortune and men's eyes it will be a comforting protection.

Leaving the town, pedaling out to the house, she smiles at Sam's rural humor. She had known all along that she was fragrant. She had called Kevin and Peg right after her arrival and made the announcement. Kevin said,

"Jazus! A bun in the oven and no man in sight."

Peg said,

"How in the name of Mary will you manage up there alone?"

And Emma said,

"With saffron, juniper, trillium, and sage."

She had waited until she was a week late before going to see Dr. Rubin. Seven mornings in a row she had gone to the glossy calendar above the old, dry sink, and affixed a prominent X across each day. She enjoyed the daily, incremental excitement of marking off a full week. Of passing the calendar fifty times a day while scouring, scrubbing down, polishing, gathering up cobwebs. Glancing at the photograph of the covered bridge, letting her eye fall to the documented proof, the numerical certainty of mounting, bloodless days. But today it has been medically affirmed. Today, finally, she is moored.

Entering the yard, she follows the tracks that were made, in her absence, by the mail truck. Parking the bike, she sees a large cardboard box sitting on the back porch. Peg responded promptly to her request. Inside the house she slashes the cord, runs a knife through the masking tape, and then empties the carton, spreading the array across the kitchen counter. Michael's soufflé dish, Peg's pressed glass plates. Egg cups with shamrocks, Kevin's hand-made wooden trivet. A lace tablecloth and an embroidered tea-tray runner. These are a few of her favorite things. They confirmed her right to be in this kitchen and she handles them lovingly. She fills the sink and submerges the glass and china to soak in billowing suds. For a moment she thinks that these items are like preserved artifacts from some other era, rescued from the bowels of some ancient, sleeping ship. They asserted that the people who used them in the past had certain standards of civilization. They assured that, recycled here to New Hampshire, they would serve to civilize again.

She moves to the stove in the parlor and lays three new logs on the bed of glowing embers. She looks at the two fat books on the coffee table and smiles at their dissimilarity, their seeming polarity. They are quite bizarre together, these two fat books, and yet they complement each other entirely to Emma's satisfaction. One is the Montgomery Ward catalogue and the other is *Renaissance Madonnas*. She hears the chug as the well empties water into the tank under the house. She looks past a stand of snow-laden white pine and sees, in the distance, bundled children seated on garbage can lids, sliding over the latest powder, trying to navigate a swerve at the bottom and make a "doughnut" of the landing. She lifts the bookmark from the catalogue and has a moment of chagrin over her recent disagreement with Peg. Peg offered to inquire around the neighborhood for a second-hand crib. The Dorchester attics were full of them. Maggie Tilson would breed no more—her tubes had been tied—her crib could be had for thirty dollars. A bargain. And Kevin could scrape off the gaudy decals. But Emma didn't want a bargain. She wanted this solid oak, adjustable, four-position steel link crib. One hundred and fifty dollars, but hang the expense. She wanted this child to start off with the top of the line.

The bookmark in the book of madonnas is the photograph she stole from the St. Ronan study. She keeps it in a little three-by-five-inch wallet protector. And there they are, the two of them, behind the cloudy plastic in front of the statue of Nathan Hale. She pauses and examines the faces of the two tall men. At what point? she asks. At what age? How will the knowledge come to her? Perhaps this child will excel at math and cherish order. Perhaps it will be a solitary scribbler, given to seizures. Or will she live forever in a state of watchful ignorance, always alert for the signs? It really doesn't matter. In the deepest regions of her heart she has no preference.

And by being here, in this New Hampshire saltbox, she has saved herself from what would have been a tumultuous territorial disaster. Saving yourself, she had told Wendell, was paramount, elemental, a basically religious idea having to do with the essence of life.

Kevin said,

    "I'll build it a rocker."

Peg said,

    "I'll knit it a toque."

And Hamlet said,

    The rest is silence."

About the Author

JOANNA MCCLELLAND GLASS lives in Guilford, Connecticut. The author of *Reflections on a Mountain Summer* (1975), her most recent play, *Play Memory*, was nominated for the 1984 Tony Best Play Award; her other plays include *Canadian Gothic/American Modern*, *Artichoke*, and *To Grandmother's House We Go*.

Ø **SIGNET** (0451)

SENSATIONAL BESTSELLERS!

☐ **TRADEOFFS by Jane Adams.** Cass, Paula and Ellin are living and loving in a glamorous Manhattan townhouse they share with their men and their dreams, their triumphs and their despairs, sustaining each other through every crisis. And they're learning that trying to "have it all" carries a powerful price of its own.... (131002—$3.95)

☐ **FAME AND FORTUNE by Kate Coscarelli.** Beautiful women ... glittering Beverly Hills ... the boutiques ... the bedrooms ... the names you drop and the ones you whisper ... all in the irresistible novel that has everyone reading ... "From the opening, the reader is off and turning the pages!"—*Los Angeles Times* (134702—$3.95)

☐ **SINS by Judith Gould.** Hélène Junot was the most successful woman in the international fashion world. Her's is the story of a daring but vulnerable woman with the courage to use any means to reach the peaks of money and power, with the heart to give it all up for the love that would make her life whole.... (140249—$3.95)

☐ **LOVE-MAKERS by Judith Gould.** Their glittering hotel chain, sky-high ambitions, and sexual greed crossed all borders. They are four generations of daring, dauntless, desiring Hale women who fight with passion for what they want—love, sex, power, wealth—only to learn that the price of power is far more than they bargained for.... (140362—$4.50)

Prices slightly higher in Canada

───────────────────────────────

Buy them at your local bookstore or use this convenient coupon for ordering.

NEW AMERICAN LIBRARY,
P.O. Box 999, Bergenfield, New Jersey 07621

Please send me the books I have checked above. I am enclosing $_____
(please add $1.00 to this order to cover postage and handling). Send check or money order—no cash or C.O.D.'s. Prices and numbers are subject to change without notice.

Name_____

Address_____

City_____State_____Zip Code_____
Allow 4-6 weeks for delivery.
This offer is subject to withdrawal without notice.